ALSO BY AJ CAMPBELL

Leave Well Alone

Don't Come Looking

Search No Further

The Phone Call

The Wrong Key

Her Missing Husband

My Perfect Marriage

Did I Kill My Husband

The Mistake

First-Time Mother

Left at the Altar

All books are available at Amazon and in Kindle Unlimited

ISBN 9781838109189

This novel is entirely a work of fiction. Names, characters, places, and incidents portrayed are the product of the author's imagination or are used fictitiously. Any resemblance to actual persons, living or dead, or actual events or localities is entirely coincidental.

A FREE GIFT FOR YOU

See the back of the book for details on how to get your copy
of my FREE novella.

For the @bookstagram community

You're the best.

Your continued support means the world to me.

AJ x

PROLOGUE
15 YEARS AGO

Violet was nine years old the Christmas her mother was shot.

It was eight minutes to midnight on Christmas Eve, to be precise. She'd woken up because she needed to pee. At first she fought it, lying awake, listening to the gentle purr of her sister snoring from the bed beside her, wondering if she could get away with going back to sleep. But unable to ignore the need for the loo anymore, she discarded the duvet, flung on her bathrobe, and headed downstairs.

Garlands of fake ivy encircled the handrail of the old wooden staircase, one of the many Christmas decorations her mother adorned the house with every year. Her mother loved Christmas.

They all did back then.

As she neared the bottom stair, she heard a noise. The chink of smashing glass cutting through the silence of the night. She froze, terrified, not knowing whether to run back upstairs and risk being seen, or dart into the living room.

The disturbance was probably another of the mysterious sounds their old house was known to make. But there was no mistaking the sound of the back door creaking open. Her little heart pounded in her chest. Someone had broken in.

She should've fled back upstairs to her parents. Instead, as quick as a cat, she leapt across the hallway and into the living room. An eye-blink decision that determined her destiny.

Footsteps creaked stealthily along the hallway.

They were coming for her.

She hesitated, staring around the room that was lavishly decorated for Christmas. The gap behind the sprawling wing-backed sofa invited her to take cover. She dived inside and unravelled her body, straightening her torso to lie flat. The radiator creaked. Her stomach turned. Petrified, yet strangely intrigued, she edged her body to the end of the sofa.

Faint footsteps entered the room. The smell of sweat filled her nostrils. He was tall. That's what she recalled afterwards when she sobbed to the police. His body was all limbs. Long arms and long, long legs.

The bogeyman.

He walked directly to the sofa, stopping inches from her head, a terrifyingly close distance. Surely he could hear the thumping beat of her racing heart. She could. It sounded as loud as thunder to her young ears.

Her need for the bathroom became unbearable. She could see his outline from the beam of moonlight shining through the window, but she couldn't see his face. The material of his hoodie was pulled over his forehead, and he was wearing what looked like a scarf around his neck that covered his mouth.

He slipped a backpack from his shoulder and pulled up his sleeves to the middle of his forearms. He was wearing a bracelet. A tight, black, ornate bangle, which she somehow thought was odd at the time. He shone a light at the doors on the ugly dresser that filled the gap to the left of the holly-draped fireplace. It was where Dad stored valuables in a safe carved out of the false back of the mahogany structure: money and paperwork, their passports, and his mother's precious jewellery.

The crunch of the man's knees as he crouched down was deafening in the silence. He opened the lower cabinet drawer and set to work. The dial of the safe clicked in next to no time. This guy knew exactly what he was doing. Afterwards, the police said he was a professional. He had come with purpose.

She wanted to run – fast – back to bed, where she could pinch herself and pretend it was all a nightmare. Her belly felt like jelly, and if she hadn't been lying on the floor, she would've passed out. The intruder piled the family posses-sions into his open backpack and shoved an object into the pocket of his hoodie.

'Is that you, Violet?' a hiss came from upstairs. An urgent whisper that broke the silence. She couldn't work out if it was her mother or father. 'Get back to bed.'

The intruder shot bolt upright and paused, his eyes boring into her. At least, it felt as if they were. Her body froze. He had seen her. He was going to get her. But he quickly zipped up his backpack and darted from the room.

She scrambled out from behind the sofa and slotted into the space next to Mum's piano. In the hallway, the intruder pulled a gun from his pocket and aimed it at the silhouette of a body descending the stairs like a ghost.

The crack of the gunshot was deafening.

Violet slapped her hands over her ears, her eyes as wide as saucers.

The lifeless body crumpled down the stairs, pulling a strand of ivy in its wake. It came to an abrupt halt at the bottom, arms and legs strewn bizarrely, like a discarded broken puppet.

The intruder momentarily paused as if startled. Panicking, he secured his backpack over his shoulder ran towards the back door, as Violet's tiny bladder finally released all over the living room floor.

1

NOW

ROSE

'I don't like this. I've never driven in the snow before.' I steer the car onto the main road. Snow flutters in the air, growing heavier as we approach the road leading to the hospice. I flick on the windscreen wipers. It's growing dark, the mood sombre, the sky bearing the threat of heavy snow.

'You'll be fine. Just drive slowly.' Trepidation creeps into my sister's voice. I know what she's thinking – she should've offered to drive. I've only recently passed my test after all. And on the third attempt.

'We should look at getting cars of our own when... you know.' V pauses. 'We can sell this one and put the money towards getting one each.'

I sharply turn my head and meet her gaze. 'How can you even think about buying things with Dad on his deathbed?' The sound of a beeping horn returns my attention to the road.

V grapples with the volume on the radio playing *Hark the Herald Angels Sing*. My sister detests carols. She wishes Christmas didn't exist at all. It's the worst time of the year for her. And don't I know it. But I can't blame her. The memories are too painful. She witnessed far too much that Christmas fifteen years ago.

'We can't shy away from it, Rose.' My sister gives one of her deep sighs. 'We need to prepare ourselves.' The skies darken, casting a gloomy glow across the road. 'You heard what the doctor said yesterday,' V continues. 'Dad's cancer is far more aggressive than they first thought. It could be a matter of days.' She reaches across and squeezes my arm.

'I can't believe this has all happened so quickly.' I should be used to death. I've seen people die at work before. But this... Dad... I'm not prepared for it. 'One minute he was fine. And now we're going to lose him.' My voice breaks. 'I hope he makes it to Christmas.'

'We need to talk about Mum, as well,' V says. 'We've managed this long, but knowing Dad's not going to be around for much longer, we're going to have to work out a schedule... you know... to look after her full time.'

I suck in a deep breath and turn to glance at her. 'I've been thinking about that, too. I've been looking into...'

V holds out her hand. 'Don't go there.'

I start at the pitch of her voice. 'Come on, V. We need to be realistic.'

'No! Over my dead body,' she continues. 'We're not putting Mum into a home.'

My shoulders drop in resignation.

'We've coped well enough with Mum all these years. It's not as if Dad was the ever-present parent we needed.'

'Don't start. You know how committed he's been to his

work. He's provided for us. Besides, he's been a lot better this past year.'

'I could give up work,' V suggests.

'Or I could see if I can go part-time.'

'I'm a cleaner, Rose. My work is more flexible,' my sister says. 'We both know it makes sense for me to give up or at least reduce my hours.'

'It'll only be temporary. Until we can find a more permanent arrangement.' My hands grip the steering wheel with intensity. 'Damn. I've missed the exit to the hospice.'

A lorry joins the roundabout. I veer into the wrong lane, momentarily losing control of the car. 'The steering's not working.' I must have hit a patch of ice.

'Stay calm and go round again,' V says.

It all happens in a blur, as quick as lightning.

One heartbeat we're discussing our parents, the next, I jam on the brakes. The spongy, strung-out sound of tyres sliding across the road makes me wince. But not as much as the accelerating red Audi that joins the roundabout from the road leading to the hospice, skidding towards us.

'You're in the wrong lane, Rose! Move!' V shouts.

'Oh, hell!' I swerve.

Car horns blast, but it's too late.

An explosion of metal crunching against metal reverberates through the car.

My body jolts violently against the tightness of the seatbelt. Airbags deploy, inflating with a loud bang, smashing me like a rag doll into the back of the seat. In an instant, the airbags deflate, hissing softly as the gas escapes. Smoke curls around the dashboard. My eyes sting, and I cough like a chain-smoker.

Dad's going to kill me for trashing his car – such an odd

thought in the moment. But then I remember. He'll never find out. Not now he's so ill.

I turn to my sister. She's unconscious. 'V? V! Wake up.' The sting of bile bites at my throat. 'Oh, hell, V. I'm so sorry.'

The car's hazard lights repetitively click on and off in a steady rhythm above the sound of the radio. I reach across and prod V's shoulder. She's not responding. Smoke rises from the front of the car. Or it could be steam. The smell of petrol hits me. I panic. The car is going to catch fire and explode.

Through the haziness, the driver's door of the offending car opens. A man gets out. His Audi is now buried in the front side of Dad's car, which is crumpled down to two-thirds of its original size. Lights from the vehicles around us flash like well-dressed Christmas trees. Other drivers have stopped. People are on their phones, approaching us. The faint din of voices rises, but I can't work out what anyone is saying. It's madness out there. But inside here, it's oddly calm, as if time has slowed to allow me to become accustomed to the chaos that has erupted around us.

A beeping horn from another car startles me. 'Wake up, V.' I should've let her drive. I'm not experienced enough. 'We need to get out of this car.' I prod her shoulder again. She's not responding.

Fear rips through me. I dithered when that lorry entered the roundabout, and I veered into the wrong lane. I caused this accident. This is my fault. I remove my seatbelt and then unfasten my sister's. I need help. There's no way I can get her out on my own.

Irrational notions of burying my sister alongside my father claw at my thoughts. They won't let go. I see myself pushing Mum's wheelchair towards a congregation of mourners circling a wide hole in the ground containing two coffins laid to rest – one for my father and one for my sister. The congregation toss handfuls of earth on top – and me, two velvety red roses.

My screeching voice echoes around the car. 'V! Please wake up. I'm begging you.'

2

VIOLET

The desperation in Rose's voice screams around the car.

'I'm OK,' Violet groans. But she's not OK. Her head had thrashed sideways from the impact of the oncoming car, smashing against a hard surface with a dull thud.

Nausea pulses through her. She's struggling to breathe. *I Wish It Could Be Christmas Every Day* sings from the radio. No, she doesn't wish that. She wishes Christmas didn't exist at all. It's the worst time of the year. She hates every minute of it. It's a deafening din since the engine cut out, and is at odds with the chaos unfolding around them. She tries to move, but her head pounds with pain.

She squints. The front of Dad's car has disintegrated. Snow falls heavier, slicing across the smashed windscreen. Rose grapples with the car door. Her sister gets out and shouts frantically at a man approaching them, 'I'm so sorry!'

No, Violet tries to cry out. You should never admit fault.

Her sister should know this. But the words are trapped in the trauma wreaking havoc on her senses. They were talking about their parents. She remembers now. Their dying father. Rose hasn't come to terms that he hasn't got long. But her sister has been Daddy's girl since forever, so it's no surprise she's taking the news of their father's imminent passing harder than her.

But then, Rose doesn't know what she knows.

Her chest is heavy, her breathing laboured. A fuzzy version of her sister sways before her. She's fading. Her head continues pounding, as fear creeps through her bones. Is this how it feels when death is approaching? Is this how Mum felt that night when she lay on their hard wooden hallway floor, her body mangled and distorted? 'Mum!' The word escapes her mouth in a whisper.

Discordant voices continue. 'We need to get my sister out of the car!'

A serenity washes through her as she drifts in and out of unconsciousness. She's right. Death is calling. And she's at peace with it. Despite her short-lived twenty-four years, she's tired of life. So tired.

Rose's voice rises above the crowd. 'V!'

Violet opens her eyes wide. Rose and the Audi driver are standing by the car door. His tall frame towers over her sister's petiteness. He looks like a ghost in his hoodie, which is as white as the snow falling around him.

Rose tugs at the car door. 'What have I done?' she cries.

The Audi driver bends over. His hand reaches for Violet. And she can't believe what she sees.

Her heart thumps, briefly pumping out of rhythm.

She is sure of it. She waits.

There it is again. In her semi-conscious state, she is back

there, that Christmas Eve fifteen years ago, smelling the sweat and pine. She looks once more, just to make sure. And she knows. This is not her time. She can't leave this life yet.

The faintest of smiles trembles on her lips.

Finally, it's happened.

In the strangest of circumstances, she has found the person she has been searching for all these years. She told Mum she would. She told her she'd never let it rest until she did. And she promised Bean, too. Bean, that's what they called their unborn baby sister because when Mum told her and Rose that she was pregnant, she said the baby was the size of a bean, and the name stuck. Their beautiful baby sister who they never got to meet because of what this man did.

Her heavy eyelids droop. She wills them to remain open, despite their resistance. She stares at his face, desperate for a connection. Desperate for reassurance that she's right. Dark hair, yesterday's stubble. But it means nothing. She witnessed what that beast did that night fifteen years ago, but she never saw his face.

The temporary smoke from the deflating airbags make her eyes water. She blinks several times and refocuses on the bracelet the intruder was wearing that night. An icky sensation rips through her. She is right. But her body fails her. She hasn't got the strength to bring herself back.

A blurred white light beckons her, pulling her like a magnet towards it. The crescendo of the Christmas carol playing on the radio reaches its climax as her world turns black.

3

ROSE

'Best we get you checked out.' The paramedic gently takes my shaking arm.

'But my sister.' I resist his grip. 'I have to make sure my sister's OK.'

The same flash of fear bolts through me.

I lost the mother I knew – the woman before she was shot. My father is dying. I can't lose my sister, too.

'My colleagues will deal with her,' the paramedic says. He places a red blanket around my shoulders and guides me to one of the waiting ambulances. The guy from the Audi is sitting in the back of another, shrouded in a blanket. A police officer is standing next to him, taking notes.

Cars restart around us. People are eager to get on with their day. It's the middle of December. Christmas parties beckon, or in my case, an evening wrapping presents after visiting our father. But cars are crawling along, drivers rubbernecking at the aftermath of the accident.

'We need to get that cut checked out.' The paramedic's gloved hand touches the side of my face.

'But I need to see my sister.' My voice trembles. 'I need to make sure she's OK.'

'They'll take her to Queen's, where we're taking you. You'll be able to see her then.' The paramedic's soft, steady voice is calm and reassuring amid the madness this day has turned into. 'Please don't worry. She'll be well looked after.'

'But she was unconscious. I don't even know if she's alive.'

Another police officer appears. He can't be any older than me. He takes my details and asks if I've consumed any alcohol.

'No!'

He's going to breathalyse me, he tells me kindly but firmly.

'But I haven't been drinking.'

'You're required by law to comply.' He attaches a fresh mouthpiece to the breathalyser and hands it to me. 'Please blow steadily into the mouthpiece.'

I do as instructed.

The machine beeps. He reads the screen. 'All good.'

The late afternoon darkness throws a low glow over the scene as if I'm watching a black-and-white film. I point to the guy from the Audi sitting in the other ambulance. 'And him? The driver of the other vehicle. Has he been drinking?'

The officer shakes his head.

'I need his details... you know, for insurance purposes.'

'I'll get everything sorted for you.'

'What about the car?' I'm panicking. 'I need to call the hospice.' Desperation chokes my words. 'It's my dad, you see... he's... he's... I need to see him. And I have to know my sister's OK.'

The paramedic butts in. 'We need to get you to hospital.'

'I have your details,' the police officer says. 'We'll deal with what's happened here, and someone will be in touch. Is there someone you can call to be with you?'

I nod. Jamie. He's always there for me. He'll help me. 'I need to get my bag from the car. My phone's in there.'

'I'll do that for you.'

'It's on the back seat.'

Another paramedic appears. Tall, slim, long dark hair in a bouncing ponytail. She's wearing Christmas tree earrings that jiggle when she addresses her coworker. 'Good to go?'

The guy nods and helps me to my feet. 'Let's get you strapped in. As soon as you've been seen to, someone will take you to see your sister.'

I groan. I'm not a serious case. I know what's in store for me. I'm going to be there all night. I spent a period working in the local Accident and Emergency department when I was still at school and thought I wanted to be a nurse. Someone my auntie Audrey knows arranged some work experience for me. Ever since I was young, that's where I wanted to end up working. But, only a week into my stint, late on a Friday afternoon, a drunk turned up and beat the hell out of a nursing practitioner, and I knew it wasn't for me.

The ambulance bumps and bounces along the busy roads. A strand of gold tinsel is twirled around the headrest of the paramedic's seat beside me. She jolts and sways, completing a task on an iPad, chatting incessantly as if she's trying to keep me awake.

I find Jamie's number. He answers after the first ring. He always does. For me, anyway. I've seen him send calls to voicemail when we're together. 'I was just about to phone you. How's your dad?' he asks.

The reassuring sound of his voice makes me well up. I wish he were here. Everything is always alright when Jamie is around. 'I need your help. Something terrible has happened.' I relay the course of events.

'Leave it with me. I'll call the hospice for you and come straight to the hospital.'

'But what about the party?' He's due at a friend's birthday gathering tonight. He's been talking about the annual affair for his old school friends all week. It's one of his favourite nights of the year.

'Forget that. I'll be there as soon as I can.'

I place another call. This one is to my auntie. Dearest Auntie Audrey, my mum's sister, who lives a few streets away from us and helps us look after Mum. If it weren't for Auntie Audrey, Dad would've had to have placed Mum in a care home years ago. I relay what's happened.

'Are you both OK?' she asks.

'I am. I don't know about V. They've taken her to hospital. Can you stay with Mum until I get back? I'll get there as soon as I can.'

'No problem, love. Keep me posted.'

As I thought, A and E is packed. People who have fallen foul of the bad weather or fallen into the trap of drinking too much booze at this time of year; the elderly incapacitated from falls or wrapped in blankets, shivering from the cold; the young with ice-skating injuries. All of them waiting for several hours to be tended to.

'I'm fine,' I tell the triage nurse.

She nods curtly. 'Let me be the judge of that.'

'I really am fine. But I need to see my sister and make sure she's OK.'

After I persuade her that I honestly am OK, but not before she has carried out a set of tests, she delivers unneeded advice about head injuries. She doesn't tell me anything I don't already know. I've completed extensive first aid training for my job. 'You must come back here immediately if any of these symptoms occur.' She reels off a list before directing me to return to the waiting area to be discharged. 'I'll find out what's happened to your sister.' She digs into the pocket of her uniform and takes out a napkin scribbled with notes. It may be a written mess to me, but she immediately finds what she's looking for. 'Violet.'

'That's right. Violet Sapphire.' Panic is growing in me by the minute. 'I need to know she's OK.'

I envisage V lying on a slab in the hospital morgue. Anxiety raises its familiar head, making me overthink things. Jamie is always telling me it isn't helpful to be like this. But he's never been inside our house. And I've never told him what life is *really* like behind the closed doors of our dysfunctional family home.

4

VIOLET

Rose appears, her face flushed from the ordeal. Her eyes dart up and down the narrow A and E bed where Violet lies.

Jamie is with her. Violet doesn't like many people. She never has. Trust is one of her many issues. But she likes ginger-haired Jamie with his rich green eyes and vivacious can-do attitude. He nods hello.

Violet is thankful she has been put in a private cubicle. Mingling with the masses in the overcrowded reception area would've triggered her. She can't cope in crowded places at the best of times, especially not ones crammed with sick people.

Rose shakes her headful of dark curls. 'I thought you were dead.' Her voice is choked with guilt.

Violet rolls her eyes and smiles lovingly. Her poor sister. She's been overthinking things again. Violet can tell. Since Dad's diagnosis, her sister has turned angsty. Nearly as angsty as her, which is unlike Rose. Her sister screws up her button nose. She was blessed with their father's nose – small and delicate with a beautifully curved tip. Whereas Violet firmly believes she inherited an over-pointy ski slope of a beak from their mother.

Violet tries to sit up. 'They've taken X-rays. There's no lasting damage. They're talking about keeping me in, but I'm fine. We need to get home for Mum.'

'I've called Auntie. She's OK to stay until I get back.' Rose takes a seat. She crosses her slim legs, scrunching up the loose material of her cargo trousers and letting it go before repeating the action. Jamie stands behind her. 'That Audi pulled out in front of me, V. I had nowhere else to go.'

'I saw.' Violet doesn't mention that she had veered into the wrong lane and that a more experienced driver would probably have been able to prevent the disaster. Her sister doesn't need to hear that just now. 'Did you get the driver's details?' Violet coughs. A sharp pain stabs around her chest area. She can't pinpoint exactly where, but it's sore. 'We need them for insurance purposes.'

Rose looks up at her friend. 'Jamie's sorted it.' The six-foot-two stocky guy digs into the pocket of his jeans and pulls out a piece of paper. Violet knows how tall he is because he's the same height as their father.

'I've spoken to the police and got some details,' Jamie says. 'And arranged for a garage in town to pick up the car. They're going to assess the damage and give you a call. It could be a write-off.'

'Thanks.' Violet holds out her hand. 'Give it here. I'll sort this.' It's nothing unusual. Since Dad fell ill, she's taken charge of the family paperwork.

Rose snatches the piece of paper. 'No way. You've got

enough going on. Anyway, this is my responsibility. It's only fair I sort it out.' That's her sister all round. Rose always has been, and always will be, about fairness. Equality for everyone. And she's usually so chilled out, totally unflappable.

Violet wishes she could be more like her.

'No, Rose.' Violet smacks the side of the bed. 'No!' she snaps. She doesn't mean to, but her sister doesn't realise the importance of her getting the Audi driver's details. 'I mean it. I've been sorting all of Dad's paperwork.' Nausea wafts over her. She suppresses it, not wishing to bring attention to the fact that she feels pretty rubbish.

'Not until we know you're OK first,' Rose says.

'What's the Audi guy's name?' Violet's voice is barely a whisper. She hopes her sister will at least tell her what she's desperate to know.

'William,' Rose says. 'William Watson. He was really nice.'

She couldn't be further from the truth.

William Watson.

Violet clasps her trembling hands together, so nobody sees how much they are shaking, and she sucks the inside of her cheeks to conceal the smile her lips are desperate to form.

Never before that Christmas Eve fifteen years ago has she felt such joy. It seeps through her like the child in her that evening before their mother was shot. And she lost her baby sister.

She knew it.

In the depths of hope, as she's searched and searched all these years, she knew she'd find him one day. She promised Mum she would. And she promised her beautiful baby sister in heaven above.

William Watson.

Now she has a name, she can find out where he lives.

And she can make him pay for what he did to her and her family.

5

ROSE

I don't like the way V's looking at me. It mirrors Mum's gaunt, perished expression, as if she's looking right through me. Her face is grey and pinched, and her lips are bloodless. Jamie and I try to engage her in conversation, but she shows little interest. I know my sister. Something is playing on her mind. And it's not just the accident.

'Just go. I'll be fine,' she says. 'There's little you can do for me. I'm going to go to sleep.' Her head twitches and she closes her eyes.

Jamie and I exit the revolving doors at the end of the hospital concourse. An inch or so of snow has fallen since I arrived in the ambulance. He slips his arm through mine. Snowflakes flurry around us as our feet crunch through the snow to the car park.

'Something's got into her. I don't like it,' I say.

The snowy atmosphere muffles our voices. 'You probably

need to cut her some slack.' Jamie takes his car keys out of his coat pocket. 'She has been in a car accident, and, by all accounts, she took a pretty hefty blow to the head.'

'No, it's more than that.'

'What do you mean?'

'It's as if she's reverted to her old self. The way she snapped back there. The stubborn look in her eye.'

We locate his car and climb inside. The pungent combination of cinnamon and nutmeg from the Christmas-tree-shaped air freshener dangling from the rear view mirror is refreshing after the antiseptic smells of the hospital.

Jamie starts the engine and turns on the heater. 'Her old self?' He rubs his hands together and blows on them. 'What do you mean?'

I sigh heavily. 'V was pretty messed up as a kid. You know, what happened to Mum and all that. It affected her really badly. Understandable, of course.'

'It couldn't have been easy for you, either.' Jamie pulls out of the parking space and onto the main road.

He knows a little about what we've been through with Mum. I rarely open up to people about my family. But when we dragged V along to a house party one night, and she had one of her episodes less than ten minutes after arriving, I found myself confiding in him. Not everything, but enough.

I told him about the unlikable person my sister was before the therapy our auntie Audrey sought for us in our teens. Therapy to deal with our disturbed childhood of looking after a mum who hasn't muttered a word in fifteen years and a father who's hardly been around. It wasn't his fault. So traumatised about what happened to Mum, he took solace in his job as a self-employed salesman for global tech firms, and, right up to his pancreatic cancer diagnosis two months ago, spent many nights away.

'You're right,' I say. 'It hasn't been easy, but it's been far harder for her. I didn't witness what she did that night. During her early teens, she became obsessed with tracking down the guy who shot Mum.' I pause. 'Listen, Jamie. This is highly confidential. I don't tell people about what happened that night or about how badly it affected V. You mustn't tell anyone what I've told you.'

He turns to me, his lips parted. 'We're mates, Rose. I'd never share what we talk about.' He refocuses on the road. 'Do you think you need to get some more help? You have a hell of a lot going on.'

'I'm trying. My auntie and I have been looking at some options since Dad fell ill. I didn't want to say anything, because I haven't got V to agree to it yet. My uncle died earlier in the year and my auntie has offered to fund a place in a nursing home. He was very wealthy, so she can afford it. We went to see a lovely one yesterday – Abbeyfields – over in Radstone.'

'I know Radstone. My family lived there before we moved here,' he says.

'It'd be ideal for Mum. It was so much better than any of the other ones we've visited recently. Something has always been not quite right. You know, too far from home, the staff, the décor, or just the general vibe.'

'It must be so difficult.'

'We're never going to find somewhere perfect, Auntie said. But Abbeyfields ticked all the important boxes. The staff were lovely, and there was lots going on. But V won't even entertain the idea. She is so overprotective where Mum is concerned. I can't see her ever giving in. Over her dead body, is her attitude whenever I broach the subject. She's adamant. She'd rather die than see Mum put in a home.'

'Just give her time. I'm sure she'll come around. You're different, aren't you? I mean, not just in looks, but in character as well.'

'I know. It's hard to believe we came from the same parents, isn't it? We did, though.'

'Is there anything I can do for you?' he asks.

I smile. He's got to be the kindest human being I've ever met. 'Just be you.'

He stops in the drop-off bay at the front of the hospice. 'I'm really happy to come in with you. I don't need to go into his room. I can wait outside.'

I hug him. 'Absolutely not. You've done enough for me today.'

'I could stay in the car and take you home afterwards.'

'Honestly, I'll get an Uber. Go to the party.'

'I'll call you later,' he says.

'What would I do without you?'

He winks and give me one of his boyish smiles. 'You'd be just fine.'

I lean over and bump my shoulder against his. 'See you soon and please don't share what I've told you.'

He grabs my coat sleeve. 'You can trust me, Rose.'

'I do.' Apart from my auntie Audrey, and my sister, of course, he's the only person I wholly trust.

6

ROSE

I climb out of the car and take the snow-covered path to the main doors of the hospice. It's a listed building. Stately, with a comforting appeal despite having been converted into a place for the dying. A giant Christmas tree dominates the reception area, dressed up to the nines in fancy felt ornaments. Festive music hums in the background.

Carlos, one of the male nurses, is on the reception desk when I enter. 'I'm sorry to hear about your accident. How are you?'

'I'm OK. It's my sister I'm worried about. She had a nasty bump on the head. They're keeping her in overnight.'

Carlos is a short, stout Filipino with a broad smile and crooked teeth, who was on duty the day we brought Dad here nine days ago. V and I could no longer manage him at home. We tried, and I would've carried on, but Violet was losing patience, and I couldn't let her carry the consequences on her conscience. Carlos updates me on Dad. 'He was a little agitated this afternoon.' He hands me a pen to fill out the signing-in book.

After completing my details, I walk along the carpeted corridor, coughing at the medicinal odour, and take the stairs to room 212 on the first floor. A member of the care staff team passes me. She nods and smiles.

I pause outside the door and take a deep breath before entering.

Dad's illness has eaten away at him. He's half the man he was before his diagnosis. Sadly, the progression has been quick. Extremely quick. An unignorable pain in his back was diagnosed as a secondary tumour in one of his ribs. All they had to do was find the primary source, which they discovered in his pancreas. Within a couple of weeks, he was bedridden.

He's propped up in the hospital bed to keep him as comfortable as possible. Staff have tried to lift the mood of sadness by surrounding him with Christmas cheer – garlands of holly wrapped around the head and foot of the bed, a bright red shiny bauble hanging from the IV stand – but it only serves another dose of suffering for the grief that lies ahead.

His once full head of dark curls is now thin strands of iron-grey that don't even warrant a comb anymore. He was a handsome man when he was younger. I've seen the photos in one of the family albums Mum used to keep updated.

I swallow the ball of sadness in my throat at seeing the once strong, healthy man who I adore and have always looked up to. I know he hasn't always been around for us, leaving V and I to care for Mum while he went off working. But he was only doing his job, striving to keep a roof over our heads, food on the table, and the medical help Mum needed to keep her comfortable. It's hard to believe the ghost of the woman we once knew is going to outlive Dad. He's always been so strong. I can't remember him even having a cold. But this damn indiscriminating disease can catch even the fittest of us.

A nurse is changing his IV bag. 'Did you speak to the doctor?'

I shake my head.

She points to the bag of clear liquid on the stand attached to the bed frame. 'We're giving your father extra fluids.'

Dad coughs as if he hasn't got the energy to open his eyes but wants to tell me he knows I'm here.

'He had a CT scan this afternoon.'

I know what's coming. I've seen it before at work. The chest pain Dad has complained of that has accompanied the dry cough that's worsened each time I've visited this week. 'He's got pneumonia, hasn't he?'

She nods, her lips forming a sympathetic smile.

Dad opens his eyes and mumbles through shallow and weak breaths. His eyes droop until they finally close again.

I place my bag on the high-backed chair that I've spent many hours occupying these past nine days. Approaching his side, I take his hand. It was once strong and fleshy but is now frail and bony and cold to the touch. You don't need to be in the care profession to know he hasn't got long left with us. 'We'll get you better, Dad.' I can't believe I've just said that. Honesty is the best policy. My job has taught me that.

The nurse removes her latex gloves and apron and chucks them in the bin. 'I'll leave you alone for a while.' She repositions the control panel nearer to Dad's hand. 'Buzz me if you need me.'

As soon as she leaves, Dad opens his eyes again. They

look so large in his gaunt face that was once so strong and sure. 'I need...' He pauses to take another shallow breath. 'To talk to you.'

'Don't, Dad.' I gently squeeze his hand. 'Save your energy for getting better.' He's slowly slipping away. The thought of him finally leaving us is wholly daunting.

He faintly shakes his head. 'Let's not kid ourselves.' His voice is gravelly, as rough as sandpaper.

'Stop it.' I can't bear it.

'I've been a fool.' His words slip out between raspy breaths. 'I need you to do something for me, Rose.'

'I'll do anything for you, Dad. Anything. You know that. Just tell me what.'

'Don't...' A nasty cough quells his words. He struggles to continue.

I should tell him to rest. We can talk later. But he's left me curious. 'Don't what, Dad?'

He closes his eyes, concentrating on his breaths. 'I should've done it myself.'

'Done what?'

'Don't tell anyone.'

'Tell anyone what?'

'Stupid fool.' His weary eyes half open. 'In the eaves... cupboard... upstairs.'

He's never looked at me like this before. It's unnerving. 'You're scaring me, Dad.'

'Never tell Violet.'

'What is it?'

'Gun. Get rid of it.'

7

VIOLET

Auntie Audrey is keen to hear what's happened when Violet arrives home from the hospital. Their auntie is a good woman. Violet doesn't know what they would've done without her all these years. 'I didn't expect you back.'

She's a full-figured woman, blessed with a generous volume of shoulder-length hair styled with layers and a wispy fringe that she dyes a bright silver. Everything about her is large, from her voluptuous chest to her big heart and the bold beaded necklaces she always wears with her silver cross. A devout Christian, she throws her heart and soul into the church, when she isn't helping her nieces to look after their mum.

'Rose called to say they were keeping you in for the night,' Auntie Audrey says.

'They didn't need to.' Violet doesn't tell her auntie that she discharged herself. In fact, despite the fondness she has for her auntie, she tells her little about herself. Because, despite all the goodness in her, Auntie Audrey is a busybody trapped on a hamster wheel of gossip. Mostly, it's a blessing, listening to her rattle on about the trials and tribulations of every other soul in their small town. It grants Violet respite from the feeling that she's not as odd as others think she is. But the few clients she's managed to retain in town don't need to know her business.

'I put your mum to bed about an hour ago,' Auntie Audrey says. 'She was very tired tonight. I'll make you a quick cup of tea, then I need to be off. I'm bushed. Unless you want me to stay with you, of course.'

Her pendulum hips sway towards the kettle. She flicks the switch and walks to the table. 'Here, I bought you a poinsettia. Look after it and it should last through the festive period.' Auntie Audrey loves this time of year.

Not Violet. If she had her way, Christmas would be cancelled. Permanently.

Violet doesn't have time for tea. She's too excited for the important work to start, despite not feeling quite with it. Besides, Auntie Audrey would have gleaned everything from Rose when they spoke earlier. Violet glances at the old clock on the wall above the sink that has half the minute hand missing, so it's difficult to tell the time at certain points in the day. It's now half-past nine. 'Hold the tea, Auntie,' she says. 'I'll say goodnight to Mum and then go straight to bed. It's been a long day. You go home now. I'll be fine.'

'Are you sure? I don't feel comfortable leaving you.' Auntie Audrey gives her that look. The one that says she can read her innermost thoughts. But she can't. There's no way she could possibly know what's going on in Violet's head right now. Nobody could.

Violet placates her with the bare minimum of today's events, omitting the glee that's overcome her, and the truth she wouldn't dare to admit that she's glad that accident happened today. It's given her a new lease of life.

Auntie Audrey shakes her head. Her candy cane earrings jangle. 'Have they not given you any tablets? Nothing?'

'I need to rest. I'll be fine. Just go.'

'Well, if you're sure.' But getting rid of Auntie Audrey is never quite that easy. She always has something else to say. 'Violet, can I be cheeky and ask if you'd be kind enough to donate one of your lovely paintings to the church's Christmas auction? It's for the roof appeal.'

Violet shrugs. 'I'll think about it.' Auntie Audrey has been trying for years to get her to do more with her artwork, but Auntie Audrey is the type of person who sees everything through rose-tinted glasses, especially Violet's paintings. They're not good enough for others outside their family to view.

Auntie Audrey picks up her large leather shopper and digs about for her car keys. 'I'll stop by in the morning, as usual. Toodles.'

When the front door bangs shut, Violet heads to Mum's bedroom at the back of the house. It used to be the dining room, before Mum was shot. Back then, it was Violet's favourite room in this house. Violet's happiest memories are of their little family sitting at the old dining table. It had to be thrown out when Mum finally came home from hospital after the professionals said there was nothing more they could do for her. Time, they said. She just needed time to come to terms with what had happened to her – three broken ribs, legs that would never walk again, and the PTSD that's left her non-verbal and barely cognisant. Not to mention the bullet that took Violet's unborn sister's life.

They were never told that fifteen years later, Mum would still be needing time. The neuropsychiatrist said he had never seen a case quite like it.

They didn't sit down to dinner in this room every day back then. Only on the weekends that Dad wasn't working. That's when Mum was at her happiest. She'd dress that old table as if she were expecting royalty and serve up a dinner fit for the Queen.

Violet steps over to the bed. Mum's asleep, as is the norm at this time. Thankfully, her routine is like clockwork. At least there is some certainty about her care. But that doesn't stop Violet from checking on her every night before she heads upstairs to bed and again before she goes to sleep. She likes to observe the rise and fall of the covers because her mother's ashen face always looks dead to her.

She bends over and strokes her mother's head, as she always does last thing at night. A sharp ache in her shoulder makes her wince. She's battered and bruised, and random bouts of dizziness blur her vision, but the edge of elation is keeping her going. 'Mum,' she whispers. 'I've found him!'

She looks up to the ceiling. 'Did you hear that, Bean? I've found him.'

She kisses her mother's forehead and whispers, 'I love you.'

She returns to the kitchen and takes a packet of cigarettes from her handbag. No alcohol, the nurse told her before she left the hospital. No alcohol and no drugs. But one cigarette can't hurt. It's her nightly ritual after she's put Mum to bed. It keeps her off the funny pills.

She opens the back door to a blast of cold air. A blanket of snow covers the long lawn. Mum used to love this garden, out here at every opportunity. Even when she was pregnant, she'd be on her hands and knees tinkering with the containers and beds. She adored flowers, even named her daughters after them. And she was always filling vases with whatever was growing. But not even the spring blooms can now find a glimmer of light in her vacant eyes.

The cold of the stone step bites Violet's bum. She shivers and sparks up, taking a deep drag of the cigarette. The warmth hits her lungs, a brief distraction from the chill in her bones. She smokes the cigarette with rapid, sharp sucks. The anticipation is almost too much to bear.

William Watson.

It's time to lift the floorboards.

8

VIOLET

Violet climbs the two flights of stairs to her bedroom on the third floor of the house. The loft conversion that her parents were building when her mum was shot has never been properly finished. Her dad said his money was all wrapped up in taking care of her mum and adapting the downstairs to accommodate her requirements. But that wasn't entirely true.

With Mum no longer able to climb the stairs, the bedroom and bathroom her parents were having built up here became redundant. Dad remained in their bedroom on the middle floor. The nursery Mum had decorated ready for Bean's arrival was turned into a study. Rose stayed in the bedroom Violet and she shared, and Violet grabbed the chance for some privacy and bagged the bedroom up here. The shell that was intended as a bathroom turned into a dumping ground.

She loves it up here. It's her safe space. The place where

she can escape the madness of the world. For a long time, she made do with the greyness of the plastered walls, but at some point in her teens, she painted them black. It was just before she began therapy. Not for her, but for Rose. She wouldn't commit to it at first, but as Rose piled on the pressure in the fear that she would do something stupid one day, Violet succumbed to sitting in front of a counsellor once a week for a year. Not that it did any good. The bedlam that has lived in her head since that horrific Christmas Eve has refused to ever move out.

She enters her bedroom. There's no time to waste. She has to get it in order in here again. She needs to recreate the work she carried out years ago but lost heart with as the days turned to weeks and months and years without progress. Not that she ever gave up. She couldn't. She promised Mum and Bean she never would. No. It was more the exasperation from the unanswered questions and blank spaces between the evidence she'd collected that she couldn't bear to look at anymore.

Blank spaces she can now begin to fill.

She ties her hair that hangs long and straight to her waist into a ponytail and puts on some music. The delight of a piano concerto brings calmness. Mum used to play the piano all the time for them when Rose and she were kids. She tried to teach Violet to play at some point. But Violet could never match the way Mum's fingers glided so effortlessly over the keys, enchanting them with her immense talent. Dad wanted to sell the piano at some point, but Violet kicked up such a stink, he finally backed down.

The monitor on her bedside table alerts her to Mum coughing. She'll go and check on her again when she's finished here. She and Rose both have monitors by their beds that are connected to one in Mum's room and each night, they take turns to have them switched on so they can hear her if she needs them. Dad bought them after he stopped sleeping on the sofa bed in Mum's room, a few months after she was shot, when he resumed working away again.

Discomfort accompanies every bend and stretch as Violet takes out the crowbar from the bottom of her wardrobe and pulls the bed out from against the wall. The pain in her shoulder smarts. A muscle she must've pulled during the accident. It's making her feel sick, but determination drives her forward. With the bed far enough away from the wall, using the crowbar, she lifts the two floorboards three in from the wall.

She leans the boards against the bed and reaches inside the gap. A musky odour mixed with the earthy smell of leather wafts into the air. Her hand comes across the flannel bag. She smiles, moves it aside and reaches for the large, leather-bound scrapbook she bought from Etsy when Rose and the counsellor persuaded her it was time to bury the memories that haunted her day in and day out. It cost a fortune, but it was worth a try if it could help rid her head of the demons that had possessed her for so long. Rose thought she threw out all the scraps she'd collected over the years, but not even her sister could persuade her to go that far.

She perches on the edge of the bed and opens the scrapbook. The intense feeling of injustice she's become accustomed to rushes through her. She approaches the wall at the rear of the room and randomly, without care, peels off the pictures she has drawn over the years and tosses them on her bed. Some are pastels, others charcoal, her favourite medium. She likes how it gives a dark, intense vibe to her work that marries so well with the thoughts and images that possess her mind. Ghouls and witches, ghastly effigies of pain and anger, smudged into intricate patterns seen by no other eye.

Her breaths are erratic as she works, taking each piece of evidence from the scrapbook and reconstructing it on the wall just like it once was. Before she knows it, she's revived the past – beginning the night her mother, as they knew her, and her unborn baby sister were taken – and bringing it back to life on her bedroom wall that now resembles a police incident board.

DCI White promised they'd never stop looking for the man who stole so much from her family. And she's not talking about the physical possessions – the jewellery and the money. She doesn't care about the material stuff. She's talking about her mother and her and Rose's childhoods and her darling baby sister who she loved to the moon and back, even though she'd never met her.

But DCI White failed them all.

So Violet had no choice but to take over.

Cuttings from newspapers, printouts from the internet, photos and timelines, along with maps and a list of suspects the police systematically discarded from their investigation that dried up after five months, cover the wall in an organised mess only her head can understand.

She needs to order them so her staff can understand her when she presents this case to them.

Once satisfied, she grabs a ruler and a marker pen from her desk drawer and draws a timeline, beginning on *24th December, 2009*. She addresses the police officers blurring in front of her. It's sad the paths trauma can lead you down. 'Now, everyone, listen up.'

The officers shuffle in their seats.

'Exciting times.' Violet smiles – a beam as wide as the

wall behind her. 'We've had some new evidence come in. Finally, we have a break.' She places one end of the ruler beside a photo of her mum on the afternoon before she was shot. Her mum is in the kitchen holding two bun tins of mince pies fresh from the oven. Her cheeks are flushed, and the kitchen light shining on the crown of her long blonde hair looks like a halo.

Mum then.

She raps the ruler against the photo of her mother. 'For those new to this case, this is Melanie Sapphire. She was shot in her home on Christmas Eve, 2009.' She taps another photo of a woman sitting in a wheelchair, her hair bedraggled and her soulless eyes staring into the ether. 'And this is Melanie, a year later.' Violet points the ruler to a third photo of her in which her mother looks little different to the second one.

Mum now.

'We believe Melanie got out of bed that night because her nine-year-old daughter, Violet, had gone downstairs to use the toilet.' She clears her throat. 'Her other daughter, six-year-old Rose, was asleep in bed at the time. And Melanie's husband had got up because he heard his wife get out of bed.'

She removes the lid from the marker pen, and at the end of the timeline, she writes: 24th December, 2024. 'That's two weeks away, team. Fifteen years to the day, Melanie Sapphire was shot in her own home. A cruel act of violence that Violet, the poor, frightened child, witnessed from behind the living room door.'

An officer raises his hand.

'Yes,' Violet says, pointing the ruler in his direction.

'What's the new evidence that's come to light?' He has an Irish accent, a musical lilt from the Southwest.

Violet nods. 'Good question. We have a name. William Watson. We don't have a photo yet, but it's on its way.'

The officers before her sway unnaturally in and out of focus. 'And during the next two weeks, we're going to seek him out and make his life hell.'

She has fourteen days to exact her revenge.

9

ROSE

During the Uber ride home, I repeat Dad's unwanted revelation in my head.

My father keeps a gun in our house.

And he wants me to get rid of it.

I consider calling Jamie, but I'm reluctant to divulge the shocking news that my father has a gun stored in our house. I trust him implicitly, but I've only known him for six months, and he's heard enough already about my disturbed family life.

No. I must face this head-on while Violet spends the night in hospital. I'll find this gun he's talking about and take it to the police station.

But something tells me that wasn't Dad's intention.

I google what to do if you find a gun in a dead relative's house. I need to inform the police immediately. It's against the law to move a gun without being instructed to. I think back to when Mum got shot. I've never told V or my father this. Or anyone, in fact. But vague recollections of that night occasionally escape into my consciousness. I don't remember the incident as one clean scene. It's never a movie playing in order from beginning to end. Rather it comes in flashes, like snippets of a nightmare you can't fully remember. The screaming and yelling. An ambulance arriving. The smell of pine. Me sitting, out of view, at the top of the stairs as people dressed in green frantically tried to save my mother's life. It's all a blur.

I tried in vain to extract more out of Dad. Is the gun his? How did it get there? But it was as if he'd exhausted his energy on what he'd already told me. All he could add was that it was in a shoebox inside a blue plastic box and reiterate that I was to get rid of the unwanted weapon, and I was never to tell a soul.

I open the front door with a stomach full of unease. I pause. Mum's coat is slung over the rack at the bottom of the stairs. An old one which is as thick as a duvet that V has worn for years. I'm sure she was wearing it today. I must be confused. The doctor was insistent she stay in hospital for the night.

The house is strangely quiet. Usually, Auntie Audrey has the TV on, even when she's not watching it. She revels in all the soaps and watches them with Mum, although we don't know how much Mum takes in.

I kick off my shoes and head to the kitchen. It's in darkness. I rush to the living room. Auntie Audrey must be in there. She's not. She must've fallen asleep in Mum's bedroom. But when I look, the sofa bed that V and I take it in turns to sleep on when Mum's poorly remains empty.

Mum coughs. I find the remote control for her bed and

raise the head an inch. She coughs again and turns her head. I wait for her to settle and dig my phone out of my pocket. My call to Auntie Audrey goes to her voicemail. Something's not right. A message from Auntie Audrey awaits me. V arrived back and insisted she go home.

Frustrated, I leave Mum sleeping and head up the two flights of stairs to V's bedroom. This has scuppered my plans. I wanted to hunt for that gun tonight while she was in hospital. Get the whole thing over and done with. The junk room, with the large cupboard in the eaves, where Dad said I'd find the gun, is next to her bedroom. She'll hear me if I start messing around in there.

I rarely come up here. There's something creepy about the junk room that was meant to be a spacious bathroom for Mum and Dad that never got started, let alone finished. I stick my head around the door. The eerie cobwebs draped from corner to corner don't help. The walls remain bare plaster, with swishes of concealer covering the cracks. Numerous boxes and various accumulated pieces of junk that should have been discarded when last used – a tent, a chair with a broken leg, an old TV with an aerial sticking out the top – now block the entrance to the cupboard that I need to access.

I knock on V's door. It annoys her on the few occasions I enter without doing so. Not that I especially like venturing inside. Despite her incredible artistic talent, her work that covers the walls is macabre. If she could only turn herself to more colourful happy paintings like Mum used to paint, I'm sure it would help lift her spirit.

There's no answer. I pull the handle. It's locked. I panic. Something's happened to her. It's the concussion from the accident. I hate it when she locks the door. She used to do it all the time. Back when she was obsessed with finding the intruder who shot our mother and changed our lives forever. She never knew I knew this, but I caught her one day. I'd woken in the middle of the night and heard voices from her room that's directly above mine. People were talking normally, but one was louder. It sounded like my sister, but I couldn't be sure. It didn't make sense. She never invited people home. Even as a kid, she was a loner. She never had any friends of her own; she just hung out in the shadows of mine.

I remember getting out of bed that night and creeping upstairs, perplexed. It was her talking the loudest, but there was an Irish lilt to her voice as if she was putting on an act. Her bedroom door was ajar, which was an oddity all in itself. Violet always shut that door, and usually locked it. I peered through the gap in the door. She was standing at the far end, dressed in a police uniform from our childhood dressing-up box. The body still fitted her skinny frame, but the sleeves now stopped in the middle of her forearms. She held a ruler, pointing it at a large photo of Mum stuck on her bedroom wall and informing her pretend audience in a raised Irish accent about the events that took place at 125 Ambley Avenue on Christmas Eve December 2009.

I watched, dumbfounded, as she moved her ruler up and down the timeline she'd constructed, summarising the list of suspects, all of whom had alibis for the night in question. After she'd finished her spiel, she pointed the ruler at her imaginary audience and said, 'Any questions?'

She changed her accent to a Scottish one for her audience member, whom she later addressed as DC Naylor. 'Have you spoken to the family members?'

And so it continued until the questions dried up, and V burst into tears. It saddened me, hurt my heart, as she rarely cried. It was as if she'd used her lifetime quota of tears after Mum was shot. I wanted to go into the room. But I knew my sister. The shame of being found like that would've been too much. So I left her and snuck back to bed, never breathing a word of what I'd witnessed that night.

I can't think why she would've started all that up again.

I knock again, harder, calling her name, but there's still no answer. The fear of finding her passed out on her bedroom floor consumes me. She could be dead. A scene of police and ambulances and undertakers arriving to take away her body plays out in my overwrought mind. I will myself to calm down. I'm overthinking things again.

I knock harder and give the door a gentle kick. 'Violet.'

'What're you doing?' comes my sister's voice.

'Open up,' I say.

'I'm getting undressed.'

'I've been knocking.'

'I've had my headphones on.'

'Why did you come home? You were meant to stay in for the night.'

'Go back downstairs. I'll be down in a minute.'

I stand, staring at the door, frustrated that it's locked. It's annoying she's got a lock at all. She fitted it years ago, saying it made her feel safer at night. But it was because she didn't want me to see what she'd done to her bedroom wall.

There's no point in arguing with her. My sister is as stubborn as a stain when she wants to be. I return to my bedroom and get ready for bed. This has been a day from hell.

Violet appears at my bedroom door as I'm putting on my bathrobe. 'Why did you leave the hospital?' I ask. 'They told you to stay in for the night. They don't keep people in for nothing these days. You could have concussion.'

'I'm fine. Did you get any details about the driver?'

'What?'

The muscles in her neck tense up as she clenches her jaw. 'The guy who drove into you. William Watson. I'll need to dig out the details of Dad's insurance company in the morning and give them a call.'

It's an odd request at this time of night. And she hasn't even asked how Dad is. I delve into my bag. 'Dad wasn't great.'

She presses the heels of her palms into her eyes.

'V, did you hear me?'

She drops her hands and stares at me. 'Sorry?' Her face is so pale.

'I said Dad wasn't great.'

She nods, her expression blank.

'Are you feeling OK? Perhaps you should go back to the hospital.'

'Stop fussing. I'm absolutely fine.'

I fish around in my bag and hand over two pieces of paper. One with the details of the driver of the car that ploughed into us. And another on which Jamie has scribbled details that he gleaned from the police officers he spoke to at the hospital. 'Here you go.'

'The insurance company will provide a rental car,' she says.

'Do we need one?' I ask.

'Yes,' V replies. 'You can drive my car, and I'll use the rental. Then we both have cars.' She almost snatches the piece of paper as if she's eager to get hold of it. She glances at it. 'William Watson of number 12 the Ridgeway, Radstone.'

'You sound as if you know him.'

She shrugs. 'Never heard the name in my life until today.'

10

VIOLET

William Watson!

The name is now ingrained in her head.

Violet returns to her bedroom and locks the door behind her. She hasn't locked it for a while. She hasn't needed to. Everything has been stored away. But the time has come for her to turn that key every time she's in here, and every time she leaves. She stares at her bedroom wall. It's refreshing having all the evidence out on show again.

She switches on her computer. It's an ancient model she inherited from her father when he upgraded to a laptop. While waiting for it to load, grinding and whirring like the family's old coffee machine, she unfolds the piece of paper Rose gave her. Her heart races.

William Watson. The man she's been looking for all these years.

It doesn't make sense. How can Rose have driven into the

man who shot their mum all those years ago? It's too much of a coincidence that he was on that roundabout at the same time as them. But coincidences happen. And she knows it's him. She doesn't remember his face. She never saw it. But there was no mistaking the unique eagle tattoo enwrapping his wrist. The one she'd mistaken for a bracelet in the darkness that night he shot her mother. It was an easy error for a nine-year-old to make. The tiny ornate etchings, creating the intricate bodies of the line of birds of prey, are exquisite.

The computer beeps, and the screen lights up. Violet clicks on Google and types *Radstone* into the search bar. She squints at the screen. It's a small town about twenty-five minutes away. So what was William Watson doing here in Stanwell today? She finds the house on Google Earth and zooms in. It's large and detached. He's got money, this guy. She grits her teeth. Wealth that came from what he stole from her parents.

She replaces the address in the search bar with *William Watson*. She finds him in a heartbeat. There he is: a thirty-one-year-old owner of a scaffolding company. She performs a quick calculation. That made him sixteen when he burgled this house and shot her mother. She shakes her head. Sixteen years old. He was so young, he must've still been at school. He must've been working for someone. The taste of bile burns the back of her throat. It's hard to imagine. But it's not unheard of for such young people to be involved in serious crimes, especially these days. The daily news she reads online is littered with muggings and stabbings and acts of arson, all carried out by minors.

Disturbed kids from dysfunctional families.

Violet snorts. A bit like her.

She follows the link to William Watson's Facebook page.

His profile picture shows him holding hands with a woman as they stroll through a park. A small kid straddles his shoulders. The woman is pretty. She squints, bringing her face closer to the screen. Blue-eyed, blonde-haired, rosy-cheeked pretty. Just like Mum used to be. Not only does her memory tell her so, but also all the photos that line Mum's piano in the living room.

She rolls her fingers over the computer mouse, scrolling through his posts. Apart from the occasional photo of him and his wife, Tiffany, and their son, Leo, he mainly uses his page for business purposes. Unless you need scaffolding, there's little of interest. But Violet can't help returning to the personal photos, pausing to stare at the happy family.

It's not fair.

He doesn't deserve to be happy.

She stares at his profile picture. 'William Watson! How could you have lived with yourself all these years?'

She prints off a copy of the Facebook header, hoping Rose can't hear the printer spring into action. While waiting, she finds a pair of scissors from the drawer. When the printer spits out the piece of paper, she cuts out the picture of William Watson and sticks it to the timeline on the wall, next to today's date.

Standing back, she considers her options.

She could go to the police. Turn him in. But the police have been useless all these years. Utterly useless. She simply doesn't trust them with the new evidence.

No. She has better plans for William Watson.

Plans that she's been fantasising about all these years.

And with the fifteen-year anniversary fast approaching, the timing is just perfect.

11

ROSE

I drift in and out of bouts of disturbed sleep plagued by nightmares. In one, V found Dad's gun before me. She used it. But the face of the person she shot remained hidden in the shadows of our house. I woke up in a sweat, panicking. For a split second, I thought it was real. She'd actually got hold of Dad's gun. God forbid. But it was only the sick nightmare playing tricks with my mind. She doesn't even know the gun is there.

I'm exhausted when Jamie picks me up to take me to work.

'You look like crap,' he says as I climb into the car.

'How kind of you to say so.' He's the only person who could make me laugh with the way I'm feeling. My stomach won't stop turning. I can't believe what Dad has asked me to do.

'How's your dad?' he asks.

'Not good.' My voice breaks. 'I don't think he's going to make it to see Christmas.'

'I'm sorry, hun.' He reaches behind and plucks a green and white paper bag from the back seat. 'Here you go. This'll cheer you up.' He opens the bag. 'You said yesterday that you haven't had a mince pie this year. That's sacrilege. So, I bought us one each. They were fresh out of the oven.'

'It's a bit early for me.'

'Nonsense.' He waves the contents under my nose. 'Eat.'

I take a bite. The buttery pastry crumbles and melts in my mouth.

He shoves the other pie between his lips whole and pulls onto the road. After swallowing his mouthful, he says, 'You should've taken the day off.'

I stare at the garish bauble hanging from the rear-view mirror. 'I'd feel too guilty.' It will increase the heavy load staff are already carrying on their shoulders. Besides, I love my job. And, although it saddens me to admit, I'd rather be at work than at home. Especially during the festive season. It's the only opportunity I get to properly celebrate Christmas. 'You know what it's like when someone's off sick.'

'Your soul is purer than the driven snow, Rose Sapphire.'

'What a cliché! And by the way, it's brown horrible slush, look at it.'

He laughs. 'How are you feeling after yesterday?'

I touch the cut on my face. The only visible evidence of the accident. It's sore, but it'll heal. 'Apart from not wanting to drive ever again, I've come out pretty unscathed.'

'You need to get driving again straight away. Get back on the horse and all that.'

I pull down the sun visor and peer at myself in the mirror. He's right. I don't look good at all.

He turns into Chase Hill, the nursing home where I've worked since leaving school. My nursing assistant role is varied. No two days are ever the same. Jamie is the activities supervisor. He pumps the feel-good factor into the place, organising daily events from wheelchair yoga to outings to the cinema or local places of interest to keep the residents active and entertained. He's like the resident Santa. Everyone loves him, and he's particularly good with the younger people, many of whom have horrible diseases and disabilities that limit their lives.

Chase Hill is vibrant with festive cheer, courtesy of Jamie, who is a self-confessed Christmas junkie. His enthusiasm for this time of year is infectious. If it weren't for Dad's deteriorating health, this would be the best Christmas I can ever remember. Usually, it's a pretty miserable affair. On Christmas Eve, V turns inwards, as if the day triggers unwanted memories she can't fight, and Mum shuts down, refusing to eat, her way of showing awareness that another year has passed since that catastrophic night. She refuses to get out of bed, planking when we try to get her up. So for two days she stays there with me trying to prevent her developing bed sores between cooking the Christmas meals. Dad, when he's there, and V aren't much help. Christmas reminds them too much of what happened to Mum, as well, and they've never been able to fully celebrate since the events of that horrific night. Often, Dad has worked away. And the most I can get out of Violet is to sit on the sofa in Mum's room with me and watch a festive movie.

I love working here. Before Dad fell ill, I even put my name down for an early morning shift on Christmas Day. Only for a couple of hours, as Auntie Audrey is spending

Christmas Day with us this year as it's the first year without my uncle.

A large artificial tree dominates the reception area, adorned with all the frills and fancies of Christmas: tinsel and baubles, lights and bows, and a giant fairy towering over the grand affair. But the thought of what my father has asked me to do mars the festive cheer.

Jamie breaks into song at various intervals. His voice echoes up and down the hallways as I commence the morning drugs round with one of the nurses. His singing is like a happy radio station constantly playing, but not even this soulful sound can lift my spirits today. My mind is too occupied with how I'm going to find this gun with V being around. I'll have to do it when she's at work one evening.

I can't bring myself to even think what it could have been used for. I push the fleeting unimaginable thought of it playing a part in my mother's demise to the back of my mind. I can't torture myself in that way.

Just before lunch, the staff manager calls me into her office. She's an imposing Greek woman, built like a nuclear bunker. But inside, she's as soft as sand. 'I heard about your accident yesterday and about your father.'

Thanks, Jamie.

'How is he?' she asks.

I summarise my father's condition, trying to fight the tears. The lack of sleep has heightened my emotions.

'If you need to take time off, then just let me know.'

'That's kind of you.'

'In fact, finish early today. You look exhausted. I'll arrange for one of the evening shift workers to come in earlier. Go and spend time with your family.'

'I'm not sure I'm going to be able to work on Christmas Day now.'

'I'll bear that in mind when I'm doing the rotas.' She ushers me out of her office with a flick of her hand. 'I mean it. Go home.'

I can't tell her how much the thought of going home depresses me even more.

12

_____

VIOLET

The dull ache in her neck ever present since the accident has spread to the right side of Violet's head, and spells of dizziness accompany intermittent episodes of nausea. She's finding it hard to concentrate. Perhaps she should've stayed the night in hospital. But there's no way she could have left Mum.

She sits in her car, freezing. The heater is broken, and she hasn't had the money to have it fixed. She calls Cressida, whose four-storey terraced house on the opposite side of town she cleans once a week. 'I'm sorry. I can't come in today.'

She left school at sixteen. It wasn't technically allowed, but shortly after her fourteenth birthday, she started skipping school, and everyone slowly gave up on her. All she wanted was to be at home with Mum. But by mutual agreement with Dad, if she at least got a part-time job, he would stop trying to force her to go to school. So she started working for Shiny

Surfaces, cleaning in the local primary school between five p.m. and seven p.m. each day, and has never left. There's something calming about the monotony of vacuuming, mopping, and dusting, where she can lose herself in her own little world.

Word soon spread that she was good at what she did, and Auntie Audrey found her another cleaning job one morning a week for a lady from her church. The private clients grew until every weekday morning was full. For all her faults, Violet Sapphire is reliable and is told her attention to detail is admirable.

'What's wrong?' Cressida asks in her well-spoken voice.

'I was in a car accident yesterday. And my father's sick.' She explains the situation. 'I don't think I'll be back before Christmas.'

She should be used to lying by now. Her life is a lie. But despite this, she doesn't like letting people down. It's something her father instilled in her. Not because he lectured her on always acting with morality, but because he taught her how it feels when someone you rely on badly disappoints you.

'An accident! Are you OK?'

'Yes. I just hit my head. It's not too bad. But I need to be with my father.'

'It can't be helped, dear,' Cressida says. 'Please keep me posted.'

Violet delivers the same message to her boss, Pete, at Shiny Surfaces. He's understanding and tells her to stay in touch.

She finds Google Maps on her phone. Her head pounds. She should probably get it checked out. That's what the nurse said, if she recalls correctly. She wasn't really listening. She just wanted to get home when the woman was banging on about avoiding heavy machinery and getting plenty of rest. Rest. That's the last thing on Violet's agenda.

She's already mapped out the twenty-five-minute journey to Radstone. She still can't believe that the man responsible for her family's horrendous fate lives less than half an hour away. She tunes into Classic FM and backs out of the driveway. There's something cathartic about listening to classical music while plotting her retribution. Even if the channel does play intermittent Christmas-themed music.

Will Watson is going to pay.

Driving conditions are poor. The snow has thawed, leaving a slushy mess on the roads. But more is due soon. She yawns. She stayed up late last night, into the early hours, googling the hell out of William Watson – Will, he calls himself – but found little other than links to his business, so she concentrated on his Facebook page, staring at the photos of him and his family as she made her plans.

Plans for her family's revenge.

Someone has to do it. Mum can't. Neither can Dad, now. And Rose... well, her little sister is just too nice.

She arrives at the Ridgeway a little after ten a.m. and parks alongside a line of trees. The row of houses on this section of the road are semi-detached, double-fronted Edwardian dwellings with evergreen bushes separating the sizeable driveways. She glares at number 12. The windows all have those expensive, shiny shutters, and she can just about make out the fancy Christmas wreath on the elaborate front door that is fringed with two narrow vertical stained-glass windows.

A shiny black SUV is parked in the driveway. It must be his wife's car. Or it could be a rental car. Will's car would have been taken to a garage to be fixed. Dad's car is unrepairable, which doesn't surprise her. When she spoke to the insurance company this morning, they told her they are arranging a rental car.

She's mesmerised. For so long, she's fantasised about being in this position – sitting outside the house of the man who ruined her life. Night after night, she's lain in bed, studying the shadows cast over the ceiling, and at some point, the newspaper clippings and photos of Mum's case, wondering if she was kidding herself that it would ever happen. But it has. And it feels better than she ever imagined. The power she now holds is like a knife with a newly sharp-ened blade.

After about fifteen minutes, she restarts the engine and drives to the end of the road, turns the corner and heads to the road that the houses back onto. It's more of a dirt track than a road and overlooks a golf course that leads to a forest area.

She counts the houses and calculates which house is number twelve. It has a smaller back garden than she thought it would. That's because the house has been extended. But then, with a forest on your doorstep, who needs a big back garden? Her hands grip the steering wheel tighter and tighter until they hurt. Will Watson really has done well for himself.

She parks the car farther up the road and gets out, opens the boot, and puts on the old hooded puffa coat that used to be Mum's. She hasn't had it cleaned since her mother last wore it when Violet took her to a hospital appointment earlier in the year, and it still smells of her Britney Spears perfume. From the pocket, she takes out her hat, a plain black knitted beanie, and puts it on, tucking her long locks down the back of the coat.

She creeps along the back of the houses, slowing her pace as she approaches the garden of number 12. She's tingling inside as if she's got pins and needles in her belly. The gardens all have picket fences or no fence at all. It's not great for security, but it's pretty secluded around here and the house owners get the beautiful view that stretches beyond the golf course to the fields and forest beyond.

A small trampoline and a kiddies' swing dominate the garden, along with a hot tub and one of those luxury garden sofas that is covered with waterproof sheeting. Violet clenches her jaw. Will Watson really has made it big.

The extended part of the house provides a large kitchen/breakfast room with bifold doors stretching along the back, which afford stunning views from the dining table.

Will's wife, Tiffany, is flitting around the room in a designer tracksuit – one of those with the brand scribed across the butt – while Leo plays by the bifold doors. A vast array of multi-coloured fairy lights, which must have taken an age to put up, extend from the kitchen to the breakfast area and across to the impressive Christmas tree in the corner. Next to the tree is a wood-burning stove.

It looks like a scene from *Home Alone*.

Violet's heart skips a beat. She gasps out loud.

She never gleaned this from the photos on Will's Facebook page. But there's no mistaking it.

Tiffany's belly is swollen.

The same as Mum's was on the night she was shot.

It changes everything.

13

ROSE

Dad's condition has deteriorated. I see it in the greyness of his face. 'The doctor will come and speak to you soon,' the nurse looking after him says when she has briefed me on the night he had.

I sit by his bedside and take his hand. Dark veins protrude through the paper-thin skin. The smell of impending death hangs in the air: a sweet, dank smell I'm well acquainted with, but not from a family member. 'Can you hear me, Dad?' I gently squeeze his hand.

He grunts.

'V was there when I got home last night, so I couldn't look for this thing you asked me to.' I can't bring myself to say the word. It seems surreal sitting here talking about a weapon with my father. Our conversations usually centre around football or the films we watch together. I should probably use the past tense here – watched together –

because if I think back, it's been a long time since we did that.

He grunts again.

'Dad, listen. I looked it up. I can't take the... this thing... to a police station. I'd get into trouble. I need to call the police and get them to come and remove it.'

'No.' His eyes open. They're now well sunken into his face. 'Throw...' He stops to take a breath. 'In river.'

'What's the story behind it, Dad?' My voice trembles. 'I have to ask you. Was it the gun that was used to shoot Mum?'

He looks at me in horror. If it's the last look he ever gives me, I'll never be able to forgive myself. 'Just do... do as I say.'

Auntie Audrey is sitting with Mum watching TV when I get home. 'Where's V?' I ask. 'She should've been home by lunchtime.'

'She asked me to stay for a couple of hours longer. I didn't have anything on until later, so I didn't mind.'

'Where's she gone?' My sister never goes anywhere other than to work.

'She never said.' Auntie Audrey stands. 'Come into the kitchen for a minute.' I follow her. 'Have you spoken to V about Abbeyfields?' she asks.

I let out a low groan. 'I broached the subject just before the accident. But she shut me down.'

'But it's like it was meant for your mum. And they've got a place. They don't come up often. We'll lose it if we don't secure it. She could move in after Christmas.'

I shake my head. 'I can't see V ever agreeing to it.'

'Well, she needs to. We have to be realistic, Rose. I'm not getting any younger, and with your father no longer around, we can't carry on like this. And you young girls have lives to lead.'

'But V doesn't see it that way. You know that. Mum is her life. She even suggested giving up work to look after her full-time.'

A look of exasperation shines across Auntie's face. 'That can't happen. She wouldn't be able to cope. Let me have a word with her.'

'Can you stay with Mum for a little while longer? I need to do something.'

'I need to get to church. It's a busy time of year.'

'I won't be long.'

She shoos me out of the room with a flick of her hand. 'Go on... go and do what you need to do.'

I phone V as I'm running up the stairs. I'm not sure she should even been driving so soon after the accident. The call goes to voicemail again. Where the hell is she? I dump my bag in my bedroom and head upstairs to the top floor.

I stand in the doorway of the junk room, staring at the mass of clutter I need to wade through to get to the cupboard in the eaves to find this gun. I don't even know where to start. At the beginning, Jamie would say. Start at the beginning.

I need to clear a path to reach the cupboard, but that's going to take time, and I don't know how much I've got. V could be back at any time.

I take a deep breath. The sooner I find this gun, the sooner I can do something about it.

14

VIOLET

Tiffany leaves the room.

Violet enters the garden, sliding alongside the hedged fence to stay out of sight. Her pulse is beating in her throat, making her feel heady. She's enjoying it. The fear and gratification mixed together for what the next thirteen days hold make for a cocktail of pleasure she didn't anticipate tasting quite so delicious.

A tall storage unit stands beside the hot tub. She slips to the side of it, where she gains a satisfying view of the illuminated kitchen/breakfast room. It's a modern and spacious room, featuring white glossy units and a massive double American-style fridge/freezer unit. Two skylights afford plenty of natural light, and a long wide table sits parallel to the bifold doors.

She stares at Leo playing with a train track assembled on a rug on the tiled floor. She doesn't have time for kids, but she has to admit he's cute, sitting playing innocently in his own little world in his baggy jeans and stripy jumper.

A truly wicked thought chips away at her dark mind. How easy would it be to take a kid?

Leo pushes a train and its cargo backwards and forwards along the blue plastic track. 'Choo-choo,' Violet whispers.

Tiffany reappears, a caramel wool wrap coat now covering her swollen belly. She talks to her son and hands him his coat. He objects. She picks him up. His little feet kick in protest. She kisses his forehead and cuddles him, calming him against her chest. She appears to be singing to him, her head bobbing from side to side as her lips move. He finally surrenders and allows her to put on his coat.

Violet grabs the side of the storage unit and takes a few deep breaths. Her heart beats loudly, pulsing in her ears as she watches the mother-and-son show.

It's sickening.

That's what this woman's husband stole from her mother, stole from them all – the life of her baby sister growing up.

Tiffany turns as if she feels her presence. Violet darts backwards, praying she hasn't been seen.

The bifold doors swish open. 'Hello?' Her voice is soft and cordial as if she's greeting a friend. 'Is someone there?'

She mustn't find her. It'll ruin Violet's plans, and all this will have been for nothing. Violet takes a few more steps backwards and slots into the space behind the storage unit, where the thorns of an overgrown blackberry bush have overcome the side of the wooden structure.

'Hello,' repeats the friendly voice. The heels of her boots clickety-clack along the patio toward the storage unit and stop.

'Who's there, Mummy?'

'The bogeyman,' Violet says, lower than a whisper, stifling a nervous chuckle.

'No one, darling.' Tiffany's boots scratch on the ground. 'Come on, let's go. We're going to be late.'

Footsteps click back to the house. The bifold doors swish and clunk. Violet waits a couple of minutes before sneaking from the back of the unit and slowly peering around the side. The kitchen now stands in darkness. Tiffany and Leo are on their way out.

Violet nimbly slips back along the hedged fence and dirt path to her car and returns to the road that the house faces onto.

Tiffany talks to Leo as she straps him into his car seat. Or, perhaps, she's still singing. It's as clear as the desire for revenge infesting Violet's soul that this woman is a good mum. Like hers once was.

Early memories of Mum come rushing back to her. As usual, they're overwhelming. Mum singing to her and Rose during their evening bath. Mum picking flowers from the garden and arranging them in a vase on the kitchen table.

The bitter resentment that inhabits Violet's core is as ingrained as the Christmas Eve her mum was shot.

Once Leo is settled, Tiffany trots to the front door, checking she's locked it. She hurries back to her car and turns and pauses, glancing up and down the road. She shakes her head, gets into the car and backs out of the driveway.

Violet is careful to tail her, remaining two cars behind. She's unsure yet of exactly how this is going to play out. But she's made a start, and she has an end game. She just needs to figure out the middle, creating as much pain and torture as possible before she gets there.

Tiffany drives to a leisure centre, parking in a mother and child bay.

But it's not a council-run leisure centre like the one in town where Auntie Audrey used to take Violet and her sister swimming when they were little. The grotty one where other people's hair stuck to your feet in the showers. No! This is one of those private facilities where the joining fee probably costs more than Violet's monthly salary.

Violet slots into a space on the other side of the car park. She removes her hat and coils her hair into a bun at the nape of her neck. No one would ever guess how long it really is. She wraps Mum's oversized duvet coat around her and hurries to tail Tiffany and her son to the large, purpose-built building.

They enter the sliding doors, pass through a turnstile and follow a sign that says *Nursery*.

This is perfect.

Violet approaches the receptionist at the front desk. 'Can I help you?' the bubbly woman asks, her girly voice squeaky and grating. She looks and sounds as if she should still be in school with her slight frame and beautiful clear complexion. The kind of skin Violet has always envied. The spots that plagued and pained her early teenage years have never gone away.

'I'm interested in joining the gym,' Violet says.

The woman hands her a leaflet and points to a website marked on the front. 'You should find everything you need there.'

Violet studies the leaflet. 'And you have childcare?'

The two dark bunches of hair protruding from the sides of the woman's head swish as she nods. 'Yes. A nursery for twelve weeks to four-year-olds. But it's popular, so you have to book.'

'I'm keen to join as soon as possible. Could I get a tour?'

Now she has the woman's interest. Violet never was a timewaster.

'Sure. I'll see if one of our membership managers is free. What kind of membership are you interested in?'

Violet shrugs.

'We have monthly programmes: gold, silver, and a more basic bronze one, or a pay-as-you-go.'

'I'm not sure yet.'

The woman picks up a telephone and dials a number. 'Can I take your name?'

'Summer,' Violet blurts out. She has always adored that name. If she ever were to have a daughter, that's what she would've called her. But she never will, so it doesn't matter that she's using it now. 'Summer Smith.' Keep it simple. Her pulse is racing. She can't believe she's here, doing this. She's absolutely buzzing.

The receptionist replaces the receiver. 'My colleague is busy at present, but he could show you around in about fifteen minutes. Do you have time to wait?'

Violet nods.

The woman points to the café at the side of the reception desk. It's a hive of activity. A couple of older guys are nursing coffees, but it's mainly packed with rosy-faced women drinking yucky-looking green drinks and mums with kids eating carrot sticks or packets of crisps.

'I'll look up your membership options online while I wait,' Violet says.

She orders a black coffee and takes a seat on the edge of the gathering. She fishes her phone out of her pocket and clicks on Google. But she doesn't go on the gym website. Instead, she clicks on Amazon, searching while she patiently waits.

Her eyes widen. She didn't realise it'd be so easy. You really can buy anything on Amazon. Dropping the item in her basket, she continues searching. She also needs a pair of binoculars for her covert operation. She can't help but smile. This is going to be so much fun. A page of binoculars pops up. She selects the cheapest and places it the basket. This is going to push her into her overdraft, but she's past caring.

There's only one thing that matters now. And that's ensuring that Will Watson pays the heavy price for what he did.

Before she knows it, a burly guy called Jay appears with biceps and pecs too big for his tight-fitting T-shirt. 'Summer Smith!' He moves his mop of floppy hair from his eyes with a sharp, well-practised flick of his head. 'What a great name.' He takes the chair opposite her. 'Now, what are you particularly interested in?'

'The childcare and the gym,' she says.

'How old's your kid?' he asks.

'Oh, it's not born yet.' She lays a hand on her belly, thankful for her mother's full-length coat. 'It's not due for another four months.'

15

VIOLET

Violet runs her hand across her belly, wondering if she's given him the correct figure. Perhaps she should've said she's got another five months to go. She doesn't know enough about these things. It's her homework for later today.

Each day, she's learning how to plot the perfect revenge. It's wholly exhilarating.

'Congratulations,' Jay says. 'Do you know what you're having?'

She shakes her head. 'No. We decided to leave it as a surprise.'

'I've got a nipper myself. He's two now. Cheeky little chap, but the best thing that ever happened to us.'

People say that a lot. Prunella, one of her clients, said it only last week of her five-year-old son, who Violet can only describe as a bloody nightmare. Messy, noisy, boisterous. She can't think of anything worse than having to take responsibility for another human being. Mum is enough.

Jay continues. 'My wife was the same as you. She wanted to keep the sex a surprise, but I had to know. Is it your first?'

She nods.

'You've got so much to look forward to.'

The guy is crazy.

The tour sounds boring. It'll only take ten minutes, he tells her. 'Let's start with the nursery. See if you like it. It's a great place. I'm not just saying this, but I'd leave my son there.'

He doesn't stop talking all the way to the nursery, which is housed in a room about the size of a squash court. It's divided into three sections according to the age of the child. Babies asleep in car seats or being rocked by a staff member occupy one section. Toddlers another, and the third larger section is for the older, lively children, who are running around like headless chickens. The noise is clamorous, grating on her raw nerves. She could never work in a place like this. Give her a pair of headphones and a hoover any day.

'You may want to take your coat off,' he says. 'It can get boiling in here.'

She wraps her arms tightly around her middle. 'I'm fine thanks.'

He gives her a funny look. He finds her strange. Most people do. They always have. 'Let's take you to the baby section,' he says. 'It's probably the best place for you to start.'

This guy possesses the gift of the gab, but she's not listening. Her focus is on Leo, the offspring of the man for whom she holds such all-consuming hate. The boy is skipping about the toddler section, hand-in-hand with another kid annoyingly singing *When Santa Got Stuck up the Chimney* but getting all the words mixed up.

She has to get out of here.

One of the staff starts talking to her. Her shoulders tense. Pressure builds in her head. She can't stand the overlapping noises – babies crying, kids screaming, the staff singing – they're deafening, intense, unbearable. Her breath quickens. She needs to escape. She turns to Jay. 'It's great. Can we carry on? I need to get to an appointment after this.'

She takes deep breaths, calming herself, as the tour continues to the gym. She can't let her anxieties stop this opportunity. She can't.

She pretends to be inquisitive, asking relevant questions, but working out in front of others in a sweaty, smelly environment has never appealed to her. It's not that she's not interested in exercising, far from it. She exercises daily. Obsessively, her father says. But in the confines of her bedroom where she completes rigorous HIIT sessions where no one else can see; or she runs the streets when it's dark.

Next is the swimming pool and then the changing rooms. The tour is taking forever, but it gets interesting when Jay points to the heavy door that Tiffany has just entered. 'I can't go in there, but you could have a quick look around if you want.'

'Sure.'

She slowly pushes open the door. The heady feeling from earlier returns. A warm glow that's stirring within her.

Tiffany is standing in front of a large mirror positioned above a dressing table with padded seats and a row of hairdryers. Violet scoots behind a line of lockers. Tiffany can't see her, but Violet can see her from the mirror to the side. She's getting rather good at this spying lark.

Tiffany is wearing high-waisted gym shorts and a tight-fitting sleeveless top. It shows her perfectly formed bump. She brushes her long blonde hair into a ponytail. What Violet would give to have hair like that. She's never been able to get her lank hair to shine in that way. It's as lifeless as her mother.

The woman behind Tiffany steps into a pair of jeans and jiggles her bottom into them.

'What's happening in your world, then, Jacqui?' Tiffany asks. 'All set for the big day?'

'Hardly. I haven't even started my Christmas shopping yet. And don't get me started on Lewis. He's still giving me grief.'

'What's he up to now?'

'He's got a new business idea, so the money we've been saving to get the house decorated is now going into that.'

Tiffany rolls her eyes.

'Nice to bump into you, anyway. Fancy a coffee?' Jacqui asks.

'I can't. I'm in a rush.' Tiffany slips into her velour track-suit bottoms. 'I need to get Will from work and take him to the garage to pick up a hire car. I didn't even have time for a proper workout.'

'What's wrong with his car?'

'Did Lewis not tell you? He was in an accident.'

'Oh, no! He never said,' Jacqui says. 'Is he OK? What happened?'

'It's shaken him. A young kid cut into the wrong lane on a roundabout. He crashed into her.'

'Oh, gosh! Was anyone hurt?'

Tiffany shakes her head. 'Will spoke to the driver yesterday to check.'

Rose never mentioned that. It's weird to think she talked

to the man who murdered their unborn sister without knowing. But Violet can't let on. Rose would make her go down the proper channels – tell the police. That can't happen. In the end, what would he get? A pathetic prison sentence. No. Violet refuses to settle for that. That beast of a man deserves to suffer.

Tiffany continues. 'The other passenger got knocked out, but the driver says she was discharged from hospital, so everyone's OK. Thankfully. Will said it could've been a lot worse.'

'Good. You don't want that hanging over you when you go away,' Jacqui says.

'Exactly,' Tiffany says.

'Lewis mentioned that Will's booked the hotel. Five-star, you lucky bugger.'

Tiffany opens a compact and brushes her cheeks with rouge. She's got beautiful cheeks, prominent with a soft fullness – not all sharp and angular like Violet's. 'Yep. All sorted. We fly Boxing Day. Heathrow to Bangkok, then a quick one-hour flight to Koh Samui.'

Jacqui sighs heavily. 'Paradise.'

'I know. I can't wait. Will needs it. He hasn't had a break all year.'

Violet clenches her jaw.

'I wish Lewis and I were coming with you.' Jacqui sighs heavily. 'I'll miss not having you around for Christmas. It won't be the same. Karen said so as well.'

'We'll be together Christmas Eve and Christmas Day as we usually are,' replies Tiffany.

These two must be sisters-in-law. Violet slips her phone from her pocket and takes a photo of them.

'I hear you're flying business class,' Jacqui says.

Tiffany layers her plump lips with gloss. Violet would die to have lips like that. They're natural as well. Hers are thin and all cracked in this cold weather. 'Yep. Will was going to surprise me, but he let it slip. I'm so lucky. He's such a gem.'

Violet refrains from roaring with anger. What a wonderful picture this woman paints of her husband. When Violet knows he was responsible for the shell of a mother she once knew and the cold-blooded murder of her unborn sister.

If Tiffany Watson thinks they're swanning off to Thailand for Christmas, she's got another think coming.

16

ROSE

The room is in darkness, and the air is stale. I turn on the light, a single dull bulb that barely carries a whisper of light. I'm not sure at what point it became a dumping ground in here. Probably when Dad realised that Mum was never going to make it up here again.

I need to be quick. V will be home soon.

I try to climb over the clutter to reach the cupboard in the eaves, but it's pointless. Painstakingly, I move stuff aside. So much stuff. Boxes, bags, crates and cases, and an array of miscellaneous equipment, most of which needs to be chucked out. I come across a random box of Christmas decorations. Removing the lid, I sift through the baubles, ribbons, bows and shiny tinsel. I've never seen all this before. I move the box to the entrance. If it doesn't cause a drama, perhaps I can get them out and we can decorate the place a bit. Or I could always give them to Jamie to put up at work.

I come across a large suitcase. Curiosity gets the better of me despite time not being on my side. I drag the heavy load to the small rectangular landing outside the room, next to my sister's door, and click open the clasps. It's packed with Mum's clothes. Some of them I recognise from the photos in the living room. They must've been up here all this time, and none of us realised. Mum might love to see all these again. Not that she could wear them. She's the shadow of the bouncy bosomy woman I remember from back then. I pick up a dress. These clothes would fall off her bony frame.

My pulse races as I cautiously push aside more cardboard boxes and plastic crates labelled in Mum's handwriting: *Girls. Photographs. Easter. DVDs. Toys. Books. Sleeping bags. Jerry. Jerry.* I never thought that name suited our father.

This is pointless. We might as well chuck the lot of it out now. Apart from the clothes in the suitcase, this is never going to be given a second look. I shift a couple of boxes to join the suitcase on the landing to create more room.

I need to be careful. If V comes home before I've managed to get to the cupboard, she'll wonder what I'm looking for. I can't lie. As soon as the smallest of fibs leave my lips, a flush of red creeps up my neck, and before I know it my face resembles a bruised tomato.

I pick up an old bulky computer that looks like something from the Dark Ages and place it atop a pile of boxes. Another item that belongs in a skip at the dump. I move aside a corner table and an old floral tablecloth wrapped around a cardboard roll that's vaguely familiar.

Finally, I've carved a path to the cupboard. But when I go to open the door, I find a padlock fastening the two metal handles. I pull it, hoping it might give. Perhaps I can somehow force the door off the hinges. I tug the handle again, but it's no good. Exasperated, I swear out loud. Dad's going to have to tell me where the key is.

As quickly as I can, I return the items from the landing to the junk room. I wipe a layer of sweat from my forehead and stand back momentarily to peruse my labour. There's now clear access to the cupboard, but, honestly, it doesn't look much better than when I started.

I leave the room, closing the door behind me. I lace my hands on top of my head and exhale, wondering how I'm going to get into that cupboard, when a sudden voice scares the hell out of me.

I turn to my sister standing on the landing.

Her tone is accusatory. And so is her expression. 'What the hell are you doing up here?'

17

VIOLET

Violet runs to her bedroom door. She's sure she locked it. She used to make sure she did all the time but she got out of the habit when she transferred the contents of her bedroom wall to the scrapbook and hid it away. It's unlocked. She turns sharply. 'Have you been in my room?'

Rose steps backwards. 'You know I never go in there. I was looking at what was up here. I thought it was about time we had a clear-out.'

Violet eyes her suspiciously. Her sister has always been a crap liar. Rose is too pure to lie. 'Haven't we got more important things to deal with at the moment?'

Rose slaps her hands on her face, no doubt to hide her flushed cheeks. 'I've found a case of Mum's old clothes.' She beckons Violet into the junk room and points to a suitcase at her feet. Squatting until she's sitting on her haunches, Rose unzips it. 'We could take some of these down to her.'

Violet sifts through the dresses, skirts, and tops. 'It's summer stuff. And anyway, none of it would fit her anymore. They'd fall off her.'

'Where've you been all day?' Rose asks as they leave the room.

'Work,' Violet says. 'And I popped in to see Dad.' It's sad it's come to this – both of them having to lie. They've always been close. Lies split families apart. Their father taught Violet that.

'So did I,' Rose says. 'Listen, we need to finish that conversation we had in the car.'

'Which one?' Violet asks.

'How we're going to cope with Dad no longer around. You know, with Mum.'

'I'll give up some of my morning clients, and we can ask Auntie to help out more for a while. She won't mind until we can get something more permanent sorted.'

Her sister does that thing that annoys Violet, shrugging her shoulders and dropping her head to the side. 'And what is something more permanent, exactly?'

'I don't know yet.' Violet can't think beyond Christmas Eve. Nothing is going to matter after that. 'Let's get Christmas out of the way first.'

'Why?' Rose's voice softens. 'Mum should be in a home, V. She needs more than we can give her.'

Violet clenches her fists. 'That's not true. She's well looked after here. We can't dump her in a care home. She could die. If that's going to happen, it's going to happen here.'

'We wouldn't be dumping her. We can still see her. Every day, if we want to. We can't carry on like this. Auntie Audrey is exhausted. I'm exhausted. And so are you. We've found this lovely home, Abbeyfields, about half an hour from here.'

There's no way Violet is having Mum leave this house.

Rose won't let it drop. 'The staff are lovely – really lovely. And the facilities are good. She'd have everything she needs.'

'I phoned the insurance company this morning.'

Rose sighs. 'V!'

'They're arranging a hire car.'

'V!'

'I'll take it, and you can drive mine until we're in a position to get something more permanent in place.'

Rose sighs, exasperated. 'I'll go and relieve Auntie and make an early dinner. I think I'll do omelettes. OK for you?'

'Whatever.'

Violet heads to her room, dumps her bag on the floor and changes into her gym kit. Her leggings feel looser than usual, her hip bones jutting into the soft fabric. She starts her computer, loads her HIIT workout onto the screen and jogs on the spot. But two minutes into the routine, the room spins. She's going to pass out. She stumbles to the bed. Her head pounds. Perhaps it's the aftermath of the accident. She gives it a few minutes of controlled deep breaths and tries again. Never a day goes by without a workout. Never. But she doesn't even feel strong enough to go for a run tonight. But she can't miss it. Perhaps she'll be able to cope with a brisk walk. She'll have to go for an hour, though, to burn three hundred calories.

She stands, but her legs are too wobbly to continue. Nothing normally interrupts her daily workout. Nothing. She even persists when she's got a fever. But she can't face it tonight. It must be the stress of the past twenty-four hours. A lot has changed.

She walks to the window and pushes it open wide, sticking her head into the chill of winter. The freshness imbues her mind. She takes deep breaths, willing herself to stay calm. She's got everything under control.

After closing the window, she slips into a tracksuit, shivering despite the extra layer. She sits at her computer and loads the photo she took of Tiffany at the gym. That woman really is beautiful. How can a man like Will Watson have everything? Everything.

But he won't for much longer.

She sends the photo to the printer and switches to Google, typing Amazon into the search bar. She checks her order. There it is. Good. Delivery is due tomorrow. Then the fun can truly begin.

The printer coughs and spurts before spewing out the photo onto the floor. She picks it up and walks over to the wall, where she tacks it beside the photo of Will Watson. From her desk drawer, she grabs a marker and draws a thick black circle around the photo of Tiffany Watson.

Fifteen years ago, she learnt that the best way to hurt someone the most is to harm the ones they love.

18

ROSE

The gun is constantly on my mind. I have to find it. Before someone else does.

I settle Mum in her room, listening to an audiobook on her iPad. It's a feel-good love story she might enjoy. She stares at her hands, twiddling her thumbs in circles. We're not sure how much she takes in, but it's better than her sitting in front of the TV all the time. I sigh heavily. She needs more than this. If she were in a nursing home like Chase Hill or Abbey-fields, there'd be a Jamie who'd organise daily activities. She'd have a far better quality of life than V and I can give her here.

I remove my phone from my jeans pocket and google *how to break a padlock*. A claw hammer or a heavy pair of pliers will do the job, it seems. I step out of the back door and into the garden. My breath fogs the air as I walk to the shed at the far end of the garden. Cigarette butts litter the step leading up to the door. V is smoking a lot lately. More than she used to.

The light is dim, and it smells faintly of petrol from the lawnmower. I frantically search for Dad's toolbox, finally locating it on the bottom shelf of the large unit that fills the length of one wall. I hunt through the contents. The claw hammer is easy to find. But I can't find a pair of pliers anywhere. I shake with the cold as I search the rest of the shed. I haven't got a hope in hell. It's as much of a mess in here as it is in the junk room.

I return to the house and run upstairs to place the hammer on the floor inside the junk room. I knock on V's bedroom door. She unlocks it and pops her head out of the gap.

'Can you come down and watch Mum for a while? I need to do a few things.'

She nods. 'I'll be there in a minute.'

I return to the kitchen and chuck three potatoes in the microwave and beat seven eggs in a bowl. Three eggs for me and two each for Mum and V because neither of them will eat a bigger omelette. If either of them will eat anything at all.

V appears. She's pale. So very pale.

'I've put some potatoes in the microwave, and there's some leftover salad in the fridge,' I say. 'It'll be ready in fifteen minutes.'

'I'll do Mum's medication.'

'I'll be back in a second.'

'Where are you going?' she asks.

'I need to send an email about something that happened at work today.' I hurry out of the door before she can see the redness that's making its way to my cheeks.

I bolt to the top of the house, slip into the junk room and

shut the door, pausing to catch my breath. I grab the hammer. I need to be quick. With one hand, I hold the padlock to the cupboard and pull the shackle to loosen the tension. With the other, I try to prise the padlock free, but I haven't the strength. I resort to repeatedly pounding the side of the lock. The clanging sound of metal on metal grates on me, reminding me of the cars in the collision.

The padlock is not giving. I'm making too much noise, and it's not even making a dent. I try harder, anxious my sister will come up to see what I'm up to. My hand slips. I smack the hammer onto my finger, catching the nail. This is no good. I need to find another way.

Abandoning my fruitless endeavour, I run downstairs and call Jamie. He picks up straight away.

'Could you do me a favour?' I say.

'Anything for you, Titch.' Titch. It's the name he gave me on the first day he joined Chase Hill because he said he'd never met anyone so short. At first I was insulted, but not for long. Jamie is one of those people it's impossible to stay angry at for long.

I can't ask him if he's got a pair of wrenches over the phone. 'My sister's not working tonight, so I thought I'd go and see Dad again. I don't suppose you'd give me a lift?'

'What time?'

'Six-thirty.'

'I'll be there.'

I return to the kitchen and cook the omelettes.

V wheels Mum's chair up to the table. Mealtimes are a stressful affair. V insists on feeding Mum. She says I do enough caring for others during the day. But that's a lie. It's because she transfers most of her dinner to Mum's plate and blames Mum for barely eating anything. She must think I'm stupid. But I look the other way. Food has always been a tricky subject where my sister is concerned. It's not worth upsetting her. She's scary when she's upset.

I serve up dinner. Mum drops her head to her chest.

'You've got to eat, Mum.' V digs a spoonful of the inside of her potato from its jacket, thinking I don't notice. She lifts Mum's head and tilts the spoon to her lips. 'Come on, have a mouthful for me.'

Mum opens her mouth and accepts the food, chewing it with her mouth open. I smile and nod encouragingly.

'Want a drink?' V picks up Mum's sippy cup, a plastic beaker with a hole in the lid for a straw. She holds it to Mum's lips.

Mum takes a sip. She coughs. Liquid dribbles down her chin.

V wipes it away with a piece of folded paper towel. 'I'm sorry, Mum. Were you not ready for a drink? How about a piece of omelette?' V slices into her own omelette and feeds it to Mum before cramming a lettuce leaf into her own mouth.

The doorbell rings.

'That must be Jamie.' I get up from the table.

'How long will you be?' V asks. 'I want to go for a run tonight.'

This could work to my advantage. 'Sure. I'll be back around eight. Does that work?'

She nods.

With her out of the house, I can get on with finding this bloody gun.

19

VIOLET

The front door closes.

'We're on our own now, Mum.' Violet picks up the piece of omelette that has fallen onto her mother's lap.

A slow, short, low moan leaves her mother's mouth on a cloud of breath.

'Finally, we can talk.' Violet tucks her hair behind her ears and listens. There it is. The words only she can hear. Dad and Rose have always said it's in her imagination. Mum has never muttered a sound as far as they're concerned. Auntie Audrey is the same. But they're wrong. Very wrong.

Mum talks to her. But in a language only they can understand. If only the others would listen and treat her the same as Violet does. Then she'd talk to them, too.

When she was twelve, Violet got a Saturday job, cleaning for the lady who then lived diagonally across the road. Auntie Audrey arranged it. She said it would be good for Violet to get out of the house at the weekend. Violet saved all the money she earned and when she had enough, she bought Mum a new dress. A floral A-line one that is still Mum's favourite, Mum always tells her. Violet's smile had lifted to her eyes when she pulled it out of the carrier bag, and Mum smiled, too. Not a proper, cheek-lifting grin, but the corners of her lips definitely rose when she held it in front of her. And then Mum said, 'Thank you,' as clear as a summer's day.

Her father was there. 'Did you hear that?' Violet said with the deepest joy. 'She smiled and she thanked me.'

'I don't think so, dear.' Her father turned and left the room.

That was the first time she tasted the seed of hatred that would grow into the visceral loathing she has for her father.

Violet stabs a fresh piece of omelette with the fork and lifts it to Mum's mouth. Her mother chews it one hundred times. Violet knows because she often counts. She chews every piece of food the same number of times as if she knows this is her safety cutoff. It's why every meal takes so long.

When they were at school, word got around that Rose and she were child carers. It didn't seem to get in Rose's way. She thrived at school. But Violet? She got lost in her own world of make-believe friends. It was a safer place to be.

'I still can't believe it, Mum. I've found him. I've actually found him.'

'You found him?' her mother adds. She continues chewing, staring at her hands, tapping her thumbs together. She speaks with a soft Irish lilt. It used to be much stronger. But that's because she hasn't been back to Ireland for fifteen years. She used to take Rose and her three times a year – every Easter, summer and Christmas – when they were kids. Violet can't remember their father ever accompanying them on one of those trips. Most likely, he didn't. They stayed with their grandparents on the Atlantic coast who sadly passed away within a year of each other, shortly after Mum was shot.

'Yes, the guy who did this to you. I told you, didn't I? I told you and Bean that I'd find him one day.'

Mum stops chewing and lifts her head. Her eyes flutter.

'You understand, don't you?' Violet says. 'You know what I'm talking about.'

'You're a good girl, Violet Sapphire.'

Violet loves the way the tone of her voice rises and falls. It's like a gentle tune you never grow sick of listening to.

She takes her mother's hand and squeezes it. 'Oh, Mum. I've never given up on you, you know that. I've kept my promise. Do you remember when I was young?'

The blank expression remains, but Violet can see it in her eyes. A glint of understanding others would deny is there.

'I was about eight, Mum. I entered that colouring competition at school. But I didn't win. That girl Alexis Cavendish won it. The one with the long blonde hair she wore in two fat plaits. She won everything. I was so upset. You must remember. I cried for hours. Never give up, you told me, Mum. Never. Life throws you curveballs, you said to me.'

'Curveballs, yes.'

'It's the strongest who come up trumps in the end. All you've got to do is keep going. Well, I haven't given up, Mum. And finally, I've found him.'

'You're a clever girl, dearest Violet. I always knew we could rely on you.' Her soft Irish twang wraps around Violet's heart.

Violet pops a piece of potato skin into her mouth but spits it out. She can't eat that. She hasn't exercised today. She'll save it and have it later if she makes it out for a run.

'And I can't believe he lives less than half an hour from here. Can you believe that?' Violet takes a chunk of butter from the dish in the middle of the table and uses it to mash the potato into a mushy paste. Sometimes, but not always, softer food aids Mum's swallowing. 'Have some more, Mum. You've hardly eaten anything. We need to build up your strength.'

'Good girl.' Mum accepts another spoonful of the mashed potato, masticating it around her mouth.

'And get this, Mum. Guess what else I've found out. His wife is pregnant.' Violet's neck muscles tense. 'They're going to have another baby.' She takes a deep breath in and out of her nose. 'It's not fair, is it? They live in this big, posh house.' She shakes her head. 'And they're swanning off to Thailand for Christmas. Well, they think they are. But they're not.'

Mum's chin juts forward. 'What are you going to do to them?'

'I'm not exactly sure yet, but I'm working on it. But don't worry, Mum. I've got thirteen days. Thirteen days to work on my plan. And believe me. The outcome is not going to be pretty.'

Violet takes some more butter from the dish, mashes it into the potato, faster and faster, until it turns to a sloppy mess.

'I told you and Bean I'd never let you down. He's going to pay for what he did.' She grabs a square of paper towel and wipes a smudge of potato from her mother's chin. 'And he's going to suffer far worse than any of us ever have. Because there'll be no one to look after him like I've looked after you all these years, Mum. No one.'

20

ROSE

Carlos is manning the front desk again when I arrive at the hospice today, typing on a keyboard in front of a large computer screen. He hands me a pen. 'You know the drill. Give me a scribble of your name and initials.'

I write my name and time of arrival and am about to sign my initials when I stop. That's odd. I run my finger down the page, rereading the names above mine.

'Has my sister been here today?' I ask.

He frowns. 'I haven't seen her, but I've not long come on duty. If she was here, she would've had to sign in. Like I said, you know the drill,' he says again with a knowing smile.

I check again. I can't understand why she would've lied.

The sweet waft of cinnamon morphing into the smell of fish and boiled cabbage makes me gag as I walk along the corridor to Dad's room. A sense of foreboding accompanies each step. Each time I arrive here, I wonder if it will be the last.

Dad is asleep, his head elevated. The nurse smiles and resumes tapping the screen of an iPad. 'He's been asleep most of the afternoon.'

'Did my sister come and see him?' I ask.

'You'll have to check at the front desk. I've not seen her.' She finishes her tasks, reminds me where the call button is and leaves us alone.

I nudge his arm. 'Dad, I need to speak to you.' This is far from ideal, but I need answers. 'You've totally stressed me out, Dad.' If he can hear me, he must be able to detect the distress in my voice. 'There's a lock on that cupboard door in the junk room.' I prod him harder. 'Dad, I need you to wake up. I need to know where the key is.'

There's no response. I pace the room. I'm used to stress at work. I've been there when a resident had a stroke. And when one ran away and I had to chase him down the High Street. I've witnessed residents dying. But this is personal. It's stress on a whole other level.

The silence is unbearable. I pick up the remote control and switch on the TV, flicking to the news. He always watches the news, but his eyes remain closed. 'Dad, I need you to tell me where the key is to that lock. Please, Dad. Please.'

I continue trying. But it's no good.

After twenty minutes, I give up.

'Let's go for a drink?' Jamie says when I climb into his car. Thankfully, he's left the engine running, and it's warm. 'You look like you need one.'

'I need to get back for V. She wants to go out for a run.'

He pulls a face. 'Are you serious? In this weather?' He starts the engine and steers onto the road.

'She'll run in any weather.'

'Is she mad?'

'I need your help.' I blurt it all out before I can stop myself.

'Jeez, Titch. That's a big ask of him. Why don't you take the gun to the police?'

'He obviously doesn't want me to.'

'Why do you think he even has a gun in the house?'

'Perhaps it was to protect us all after what happened to Mum.'

'I'm not being funny. I know he's your dad, but he shouldn't be dragging you into all of this.'

'And now I've dragged you into it.'

He raises his hands. 'I don't know what you're talking about.' He winks. 'You never said a word to me.'

'Where can I get a pair of wrenches from?' I ask.

'I could swing by mine and see if my dad's got a pair.'

'Don't tell him what you want them for, though, will you?'

He joins his forefinger and thumb together, runs them across his lips and pretends to zip them up.

My body stiffens and remains tense all the way to his home, a small semi-detached house where he lives with his mum and dad and five younger sisters. A set-up he affectionally calls 'hell' at times. It's a squeeze. And the shoes. They're everywhere. And he often arrives late for work because he's had to wait to get into the shower.

Before Dad fell ill, Jamie and I discussed becoming flatmates. He found a place. A small two-bedroomed flat on the edge of town, which would've been affordable. He was more than keen, and so was I at first. It was as if I enjoyed the dream of moving away from home. But even if Dad hadn't ended up in the hospice, when push came to shove, I don't know if I could've left Mum and V. Mum's too vulnerable, and even though she'd vehemently deny it, so is my sister.

'Be back in five,' he says and clambers out of the car.

I sit waiting for him, wringing my hands in my lap. I desperately want to get this over with. Get that bloody gun, take it down to the river and be done with it. Perhaps I shouldn't have confided in Jamie. It could only complicate matters. But I was desperate. I *am* desperate.

His heavy frame bounces back into the driver's seat. He places four metal objects in my lap. 'Two wrenches for Madame. A pair of pliers, and if all else fails, a club hammer.'

'You're a star.'

He mock salutes me and drives me home.

Violet is dressed shoulder to ankle in Lycra, a woolly hat and running shoes. 'Mum's watching *EastEnders*,' she announces before heading straight out into the cold night air.

Jamie shivers. 'Your sister sure is crazy.'

I lead him upstairs to the junk room, telling him that my sister's daily exercise is as routine as her brushing her teeth. The tools scrape together in his hands, grating on my frailness. I point to the cupboard in the eaves. 'It's over there.'

He treads along the path I've created between the clutter and kneels by the cupboard door, hooking the heads of the wrenches over the sides of the shackles. Clunk, one mighty force of the handles and job done. He shakes the lock loose.

Rushing to kneel beside him, I open the cupboard door. A strong, musty smell hits me. I find the light swich, but the bulb must have blown. 'We're looking for a blue plastic box along the back wall.'

He pulls his phone from his jeans pocket and shines the torch inside the tight space.

Boxes, crates and bags line the outer walls, leaving a narrow corridor for me to crawl inside. 'I'm going in,' I say.

'Why don't you let me, and I can pass stuff out to you? If I can squeeze in.' He crawls in at a push.

'We're looking for a blue plastic box,' I repeat.

He rummages around. 'Here it is.'

I peer inside. He angles the phone light to a blue box hiding in the corner beneath some clutter like a dirty secret.

He shifts aside boxes and bags. When he gets to the blue box, he passes it to me. He crawls out of the space, dripping with sweat.

'There should be a shoebox inside.' I unclip the lid and rummage through the contents – mostly paperwork – until I come to the shoebox I'm looking for. I swallow the ball of unease clogging up my throat. 'This is it.'

My hands shake as I lift the lid.

21

VIOLET

Violet pounds the streets but can't find her rhythm. Each step is laboured as if she's running with weights attached to her ankles. Not even the Christmas trees now fronting the living room windows of many houses can distract her. She hopes she's not coming down with something. She's got far too much to do. Far, far too much.

Most nights, after a gentle jog up and down the street and a few dynamic stretches to warm up, she laps the block three times, aiming to complete a three-mile loop in under half an hour. But tonight, she's flagging. The first lap takes just shy of twelve minutes, and she has to stop to catch her breath. Her chest is tight, and her head is fuzzy. She leans against the cherry tree on the opposite side of the road to home. It's this cold air. A minute break, and she'll be ready to go again. The lights on the third floor of the house catch her attention. She turned the landing light off. She knows she did. Damn. Rose must be up there.

She abandons her run and powerwalks back toward the house. But even that pace is too fast, so she slows to a walk. An Amazon delivery guy greets her at the front door and hands her a parcel.

She smiles.

Fantastic.

Her purchases have arrived. Bubbles of excitement pop inside her belly.

EastEnders blares out from the TV – arguing, screaming, and shouting – sounds so familiar at this time of the evening. She waves the parcel at her mother. 'Look, Mum. They're here. My plan is slowly coming together.'

She dashes to the kitchen and grabs a pair of scissors. Returning to the living room, she runs the blade along the brown tape wrapped around the edges of the parcel. 'Here we go.' The elation is overwhelming. She can't wait to see it for real. But when she opens the box, disappointment strikes.

'Damn. I wanted to pay Tiffany a visit tomorrow, Mum. But only the binoculars have arrived.'

'Where's the other item?' Mum squeaks.

Violet checks her phone. 'It's due out for delivery tomorrow.' She lets out a long, slow groan. 'It looks like I need to be patient, Mum. Patience is a virtue. Do you remember you always used to say that to us?'

'I do.'

Violet bites her lower lip as she removes the binoculars from their casing and weighs them up and down in her hand. She can't believe how light they are. 'It'll be fine. I'll still go there tomorrow to continue my homework.'

Her plan for the morning will have to wait another day.

Rose. The box has distracted her. She's not thinking straight. 'Where's Rose? She was upstairs.'

Mum grunts.

Violet meets her sister and Jamie descending the stairs. They stop, alarmed as if she's caught them doing something they shouldn't. Jamie is carrying some kind of tool. He puts it in the kangaroo pocket of his hoodie. A cringy sound of metal on metal scraping together tells Violet it's more than one. 'What are you two doing?' she asks.

Rose's cheeks redden. Whatever her sister says is going to be a lie. 'We...'

Violet clenches her fists. 'Have you been in my room?'

Rose glances at Jamie. 'No!'

Jamie pulls a couple of wrenches out of his pocket. He is so tall. It could be their father standing there, towering over her sister.

Violet's first thought is he's used them to get into her bedroom.

'Rose asked me to look at the bathroom tap,' Jamie says.

'It wouldn't stop dripping,' Rose says.

'All fixed,' Jamie says in his sing-song voice.

Violet steps sideways. They hurry past. The waft of Jamie's aftershave hits her like a wave of broken promises. It's the same aftershave Dad used to wear.

She runs to her room and checks the door, relieved to find she did lock it after all. She dashes to the junk room, turns on the light and peers around the muddle. Something's different to when she was in here earlier. She sniffs. Jamie's aftershave wafts in the air. She grimaces, flapping her hand in front of her face.

Boxes have been piled on top of each other as if to clear a space. The area in the far corner piques her attention. She zigzags around the clutter towards the boxes, tripping on a metal pole sticking out from beneath the disorder. When she reaches the cupboard in the eaves, she stops and glares at the familiar-looking shoebox sitting on top of the blue plastic box.

She returns her interest to the cupboard door, wondering how Rose and Jamie got in there. The lock has gone. She hunts around the floor. And there's her answer – the warped chunk of metal by the corner of the door.

She hurries to her room, unlocking the door and locking it after her. Her head is pounding, and she feels dizzy. This is not good.

She needs to be on top of her game.

She heads to her bedside cabinet. The bottom drawer is open. That's strange. She shrugs. She must've left it open. A quick search inside leads her to the key to the cupboard in the junk room that Rose must have been looking for before they resorted to smashing the lock.

The need to check all is in order consumes her.

She needs to see it, feel it.

She grabs the crowbar from the wardrobe and, pulling the bed out from against the wall, she prises up the two floor-boards three in from the wall. The usual musty smell hits her. She's being irrational. There's no way Rose could ever find this.

She leans the floorboards against the bed and digs her arm into the opening, feeling around until her hand touches the smooth cloth. She breathes a deep sigh of relief as she drags out the flannel bag. Opening it, she empties the gun onto the wooden floor. The relief is overwhelming. She picks it up and examines it.

Dad must've told Rose the gun was in the cupboard in the junk room. She bets he asked her sister to get rid of it. Little does he know, she found it ages ago. He underestimated her. He always has done.

She hates that man more than ever.

22

VIOLET

Prunella De Vries is a social influencer entrenched in the fashion industry. Once a week, Violet cleans her three-bedroom penthouse apartment that overlooks the river in the centre of town. Violet has cancelled all her other morning clients. But not Prunella. This one is too valuable for her end game.

One of the bedrooms is dedicated to Prunella's clothing and accessories. Cleaning this room is the highlight of Violet's week. She spends nearly half her four-hour slot in here. It takes close to an hour, sometimes more, simply to gather the clothes from the floor, and those draped over every piece of furniture, and hang them all up in the floor-to-ceiling wardrobes that line two walls of the room. Then there's the jewellery and accessories Prunella leaves scattered over the large dressing table that runs the length of the far wall.

Prunella is half-Dutch and half-English and moved to the UK to further her career. The melodic tone to her accent is charming, and she loves to talk, a quality that, along with her dynamic and expressive creative style, has helped her build millions of TikTok followers. She talks in third person, a trait Violet found annoying at first, but one she's come to find endearing.

Every week, while she cleans her flat, if Prunella is there, they have a one-sided conversation, with Prunella doing all the talking. Violet doesn't mind. Being here is a distraction from the monotony of life. Sometimes, when Prunella is out on a job, Violet pretends it's her place. On a bright day, she'll make a cup of coffee and take it to one of the comfy chairs outside. She rests her feet on the balcony and smokes a cigarette, like Prunella does, and Violet wonders what it must be like to live such a charmed life.

Prunella bursts into the dressing room while Violet is picking up a hot-pink jumpsuit that's draped over the dressing table chair. 'Prunella doesn't know what she'd do without Miss Violet, you know.' She floats from wardrobe to wardrobe. 'Prunella needs Miss Violet more. Come and work here two mornings per week. Three. She give Miss Violet three mornings' work.'

Violet smiles and, sliding open the mirrored wardrobe door, she grabs another hanger. 'I can't,' she says. 'I have other jobs.'

'Prunella pay more. Make it worth Miss Violet's while. She means it. Make it four mornings per week. Five if Miss Violet wants.' Prunella theatrically throws her arm around the room. 'Then it won't look such a mess in here all the time.' She removes an emerald-green floaty dress from the wardrobe and holds it against her tall, slender frame. 'What do you think, Miss Violet? Prunella's outfit for today?'

'Where are you going?' Violet asks, intrigued. Once, when Prunella was out, Violet perused her diary that she'd left open in the kitchen, wondering how it would feel to attend so many meetings and lunchtime appointments at top-notch restaurants and fancy cafés.

'To a new client.' Prunella taps her lips with her forefinger. 'But Prunella can't tell Miss Violet. Big client. Famous client. Maybe tell soon if she's allowed.'

Prunella drops the dress on the floor and zips through the two hundred or so hangers in one of the wardrobes. The gentle, rhythmic scrape of the hangers moving along the rail is mesmerising. 'Ta-da!' Prunella whips out a white trouser suit. 'More professional.' Resting the suit over the dressing table chair, she sits down and places a headband over her hairline. She glances in the mirror. 'First Miss Prunella must make face pretty.' She taps the screen of her phone. 'We need music. Music good for the soul, eh, Miss Violet?'

Christmas music plays through the speakers on the wall, grating on Violet like when Dad scraped his cutlery on the plate when he ate. She inwardly groans as she continues clearing the mess from the floor.

Prunella applies her make-up. 'We need to decorate. Miss Violet help. Prunella loves Christmas.' She turns up the volume on her music system.

A rendition of *All I Want for Christmas is You* hammers out, erupting in Violet's eardrums. The kick-drum beat blasts through her. She can't stand it. 'Not today!' she shouts over the din. Her head is about to explode. 'I haven't got time.'

She hurries from the room. She'll have to return to the

mess when Prunella is finished in there. She takes her cleaning kit into the kitchen, which is as disorganised as the dressing room. A political news story is on the radio. She turns it down. Her head is thumping. Usually, she loves being here, but today, she just wants to go home to work on her plan. She's got twelve days to go, and she needs to make it perfect. No stumbling blocks. No loose ends.

As usual, dirty cups and used plates are piled upon the marble worktop. Violet stacks the dishwasher when Prunella reappears in her white suit, carrying two large plastic tubs. The trousers are three-quarter length, and so are the sleeves. Hardly the outfit for a winter's day, but at least she has chosen slightly more suitable footwear. If you can call a pair of orange boots with platform heels suitable for a snowy day. She has swept her long red hair on top of her head, except for a few curled strands that frame her perfectly made-up pretty face. Violet sighs. She always feels dowdy in comparison to her chicness.

'Lovely clean kitchen.' Footprints trail Prunella along the wet floor Violet has just cleaned. She dumps the tubs on the work surface. 'Here decorations. We make the place like a, what do you call it? Groggo?'

'Grotto,' Violet offers.

'Look, chocolate.' Prunella produces a tub of Quality Street and offers it to her. 'Help yourself. Eat and be merry.'

The colourful foil-wrapped chocolates are tempting. Violet shakes her head.

Prunella shoves them further under her nose. 'You must. It's Christmas. Miss Violet too thin.'

'No!' Violet shouts.

A look of offence appears all over Prunella's pretty face.

She retracts her offer and slams the lid back on the tub. 'Sorry.' She gives Violet *that* look. One of pity that people have been giving her since she was nine years old. They don't mean it. And if she tackled them on it, they'd deny it – say it's in her frenzied imagination. But she sees it – the heavy gaze, the mouth downturned, the eyes that linger.

'Miss Violet want coffee?'

Violet shakes her head. She'd rather have a cup alone when her client is out.

'Listen. Listen.' Prunella turns up the radio, swamping the awkward atmosphere as she makes Violet a cup of coffee anyway with her posh machine that takes capsules.

A serious-sounding woman is reading the news about a child who's been abducted. 'Poor, poor child.' Prunella shakes her head and hands Violet a cup of coffee. 'Poor parents. If that happened to Prunella, she would die.' She's referring to her son, whose messy bedroom Violet also cleans when she's there. 'Child gone for two days now.'

'That's terrible.' Violet grabs the worktop, thinking about Will and Tiffany's sweet little Leo playing with his train track on their kitchen floor.

Prunella's comments serve to show how beautifully ghastly Violet's mind is.

'Bye-bye, Miss Violet. See you next week.' Prunella waves and disappears.

Violet waits for five minutes and returns to Prunella's room with her bag. She rummages through the wardrobe. There we go. She pulls a pair of black trousers off a hanger. Just what she's looking for. She stuffs them into her bag. Next, she needs a top. She scours the hundreds of items in the drawers below the wardrobes, and tugs out a cream jumper.

Exactly what she needs. She stuffs it in her bag to join the trousers with nothing but sweet little Leo on her mind.

Nothing could hurt a parent more than for something to happen to their child.

23

VIOLET

'Have some more tea, Mum.' Violet guides the sippy cup to her mother's mouth.

Her mother turns her head. Ever so slightly, but enough to tell her she doesn't want any more. 'No. No,' Mum says in her Irish accent.

'Auntie said you didn't drink all day. Please have some more. You'll get dehydrated.'

Mum parts her lips.

'I'm so excited, Mum. My plan is evolving all the time,' Violet whispers, looking over her shoulder as if she's expecting to see someone. 'Don't worry – not the end game. I know what that's going to entail. But in the meantime, I'm going to make life an absolute living hell for Will Watson.'

Mum takes a sip of tea and catches the excited look in Violet's eyes.

'Will and Tiffany's kid—' The doorbell interrupts her.

'Who can that be?' She places the sippy cup on the table. 'I'll be back in a minute.'

A solid guy, dressed in summer attire, hands her an Amazon parcel. His legs, bare below the knee, make her shiver. He clicks his handheld device against the label on the parcel, nods and leaves without uttering a word.

She closes the door, bursting with excitement, and takes the parcel back to the kitchen. 'Look, Mum, look.' But her mother has nodded off. Violet gently taps her shoulder. 'Mum, wake up. It's arrived. I'm so excited. You have to see this.'

Mum's chin falls to her chest. Violet runs into the kitchen to fetch a knife. She can't get it quick enough. She returns to the parcel and slices open the box when the front door opens and bangs closed. She groans at the sound of her sister singing, 'I'm home.'

She scans the room, wondering what to do with the delivery. No way can Rose find out what's in this box. She's about to hide it behind the sofa when Rose appears, a bag of shopping in one hand, a set of keys in the other.

Rose stares at the knife in Violet's hand. 'What are you doing?'

Violet points the knife at the box. 'I was about to open this.'

'What've you been buying now?'

She hugs the box to her chest like a baby, faking a smile. 'Christmas shopping.'

Her sister eyes her warily. 'Why did you say you went to see Dad yesterday, when you didn't?' Her voice holds an accusatory tone.

'I did,' Violet lies.

'Your name wasn't in the signing-in book.'

Violet shrugs. 'I must've forgotten to sign in.'

Lies. Lies. Lies. They carry weight where her sister is concerned and make her heart heavy. She can't stand it. She's turning into their father.

The fist of guilt grabs at her heart. It hurts. Her sister has always been the constant in her life. She hates what's happening between them. But she can't stop now. She points at Mum. 'She's only just fallen asleep.' She hugs the box tighter to her chest. The anticipation is too much to bear. 'I need to get ready for work.' Another lie strikes another blow of guilt. 'Or I'll be late.'

Rose glances at her watch. 'But you're early.'

'The garage called. The rental car is ready. I thought I'd walk and pick it up on my way to work.'

'But it's freezing out. Jamie's coming soon. I could ask him to give you a lift.'

'It's fine. The fresh air will do me good.'

'I'm going to make a shepherd's pie.' Mum loves Rose's shepherd's pie. 'Want me to wait for you?' Rose calls after her.

'No. I'll grab some when I get back.'

She races upstairs to her room and fumbles to unlock the door. She can't get inside quick enough. She locks the door and opens the Amazon box. Her hands shake with trepidation as she picks up the contents. The widest of smiles forms on her face. It's a pity she can't put this to good use until after the weekend, but patience, Violet, patience.

24

VIOLET

'Sign here.' The mechanic stabs his grease-encrusted finger at the blank line at the bottom of the page. 'Don't forget to date it. Friday 13th.' He chuckles. 'Unlucky for some.'

But not for her. For once in her life, luck appears to be on her side. She follows his instructions, her signature askew from her hand shaking so much.

'You're in luck.' He jangles a set of keys in the air. 'Santa's come early for you, Miss. There's only a Merc in stock.' A faint smell of body odour wafts from his blue overalls. He hands her the keys. 'They're usually reserved for the – how do I say this without causing offence – for the richer and older folk.' He points across the forecourt of the garage to a black Mercedes A-Class parked in the far bay. 'Have fun.'

The strong smell of leather hits her when she climbs inside. It's surreal. Only in her dreams has she thought she'd ever be able to drive a car of this ilk. It's going to take some getting used to. She nervously steers to the entrance of the garage. The mechanic waves his grubby hand and nods, smirking as if he senses her nervousness. She inches onto the pavement, looking left and right until the road is clear.

She drives slowly, her nerves skyrocketing to be in such a posh car. Prunella has a Mercedes, an SUV electric model. She once gave Violet a lift home on her way to a client as it was raining heavily. It was so eerily quiet, with none of the harsh engine noises in Violet's car. She wishes she could drive this one with the same confidence as Prunella races around the streets in hers.

When she arrives in Radstone, she edges along the unmaintained dirt track to the back of Will and Tiffany's place. It's different in the dark. The headlights of the car illuminate the potholes in the uneven surface of the road. Shadows from the branches of the trees dance and stretch. The downstairs of their house is alight. Bodies are moving around inside, but Violet can't make out who they are. She parks the car fifty or so metres away and stops the engine. Apart from the squeak of the leather as she shuffles in her seat, it's eerily quiet, but her thoughts are loud. She goes to switch off her phone, only to realise that it's not in her bag. She thinks back to the garage. She didn't get it out there, either. In her haste, she must've left it at home.

The binoculars wait on the passenger seat. She grabs them and leaves the car. A chilling wind whips around like warning fingers poking her, telling her what she's doing is wrong. She hovers near the entrance to the dark woods to settle her nerves, but they're not calming. She's as wired as a coffee addict. Nipping back to the car, she finds a cigarette. She leans against the car door and lights it, sucking deep wafts of smoke in and out of her lungs in quick succession.

A small van approaches the corner of the road. She ducks behind the Mercedes. When the van passes, she hugs her arms around her body and the binoculars in her armpit and slowly walks to the back of number 12. The air is heavy, infused with her nervousness. She stands at the end of the garden and lifts the binoculars to her eyes. A shiver runs down her spine, thrill and fear in equal parts. It's them.

Tiffany sits at the side of the breakfast bar in her bathrobe, drinking from a can and scrolling through her phone. Will stands at the centre island, slicing vegetables. He pauses to sip from his glass of red wine. A monitor like the one Violet and Rose have for Mum at home rests on the worktop. Violet glances upwards. The rest of the house is in darkness. Leo must be in bed.

Will and Tiffany chat. How she wishes she could lip read. Tiffany turns the screen of her phone towards Will, laughing. He places the knife on the chopping board and strolls over to her. Placing an arm around her shoulders, he kisses the top of her head as he studies her phone. He throws back his head in laughter.

Here they are playing happy family.

But not for much longer.

25

ROSE

'She's been having these Amazon deliveries.' I turn down the volume of the TV. 'She says they're Christmas presents, but she's lying.'

'How do you know?' Jamie asks.

I shrug. 'I can just tell with my sister. She does this head-twitching thing. Only slightly. No one else would notice. But I do. She did the same when I asked her about the signing-in book. She never went to see Dad. I can't understand why she lied to me. And, more worryingly, where else did she go if she didn't go and see Dad?'

'She's a grown woman, Rose.'

I shake my head. 'You don't know my sister!'

'OK, what's the plan?'

'I'm going to have another look for the gun.'

If I'm not mistaken, Mum flinches. I look at Jamie, but his eyes are fixed on his phone. I wipe a smudge of mash from

Mum's chin. 'Mum, remember my friend Jamie? He's going to sit with you while I do some jobs. I won't be long.' I hand the remote control to him. '*Home and Away* is on Channel Five in a few minutes. She likes watching that.'

Jamie drops onto the sofa next to Mum. 'Got to love a bit of *Home and Away*, Mrs S.'

I leave them chatting or, rather, him chatting to her, and run upstairs with the torch I located in the kitchen earlier. I check V's door. As I expected, it's locked.

I enter the junk room, step over to the cupboard and open the door. Switching on the torch, I shine it inside. 'Where do I even start?' I say out loud. This is going to take all night. I lodge the torch between two boxes, allowing me to see what I'm doing.

It's cold up here, much colder than before. But I don't stay cold for long. I crawl into the narrow space and heave the bags and boxes out of the cupboard. The first box contains paperwork, old receipts and bills, bank statements and instruction manuals for kitchen equipment. Another box contains baby clothes and toys. A wave of sadness passes through me. Mum must've been keeping these for when our baby sister arrived. It's hard to imagine her pregnant, and her and Dad's life ripped away in a split second of evil. A single gunshot and life as they knew it was over for them.

One gunshot.

I sit back on my haunches with a dreaded sense of unease. One gunshot. They never caught the culprit. Never found the weapon. Dad saw the intruder flee with it. But is it a coincidence that Dad has asked me to find a gun and get rid of it? I shake my head. Dad loves Mum. I can't remember the full extent of the night it all happened, but I've witnessed the depression he's suffered over the years. The times he's disappeared for nights on end because he couldn't cope seeing Mum the way she is. Leaving us with Auntie Audrey and, as we grew older, alone, to look after Mum ourselves.

I swallow the ball of unease lodged in my throat.

Was it depression? Or was it guilt?

The uncertainty torments me as I wade through the rest of the cupboard. It's pretty organised, but moving some of the bigger boxes proves a struggle. Disappointment after disappointment weighs me down when I replace another lid on another box without success. But the next one grabs my attention.

I open the clear plastic box. Inside is a stack of what appears to be old notebooks. I pick one up. It's a diary. I flick through it as a noise from downstairs disturbs me. It sounds like people are talking. I edge out of the space, hoping to hell V hasn't come home from work early. I step over the mess and lean over the staircase. Jamie is talking to someone at the front door. I can't work out what they're saying, but the low baritone of the exchange tells me he isn't conversing with my sister. It must be one of those charity collectors who often knock at this time of year.

The door closes. Jamie's footsteps thump up the stairs. 'Your mum's fallen asleep. I thought you might like some help.'

'Who was at the door?' I ask.

'Some carol singers. I slipped them twenty quid and told them to come back later.'

'That's very generous of you.'

He shrugs. 'It was for the kids' hospice in town. A worthy cause.'

'I'll go and get the monitor so I can hear if Mum wakes up.' I point to the junk room. 'I've found a box of what looks like Mum's old diaries. There's a heavy box beneath it that I can't move.'

I run downstairs. Jamie has covered Mum with a blanket that V crocheted for her years ago. I set up her monitor and return upstairs to find him rummaging through a box.

He holds a faded gold-plated trophy in his hand. 'Looks like I've found out what your dad could've been doing with a gun.'

I place my hands on my hips. 'What?'

He pulls out a framed photograph from the box and raises it in the air. 'It looks as if at some point, years ago, he belonged to a gun club.'

I take the photo. The frame falls apart. I remove the photo. On the back, *1978* is written in pencil. 'That was way before I was even born. I wonder what happened to the gun, then.' I let out a low moan. 'This is all making me feel sick to the core. Dad must've been mistaken.'

'Perhaps he used to keep a gun, but the drugs are playing with his mind,' Jamie says. 'That happens, you know. There was this resident in the care home where I used to work. A woman. She'd been in a horrific car accident.'

A shiver runs down my spine, thinking back to the accident the other day. It could've been so much worse.

Jamie continues. 'The craziest of stuff was coming out of the poor woman's mouth.'

'Or perhaps he got it wrong, and he put it somewhere else up here. We haven't got time now. I'll take another look when V is out.'

26

VIOLET

Rose shoots down the hallway running her hands through her hair before Violet has even had the chance to close the front door. 'Where the hell have you been?'

Violet doesn't know what to say. It wasn't her intention to stay so long in Radstone, but she couldn't draw herself away from viewing the Watsons through her new toy. It was like being glued to the screen of a good TV show. She was completely mesmerised. The man who has wrecked their lives was only metres away. She wanted to go around to the front of the house and rip his throat out.

But she has better plans for Will Watson.

'I got held up.' Violet shuts the door. The lies have started and she hasn't even removed her shoes.

'It's half-nine. You're usually home by seven-thirty at the latest. Why didn't you answer your phone? Or call, even? I've been worried about you.'

'I left my phone here.'

The lines of Rose's forehead crease. 'I thought you'd been in an accident or something. That's all we need.'

'I'm sorry.'

'Where have you been?'

Violet sat watching them, scheming, determining how best to exert the most psychological pain. What would hurt the most? Not realising at first that the answer was in plain sight.

They ate their evening meal and sat talking for over an hour, before Will washed up while Tiffany curled up on the sofa like a cat by the bifold doors and browsed through a magazine.

'I went for a drink after work,' Violet says.

'Who with?' her sister asks.

'A friend.'

'What friend?' Rose stares at her blankly.

Of course she doesn't believe her. Violet doesn't have any friends. She never has, except Rose and Mum, but they don't really count. 'Someone from work,' she says.

'I was going out of my mind.' Rose's hands flap around. 'I thought perhaps you'd gone to see Dad, but the hospice said you haven't been there.'

'How's Mum?'

'She's watching TV.'

'I'll put her to bed tonight.'

'I need to ask you something.' Rose tugs her arm. 'Come with me.'

If this is about moving Mum into a home again, Violet is going to completely lose it.

She follows her sister into the living room, where Mum is dozing in her chair. A box sits on the coffee table with several of Dad's old trophies lined up next to it. 'What are you doing with all these?' Violet picks up a faded gold gloss-coated medal.

'Did Dad use to belong to some kind of gun club?' Rose shoves a photo in a broken frame at her. Her sister is growing more and more agitated. And so is Violet.

Violet stares at the photo.

'There's more.' Rose picks up two more framed photos from the box and holds them up to show her.

'Where did you find these?' Violet asks.

'In the cupboard in the junk room.'

'What were you doing in there?' Violet knows the answer. But she wants to hear her sister say it.

Her sister shrugs. 'Having a clear-out.' Her cheeks redden.

'Whatever for?' she asks.

'I thought it was about time we started sorting out Dad's affairs.'

Her sister was looking for the gun. Violet knows she was. Dad has realised that he should've got rid of that gun years ago. Her sister would have no other reason to be up there.

'I told you that I'll do all that. You've enough going on with work.' She replaces the photos in the box and picks up another medal. 'I remember some of these being out on the mantlepiece. Mum hated them. She said they were plastic pieces of junk – not to Dad, of course.' She snorts at the memory. 'One day, when he was away on a work trip, she took them all down. I guess that's how they all ended up in storage.'

'Did he keep a gun from those days?' her sister asks.

Violet adopts an innocent blank stare. 'Why would he have? It's illegal to keep a gun, isn't it?'

Her sister's face is bright red now, confirming what Violet has thought all along. Dad has asked her sister to do his dirty work for him and get rid of that gun.

Her sister shrugs. 'I don't know. I'm just asking.'

27

VIOLET

People have often told Violet she doesn't smile enough. But today, happiness and charm exude from her like the glow of a fire on a cold day.

It feels so unnatural, but she gives herself credit for carrying it off as she stands sideways beaming in the gym mirror. She drops her head from one side to another perusing the prosthetic she ordered from Amazon. It works a treat. When she first opened that parcel last night, she beamed from ear to ear. She couldn't wait to strap it around her middle. She places her hand on her bump. She's never wanted kids. But there's something strangely satisfying about this pretence of carrying another life.

She borrowed a pair of her sister's Lycra three-quarter length leggings. Rose won't miss them. Her sister hasn't exercised since leaving school. Her work and looking after Mum are enough to keep her fit, her sister says. The leggings were too big for Violet, even with the fake baby bump tucked inside. But it's fine. She found a safety pin and used it to fasten them, making them smaller. Paired with one of her oversized T-shirts, the adjustment is barely noticeable.

Based on the internet research she carried out last night, she can get away with saying she's five months along. She read about what it's like to be at this stage of pregnancy. It took a while to get all the details straight in her head.

She's felt her baby move – gentle kicks that have brought her and her husband immense joy. She gets tired at night, but she's more energised than during the first trimester, which was a nightmare. The morning sickness. Oh! the morning sickness. She suffered dreadfully. Weeks of nausea from dawn to dusk, when she struggled to keep anything down. She lost weight. A lot of weight. But she's slowly putting it back on. Oh, and the mood swings during those first few months, another cruel ordeal. The father? Yes, her husband, Declan, works in the city. He's as excited as her about the baby. Nursery? Yes, Declan's been decorating the spare room. They've gone for a pale yellow and grey combo, then it doesn't matter if a boy or a girl arrives. They can always change it when they're a bit older.

She's rather impressed with herself with the story she's concocted.

She pops two pieces of chewing gum into her mouth. The risk of smelling of smoke from the cigarette she had before she came here is not one she can afford to take.

Tiffany is already in the gym. When she came out of her house this morning, Violet followed her here and waited in her car to give Tiffany enough time to drop off Leo at childcare and get changed. Tiffany hasn't seen her yet. Everything is going to plan.

She's hanging her coat in a locker, when the changing room door opens and bangs shut. Two red-faced women enter, discussing the steps they've climbed on the StairMaster and the number of kilos they've lifted. 'Forty? You managed forty on the lat pulldown?' one says. 'That's impressive. I can barely do twenty.'

Violet zones out. She hasn't planned a workout. Usually, she pounds the streets, but she can't be seen doing that level of exercise being five months pregnant. No, she must accept that she needs to go with the flow this morning. For someone who takes a rigid structure to life, this more relaxed approach doesn't sit comfortably with her. But she'll have to suck it up.

She ties her hair into a bun at the nape of her neck and walks to the mirror, where she applies a layer of lip gloss. Her eyes look kind of good. She's pretty impressed. She 'borrowed' some of Prunella's make-up before she left the apartment, along with the black baggy pair of trousers and an over-sized cream jumper. Trendy, and not an outfit she'd usually wear, but when she got home and tried them on, she had to admit, they rather suited her. The trousers feature a drawstring waist, ideal for accommodating her growing bump. She'll return them to Prunella's wardrobe when she's done with Tiffany. Not that Prunella will miss them. The woman must have over one hundred pairs of trousers, and don't even get Violet started on jumpers – double that number, triple even.

After putting Mum to bed last night, she spent hours watching YouTube clips and TikTok videos on how to apply eye shadow, concealer, foundation and lipstick. It was quite an eye-opener learning how to do it properly. She didn't realise it was such an art, and, actually, how hard it would be. It took some perseverance. After the first application of the blue eye shadow, she looked like she had two black eyes, And the layer of foundation made her look like a clown. She needed to be more subtle, according to one YouTuber. And she needed to moisturise those cracked lips. Advice that ultimately led her to the result she was hoping for. But the concealer, that worked well straight away. It camouflaged her spots nicely.

When she enters the gym, it's buzzing with mid-morning activity. It's an impressive set-up, large and spacious, with a selection of cardio equipment, weight machines, and a mix of apparatus and free weights at the far end. She spots Tiffany straight away, pedalling on one of a line of stationary bikes that overlook a kids' play area.

Perfect.

Here goes.

28

ROSE

I drop three slices of toast into the toaster, eyeing Mum sitting at the table. Her head has dropped to her chest.

I yawn. I took the box of diaries to my room and stayed up late last night perusing them, reading about the early years of Mum and Dad's marriage, how they met at a bar where she used to work part-time to supplement her earnings as an artist. She used to paint seascapes and sell them in a local gallery. The diary entries are meticulous, dotted with etchings of flowers and love hearts, the sun and seascapes.

It's hard to think of the near-dead woman, who I call Mum, as a free spirit. I wish I'd been old enough to remember her in those days.

I butter the toast and feed her, but she barely eats half a slice. 'Mum, I have something to show you.' I run upstairs to fetch the box of diaries from my bedroom and return to her. 'Look what I found in the junk room. I thought I could read them to you.' I remove the lid and pick up one with 1999 etched across the front. 'Your diaries, Mum. All your writing and beautiful drawings. This is the year Violet was born. Look, there's a beautiful photo of you with her just after you gave birth.'

Her eyes widen, and her shoulders shake. She does this when she's agitated. I need to calm her down before she starts to flail her arms. Too late! Her upper body goes into spasm.

I throw the diary back into the box. 'It's OK, Mum. It's fine.' I apply pressure to her shoulders and gently squeeze them. A movement that usually calms her. 'We don't have to look at them.'

Her jaw trembles. My heart goes out to her. She looks as if she's about to cry. 'Mum, Mum. It's fine.'

She glares at the box, wide-eyed. It's as if the sight of them is scaring her. If only she could tell me why.

'It's OK. I'll throw them away.' I kick the box outside the room. 'We never have to see them again.'

The doorbell sounds. 'That'll be Beth,' I say.

I run to answer the door to bubbly Beth. She's Mum's faithful childhood friend who visits without fail at this time every week for an hour, sometimes longer. It's a Godsend, allowing me an hour's breather on my day off work. She kisses me as she always does and heads through to the kitchen, continually talking.

Mum is still glaring at the box.

'She's a bit upset,' I say.

'Leave her to me.' She walks over to the kitchen table. She points to the box I brought down from the cupboard in the junk room. 'What's this?'

'Some old Christmas decorations I found.'

'I'll see if I can interest your mum in getting a few of them up.' Beth flicks the kettle switch as if she's in her own home. She nods towards the door. 'Go and do what you need to do.'

I grab the box of diaries and run upstairs to the sound of Beth yapping about the weather and how people are doing their Christmas food shopping early to avoid the impending snowstorms that are due.

Flopping down onto my bed, I open the box and remove the diary I fell asleep reading last night. There's a sense of wrongness about what I'm doing. These are Mum's private thoughts. But I'm compelled to carry on, especially given her recent reaction.

Something about them obviously disturbed her, and if this can be some sort of gateway into her subconscious, then going through them could be time well spent. A trigger, maybe a happy event, anything that may help bring Mum back to a more communicative state.

So far, these diaries have been filled with nothing but beauty and happiness. I can't understand what Mum got so upset about until I reach the end of 2008, the year before she was shot, and realise it's the last one.

Either she didn't write a diary the year she was shot, or it's somewhere else.

Or it's been destroyed.

29

VIOLET

Violet slides onto the bike beside Tiffany. The hard seat digs into her bones. She sets the dials for a slow workout. Violet Sapphire could bike ten times this speed, twenty or thirty even, but she mustn't forget, Summer Smith is five months pregnant.

Loud music plays from large speakers dotted along the walls. She can't understand how people can work out in places like this. She grits her teeth, trying to block it out and focus on what she's here for.

Violet stretches her T-shirt over her bump, patiently waiting for Tiffany to begin the conversation they're going to have. If she doesn't, then Violet will have to, but it's better for Tiffany to kick it off.

Violet doesn't have to wait long.

'Hi,' Tiffany says.

Violet turns her head.

Tiffany flashes a smile. Her teeth are beautiful: straight and dazzling white. What Violet would give for teeth like that. Her bottom ones are misaligned as if her jaw is too small to accommodate them all. Auntie Audrey took her to the dentist when she was young, but she flatly refused to have the ugly braces fitted that they advised would straighten her teeth. She was teased enough at school for the way she looked.

Tiffany nods at Violet's belly. 'So how are things going?'

'All good, thanks.' Violet points at Tiffany's bump. 'And you?'

Tiffany sits up straight, still pedalling, and runs her fingers along the inside of the waistband of her shorts. Beads of perspiration on her forehead glisten in the natural light shining through windows that stretch from the floor to the ceiling. 'All good, too.' She lifts a hand to her chest. 'Apart from the heartburn in the evening, and the need to pee all night, I can't complain.'

'How far gone are you?' Violet asks.

'Five months.'

Violet places her hands across her bump. 'Me too.'

'Boy or a girl?' Tiffany asks.

She shrugs. 'We haven't found out. My husband doesn't want to. You?'

'A girl.'

Violet clenches her jaw while forcing a well-rehearsed smile.

A girl.

Like her mum was having when this woman's husband shot her.

'Which hospital are you having it at?' Tiffany asks.

Damn. That's one thing she hasn't researched. *Think,*

Violet. Think. 'Oh, I'm having a home birth.' She makes a mental note: research home births and birthing pools.

Tiffany's mouth stretches open in wonder. 'That's brave. Is it your first?'

Violet nods. 'My husband thinks I'm mad, but it'll make the whole experience more relaxing for me to be at home. I'm not good with hospitals, you see. They make me anxious. A midwife will be with me. And my husband, of course.' She grimaces. This conversation needs steering away from her. 'And you?' she asks.

'Oh, my husband would never agree to a home birth. Will's a bit of a wuss when it comes to anything medical.' Tiffany laughs. 'He can't even deal with our son's cuts and scrapes. We're having her in the Royal Free.'

'That's where I'll end up if there are any complications.' Violet makes a mental note to also research that hospital. She hopes it's not private. That could throw up complications. 'How's your husband coping with it all?' she asks.

'He's good, when he's around,' Tiffany replies. 'He works long hours.'

'Snap.'

'What does your husband do?' Tiffany asks.

'He works for a bank in the city. What about yours?' Violet asks before Tiffany asks her which bank he works for. She has an answer – Citibank – but this conversation needs to focus on Tiffany.

'He owns a scaffolding company,' Tiffany says.

'It's hard owning your own business. My dad owned his own company and was never around.' Violet stops there. The less said about her father, the better.

Tiffany rolls her eyes. 'Sounds about right. Will works such long hours. It's caused a bit of a rift between us lately, if

I'm honest, but he's getting better. He's promised to be home by six every evening, which he has kept to for the past couple of weeks. Saying that, he has a meeting tonight, so he's warned me he can't.' She touches her belly. 'It's my second. We already have a son, Leo. He's three. This pregnancy has been a bit stressful. Actually, very stressful. Which is why...' She dips her head. '...No disrespect, but I couldn't have her anywhere but a hospital.' She lowers her voice. 'I've had two miscarriages.'

Bingo.

What a perfect opportunity for some more bonding!

'Oh, I'm sorry to hear that,' Violet says. 'I've had one, as well.'

Tiffany stops pedalling. 'Have you?' Her voice rises in intonation.

Violet forces her lips to curve downwards. She nods. 'Last year.'

'I'm so sorry. And you're still set on a home birth? How brave.'

Violet shrugs. 'Yep. Some things are meant to be.'

Miscarriages – another thing she must research.

'That's a philosophical way to look at it,' Tiffany says.

'It's what's got me through the ordeal.'

Tiffany nods. 'I could take a leaf out of your book.' She holds a hand out in Violet's direction. 'I'm Tiffany, by the way.'

Violet shakes her hand. 'Summer. Summer Smith.'

'Good to meet you, Summer. We have a lot in common.'

More than you could ever imagine, Tiffany Watson.

'We sure have,' Violet says.

'I haven't seen you here before.'

'I've only just joined.'

Weights clang around the building as they chat about the ups and downs and highs and lows of the rollercoaster of pregnancy. Violet sways the chat back to her new friend when she asks questions, and like she hoped, they build up a good rapport. Tiffany's a chatterbox, which helps. Before she knows it, Violet has been pedalling for fifteen minutes, but it's a gentle walk in the park compared to the workouts she usually does.

Tiffany stops her bike and whips away the towel that's draped over the console. 'That's me done for today.' She holds the towel over her face, soaking up the beads of sweat. 'It's been nice chatting to you, Summer. I hope to see you here again.'

Oh, don't you worry, Tiffany. You will most certainly see me again.

This is only the beginning of your worst nightmare.

30

VIOLET

Violet presses the stop button on her bike. 'I'm done here, too.' She fakes a laugh. 'I'm under strict instructions from my husband to take it easy the first few times.' She throws Tiffany an endearing wink. 'But I think I'll sneak in a few weights.'

'I'm going to get changed,' Tiffany says. 'Hopefully, see you around.'

'Sure.'

'Call me Tiff. Everyone else does.' Tiffany flashes her perfect smile and wishes her goodbye.

Violet wanders around the weight machines, looking for one that a pregnant woman would find manageable. The chest press machine appears a suitable option. She places her towel on the seat and sits, but she doesn't lift any weights. She's pumped enough as it is. Pumped full of adrenaline on what she's achieved... and for what's to come.

She opens Google on her phone and searches for home births. She needs to know what she's talking about for when Tiffany asks her more questions.

Because she will.

She checks the Royal Free. Thankfully, it's not a private hospital. She reads about birthing plans and birthing pools for the most positive experience, and the required alternative in case everything goes tits up, and she needs to get to hospital in an emergency. And it's not a given. If her pregnancy develops any complications or her baby turns from a head-down position, then all bets are off.

She peruses miscarriages. Because it's another subject that's bound to come up again at some point. She prepares a story for when that time arises. Hers started with stomach cramps that became unbearable. She thought it was food poisoning at first. She should have known, eh? But she never suspected a thing until she passed some blood. That's when Declan insisted on taking her to hospital. They scanned her, prodded and poked, and took bloods, before declaring her baby had died. Declan took it hard. It was an emotional time for both of them. No, they never found out why. It was one of those things.

Abandoning her plans to lift a few weights, she heads back to the changing rooms.

Tiffany has showered and changed into maternity jeans and a Christmas jumper that fits snugly over her neat bump. 'Hi, again,' she says. 'Enjoy the rest of your workout?'

'I didn't do much.'

'Listen, I'm taking Leo to the café for a quick bite to eat if you'd like to join us.'

Violet smiles. She can't believe her blessing. This woman

is playing right into her hands. 'Sure. Why not?' she says. 'That workout has made me rather hungry.'

Tiffany grabs her bag. 'Great. I'll collect him and see you down there.'

Violet grabs her belongings from her locker, hardly able to believe her good fortune. Her mind is racing, and she's tingling inside. Tiffany is making this far easier than she could ever have hoped for. She's in control here. And it's proving to be even more fun than she thought.

She finds a private changing cubicle and throws on Prunella's trousers and cream jumper. The bump has slipped slightly, and it's a little sweaty around her abdomen, so she tightens the belt. That's better. She checks herself in the mirror. This bump thing suits her. No it doesn't. The change is in her face. It's all the make-up that suits her.

The café is as busy as it was the other day, the gentle buzz of chatter and the squeals and shrieks from toddlers filling the air. Tiffany's already here, drinking a glass of what looks like hot chocolate and feeding cheese curls to her son. She waves, beckoning Violet over to their table. 'I've got you a chair.' She points to her son. 'This is Leo.' Despite the orange crisp smudge lining the boy's upper lip like a moustache, he is cute. As cute as kids go, that is. 'I didn't know what to get you, and Leo was hungry, so I went ahead.'

'No worries. I'll grab a drink,' Violet says.

She orders a caffeine-free coffee from an orange-haired woman who is serving behind the counter. Her dark eyes are rimmed in black eyeliner that is effective. Violet might give that look a go with her newfound make-up application skills. 'Milk?' the woman asks.

She's hardly burnt any calories this morning. 'Black, please.' She turns and eyes Tiffany, who is talking to someone on her phone, laughing. She's so pretty. Violet can't help but think it's kind of a shame, with what she has planned.

The server slides the drink across the counter, and Violet returns to Tiffany and Leo. But a woman has joined them, perched on the spare chair with a toddler on her lap. Tiffany introduces the two strangers. Violet cringes. Meeting other people is not part of her plan. As if she senses her discomfort, the woman jumps up. 'See you around, Tiff. And thanks again for your help. You're a lifesaver.'

'Anytime,' Tiffany says.

'The world needs more kind people like you in the world.' The woman nods at Violet and departs.

A sudden pang of guilt claws at Violet's chest. She shouldn't be doing this.

Nonsense. She tells herself to shut up. This isn't about Tiffany. It's about her husband. She needs to understand who she's married to.

'I like your jumper,' Tiffany says. 'Trendy. Where did you get it from?'

Butterflies flutter beneath Violet's fake belly. She tries to think where Prunella could've bought it from. She should've read the label. There's so much to think about. 'A friend gave it to me. I'm not sure where she bought it.'

Tiffany takes a sip of her hot chocolate. 'Nice friend.'

Leo bangs his iPad screen and laughs. 'Look, Mummy. It's Farmer Christmas.'

Tiffany laughs affectionately and ruffles his hair. 'It's Father Christmas, darling.'

'Is he coming tonight?'

Tiffany gives him a mother's loving smile. 'No. Not today. I told you this morning, remember. It's next week.'

'You've got another eight sleeps.' Violet smiles. Nine days to go, eight more sleeps.

'That's forever,' the young kid says.

'Don't worry,' Violet says. 'It'll pass quickly. Before we all know it, it'll be Christmas Eve, and you'll be putting out a mince pie for your Farmer Christmas and a carrot for his reindeer.'

Eight more sleeps before she can seek her revenge.

Violet takes a sip of coffee. It tastes as rich as revenge.

A woman appears. She has the lined and yellowing face of someone who has smoked a million cigarettes, and she reeks of smoke. Even Violet can smell it. 'Morning.' The woman plants a kiss on top of Tiffany's head.

'Nana.' Leo bangs the table in delight.

'Hello, gorgeous.' The woman kisses his head.

'Karen, meet my new friend, Summer,' Tiffany says. 'Summer, this is my mother-in-law, Karen.'

So this is the woman who birthed that monster. Anger and revulsion mount inside her. The urge to scratch this woman's eyes out consumes her. *Control, Violet, control. All good things come to those who wait.* She places her hands beneath her legs.

'I'm not staying,' Karen says. 'I've just been to my class.'

'How's it going?' Tiffany asks.

'I'm working my way to quitting on the first of January.'

'You can do it.'

'I need to get to work,' Karen says. 'I'll pop round tomorrow.'

When Karen leaves, Tiffany says, 'She's doing a stop-smoking class in the Community Hub.' She lowers her voice. 'I'm so pleased because she smokes like a chimney.'

'Do you get on with her?' Violet asks. She has so many

questions. The desire to learn more about Will Watson and his family is all-consuming.

'I do. I love her dearly. She's a very sweet woman.' Tiffany asks more about Declan.

Violet turns the conversation back to her. 'Where do you get your maternity jeans from? Mine shrunk in the wash and I need to get some new ones.' It's the best she can think of off the top of her head.

'I've got loads of them. When I was pregnant with Leo, friends kept giving me their old ones, and I've bought a few new pairs this time around. I must have about ten at home. I could give you enough to see you through the rest of your pregnancy if you want.'

'Really?'

'Sure. If you don't mind second-hand clothes. They're all in great condition.'

'Not at all,' Violet says. Her stomach flips in excitement. She can't believe how well this is going. 'Sounds great.'

'What are you up to after this?' Tiffany asks.

'I'm going home.'

'Come back with me, and I'll dig out a few pairs for you.'

Sometimes things are meant to be.

This has all been far, far easier than she anticipated.

And she's loving it.

31

ROSE

I can't understand what could have happened to the 2009 diary. It seems odd that Mum wrote diaries for so many years, and in so much detail, but she didn't write one the year she was shot. Perhaps Dad found it after the shooting and discovered personal stuff she'd written that, for some reason, he didn't think she'd ever want anyone else to find. Maybe he still has it somewhere. In the cupboard in the eaves, perhaps, where he appears to have hidden all his other secrets.

I open up the 2008 diary. It starts with the same theme as the others: stars, beautiful flowers and hearts etched around the written entries.

Her love for me and V is evident in the time she devoted to us. I ache for what could have been. Photographs randomly appear of her engaging in activities with us. She put all her creative skills to play, teaching us to draw and paint, bake cakes and decorate paper plates to look like bunnies for Easter. Strangely, though, there are few of us with Dad. I know he worked away a lot, but I would've expected more of us as a family.

Mid-June, the niceties take a turn. Each page shocks me a little more. Passages of writing are scribbled out, and the charming etchings morph into images of the devil, fires and men hanging from the beams in our living room.

She no longer wrote about daily living: the milestones V and I had reached, the new tablecloth she stitched from an old piece of fabric she found in a charity shop, or what she cooked for dinner. As I turn the pages, her vivacious story-telling grows darker and darker, centring around her concern regarding the amount of time Dad spent away from home.

Dad's job took him across the globe, from Vegas to Toronto, Paris to Sydney. It's why I thought Auntie Audrey featured so much in our lives after Mum's shooting. Every time he came home from one of his trips, he used to bring us chocolate. I remember it so vividly. I used to climb onto his lap and he'd tell me colourful stories about all the places he'd visited.

At the end of July that year, Mum first challenged him. I gasp. She asked him if he was having an affair. He laughed at her, telling her she was being bonkers. She was the love of his life. There was no room for any other.

That August, Dad was around more. Mum was happier, it seems. But in September, what I learn shocks me to the core. After Mum dropped me and V at school on the first day of term, she visited the doctor's. She saw things. Things she knew weren't really there but that didn't stop them appearing, especially at night. Images of the devil and zombies. And she was depressed, she told him. Why? Her husband was having an affair, she wrote, and she had moments when she wanted to end her life, she told the doctor. He prescribed antidepressants and referred her for some urgent counselling.

Flowers and hearts reappear, woven around her words like a border. But in October, the entries are so heavily scribbled out that the black ink has bled through the page. It's impossible to read the words beneath.

I can't flick through the pages fast enough. November is blank. No words or etchings at all. December begins with drawings of morbid characters. It's dark and highly unsettling. I swallow hard, my mouth as dry as sand. Mum went through Dad's stuff when he wasn't around. She rummaged through his coat pockets after he returned from one of his stints away, and his trouser pockets in the laundry basket as if she were a private detective undertaking an investigation into someone else's marriage. Tiny black crosses emboldened with black ink surround each sentence.

I read aloud the entry from 5 December 2008:

He's now told me he won't be home for Christmas. He has to work and will leave the day before Christmas Eve, but I know he's going to be with her. Whoever 'her' is. But I will find her. I will. And God forgive me now for what I will do to her.

I turn the pages faster and faster.

Mum's frustration led her to self-harming in the form of starving herself. She ate only rice cakes for breakfast, skipped lunch and pushed food around her plate, pretending to eat when she sat at the dining table with V and me for dinner.

I catch my breath. It's how V behaves.

Mum noted her daily calorie intake, a number assigned to

everything that passed her lips. It was a pitiful amount. I wonder if this behaviour rubbed off on V.

When I reach the final entry of the year, the taste of toast burns the back of my throat. Mum arranged for Auntie Audrey to babysit me and V. She told her that she had to pick up some last-minute gifts for me and V, so she couldn't take us with her. But really, Mum was planning to follow Dad when he went out the day before Christmas Eve.

I turn the page. My stomach flips three-sixty. A photograph of a woman sitting on a beach with three young boys is glued on the page. And beside it an address, 23, Brook Street, Cadley.

And underneath, Mum scribbled *Gotcha.*

32

VIOLET

This is Violet's chance. Her chance to weave herself into the fabric of this family. The opportunity to find out what makes them tick – discover how she can hurt them the most. And it has happened far quicker than she could have hoped for, which is great news. After all, she's working to a tight time-frame. Christmas Eve is fast approaching.

'What about your husband? Will he mind if I come back?' she asks Tiffany on their way out of the building. Will Watson is the last person she can afford to bump into. How will she explain that the passenger in the car he ran into the other day is standing on his doormat? And now she's five months pregnant. She shudders. That simply cannot happen.

'I already told you. Will's always at work. He's never home before six.' Tiffany stops in her tracks and frowns. 'Anyway, why should it matter if he's there?'

Violet shrugs. 'It doesn't. I just don't want to get in anyone's way.'

Tiffany laughs. 'You overthink things.' She stops at her car. 'This is me.' The wind blows her hair around her pretty face like she's the lead role in a movie. She is. Violet's movie. Tiffany tries to tame her hair with her spare hand but strands fly all over the place.

Leo wriggles to escape her hold. Tiffany tightens her grip around his hips. 'Wait, darling.' She opens the car door, struggling to contain her son, and turns to Violet. 'You can follow us, but let me give you my address in case we get parted.'

'Sure.' Violet holds up her phone. 'I'll put it into my sat nav. Go ahead.'

Tiffany buckles Leo into his car seat, reciting her address.

Violet pretends to type it into her phone. 'Is it far?' she asks.

'About ten minutes away. In case you get lost, my number is...' She reels it off.

Violet could squeal with joy. A gust of wind sends a shiver through her. She didn't plan to get her new 'friend's' number, but it will come in handy. 'Thanks. I'll see you soon.'

Violet slows as she reaches the next set of lights, purposely getting stuck at a red. She doesn't need Tiffany keeping an eye on her. When she arrives at number 12 the Ridgeway, Tiffany is getting Leo out of the car. Tiffany beckons her to park in the driveway next to her. Violet pretends not to see her. The less that is seen of her car for now, the better. Instead, she parks on the road opposite a few houses away, picks up her phone and texts Auntie Audrey.

. . .

I've got stuck at work. Would you go with
Rose to take Mum to see Dad, please?

She knows it's not the best thing for Mum, but she'll understand when she explains later. This is a means to an end.

The end of the Watsons.

She texts her sister, then catches up with Tiffany as she's walking into her house. 'Take your coat off. I'll be with you in a minute. I need to see to Leo.'

Violet commits to memory the code Tiffany punches into the keypad of the alarm. One. Three. Eight. Seven. She'll be needing that.

Having viewed it from the outside, the inside of the Watsons' house is everything Violet imagined. It's not a palace, but the furnishings are opulent and luxurious, from the mammoth crystal chandelier lighting up the hallway to the floating glass staircase. A little too modern for this older-house style, but who is she to judge? Her interior design skills are about as imaginative as a moth's. It's evident money has been spent feverously. Even the vast array of Christmas decorations is somehow tasteful. Slightly garish, but in keeping with the décor.

Tiffany mouths, 'We're toilet training.' She heads to a door to the left of the entrance. Leo is sitting on a potty.

Violet jumps at the opportunity to see more of this house. 'Do you have another toilet?' She points to her fake bump. 'My bladder control is dreadful since I fell pregnant.'

Tiffany laughs. 'Tell me about it.' She points to the stairs. 'Up at the far end of the hallway.'

Violet kicks off her shoes and climbs the floating stair-case. This isn't conducive to a growing family. One wrong foot and her kids will be nosediving to the bottom. She pauses and grabs the glass handrail. Her breath quickens as the memory haunts her from all those years ago. The deafening gunshot. Mum tumbling down the stairs. Her white nightie stained with blood. Dad bellowing. A familiar bolt of pain shoots through her head. It's intense and harrowing.

'Are you OK?' Tiffany stands at the bottom of the stairs peering up.

'I'm fine.' Violet looks down. 'I got a bit breathless. It happens at times these past few weeks. I guess it's the baby growing.'

Tiffany climbs a step. 'Are you sure?'

'All good.'

'Would you like a drink?'

'Coffee would be lovely, thanks. Black.'

'Sugar?'

'No sugar. Black.'

'Maybe some sugar would do you good?'

Violet waves her away and continues to the top, where she heads towards the toilet. But she doesn't go straight there. She stops on the way at the first bedroom and quietly opens the door. It's Leo's room. Sunlight floods through the large bay window, bouncing off the matching teal-blue painted furni-ture. It's beautiful. The white duvet cover with a dinosaur print matches the curtains and rug, as well as the line of bunting running the length of the bed. A giant stuffed giraffe, its head almost touching the ceiling, stands in the corner of the room, looking over the Pyrenees of toys.

'Mummy, I'm done,' the kid shouts from downstairs. 'Look. I've done a wee.'

Violet closes his bedroom door and stops at the next room. It's a spare room, she guesses, with a double bed pushed into the corner, and a tall, narrow chest of drawers homing a large designer glass lamp.

The door to the next room squeaks as she pushes it open. Tiffany's expensive perfume, a refined hearty smell, wafts in the air. This must be the master bedroom. She pauses, listening for Tiffany and Leo's exchange from downstairs. The toilet flushes. Tiffany tells him what a good boy he is.

The same as in Leo's room, sunlight beams through the large windows. The king-size double bed takes centre stage, dressed with the best of designer floral bedding and colourful plumped-up cushions resting against the pillows. It's the same make of bedding as Prunella buys. Built-in wardrobes and cabinets painted an off-white line the walls on either side of the window and to the side of the door. The décor in this house makes their home look so shabby. She can't remember the last time Dad decorated, or rather, he got the decorators in – not since he had the dining room converted to a bedroom for Mum.

The room is like a magnet, pulling her in. She can't resist it. She steps inside and perches on the side of the bed. Her heart thumps double time. She can't quite believe it. She's sitting on the bed of the man who has wrecked her life. She runs her hand along the soft, silky duvet cover. A man's watch sits atop the bedside cabinet, along with a book on motorcycles. This is where he sleeps.

With a trembling hand, she gently slides open the drawer of the bedside cabinet. Among the contents, she comes across a remote control for the giant flat screen on the opposite wall, a phone charger, some kind of medical cream, and a pair of earphones. She picks up the remote control and slips it into her bag. The sound of footsteps bounds up the stairs. She needs to get out of here. Fast.

She steps across the hallway to the toilet, flushes the chain and washes her hands, drying them on the white Egyptian towel. It's soft and fluffy, unlike the greying, rough towels they have at home. When did they last get new towels? Never. She rolls up the bundle of softness and shoves it into her bag.

Leo runs into his room. He doesn't see her. She hurries along the landing and starts to descend the stairs when a knock at the front door stops her in her tracks. Tiffany floats along the downstairs hallway. She glances up and spots her. 'Everything OK?'

'All good,' Violet replies.

Leo comes rushing past her, waving a train. He shuffles down the stairs on his bum.

Tiffany peers through the small, narrow hallway window and gasps. 'Well, I never. That's Will's car. He must've picked it up from the garage.'

Violet stops mid step. Her pulse races, beating in her ears.

Tiffany turns to her. 'Hey, guess what? It's my husband. He's home early. You can meet him.'

33

ROSE

I reread the text from V.

> Sorry, I won't make it back in time to take
> Mum to see Dad. I've asked Auntie to go with
> you. I'll go later after work. Vx

I sigh. It's meant to be Auntie Audrey's day off. She helps us out enough.

I get Mum ready to go and see Dad, dressing her in her best dress and dabbing blusher on her cheeks. All we need to do is get her coat on.

I'm washing up when Auntie Audrey arrives. She hugs me. Her generous figure is a bundle of comfort. It always has been. 'How come V's got held up at work?' she asks before we go into Mum's room.

I shrug. 'She didn't say. I'm sorry to bother you on your day off.'

She sighs. 'Darling Rose. You've got a lot going on. I'm happy to help. Wow! You've finally got some decorations up.'

'I found them in the junk room. Beth put them up. I'm not sure what V will think.'

'Has she stopped eating again?' Auntie Audrey asks. 'She's lost more weight.'

'I wonder if she's got concussion.' I shrug. 'But she insisted on discharging herself.'

'That's V for you. She's always been stubborn, that girl. I guess you still haven't had the chance to speak to her about Abbeyfields?'

'I've tried. I don't know how we're ever going to get her to agree to it.'

'Perhaps it's best we do it together.'

'As far as she's concerned, Mum's her life work.'

'We need to find a way to make her see sense. Once she's settled, your mum will be happy in a home.'

'Can I ask you a question, Auntie Audrey?'

She lifts one eyebrow. 'Of course.'

'Were Mum and Dad happy? Before the shooting... were they happily married?'

She pulls back her shoulders. 'Wherever did that come from?'

I shrug. I want to tell her about the diaries. Discuss the photo of the woman and children I found, because it's lodged an agonising pain in my chest since I found it.

'Rose Sapphire. I've known you since you popped out of your mother's womb. What's up?'

'It's some things V has said over the years... about Dad never being around.' I shrug. 'I don't know. It's left me wondering if they were happy.'

'They had their ups and downs, as do all married couples, but they were happy.' She looks at her watch. 'Come on, I have to be at the church soon. We'd better get a move on.'

She tails me into Mum's bedroom and helps me put on her coat. Mum isn't being cooperative. 'Come on, Melanie. Help me here. Push your arm in.' Auntie Audrey turns to me. 'You can drive today.'

'Would you?' I thread Mum's other arm through the sleeve of her coat. 'I'm still a bit shaken by the accident, if I'm honest.'

'Well then you should be driving.' Auntie Audrey leans Mum forward in her chair and straightens the back of her coat. 'Get back on the horse and all that.'

'That's what my friend Jamie said.'

'Friend?' She winks at me. 'I hear he's more than a friend.'

'Who said that?'

'V thinks you're more than friends.'

'That's not true.' A wave of redness rushes to my cheeks. 'Will you drive?'

'How about I drive there and you drive back.' She peers at me with raised eyebrows. 'Deal?'

'Deal.'

We get Mum into the car. It's an effort as she hardly weight-bears these days. It's why we don't take her out much anymore. She used to love going out for a drive, but since Dad's diagnosis, she's become uncooperative when we've tried to get her into the car.

Dad is unresponsive when we arrive. Mum resists going into his room, flailing her arms like a stroppy child when I try to wheel her through the door. 'Perhaps it's too upsetting for her,' Auntie Audrey whispers. 'Why don't I take her for a walk and have a chat with her?' She shuffles me out of the way and takes the handle of the wheelchair. 'I'll take her outside for a wander.'

The nurse tending to Dad leaves the room. I sit beside his bed. There's a faint smell of body odour, which is turning my stomach, but not as much as the photo burning a hole in my soul. I come right out with it. 'Dad. You've got to help me. I can't find the gun, but I found this.' I tap his shoulder. 'Open your eyes, Dad. And look at this photo.'

He doesn't move.

'Dad! You've got to help me here. Who are these people?'

Slowly, he opens his eyes.

I hold up the photo I removed from Mum's diary in front of his face. 'Who's this woman, Dad? And who are these children?' I don't know why I'm bothering to ask him. I already know the answer.

He coughs. It's an effort. His lips remain closed, but tears escape from his eyes. They drop down his face like tears of regret.

34

VIOLET

Tiffany clicks the lock of the front door.

Violet's legs turn to jelly. Waves of nausea crash through her. She's about to come face to face with the man she's been hunting for these past fifteen years. He's going to recognise her from the accident... and now with a rounded belly. This isn't part of the plan.

Somehow, she has to make a run for it. She considers her options for her best escape route. Peering towards the back of the house, she wonders if she can escape through the bifold doors. That's got to be her best bet.

She hurries down the stairs, preparing what she's going to say to Tiffany. Her pulse is beating in her ears. This was all going to plan, but now it's all going pear-shaped. Leo rushes past Tiffany, swinging his train and heads to the kitchen.

Tiffany opens the door.

Violet's heart stops.

It's not Will standing on the doormat, but a stout man dressed in blue overalls.

She edges to the wall side of the stairs. The fewer people who see her here at the moment, the better.

The mechanic jangles a set of keys in the air. 'We've brought your husband's car back. He said to post these through the letterbox if you weren't in, but as you are, here you go.'

Tiffany takes the keys. 'That's amazing. So quick.'

'We aim to please.'

'My husband will be delighted. Thank you so much.'

The guy wishes her a good day, nods, and leaves.

Tiffany closes the door and drops the car keys into a ceramic dish filled with other keys on the glass console. When they arrived back here, she chucked her car keys in there, too. Next to the dish is a large glass vase filled with scented cream and pink roses.

Violet descends the remaining stairs, her heart still racing.

'It wasn't Will,' Tiffany says. 'It was the garage delivering his car back.' She rolls her eyes. 'Will probably slipped them some money to get it done so fast. Your coffee's ready. Go through to the kitchen, while I go and hunt out those jeans.'

Slowly Violet walks towards the kitchen, still shaking from the near miss of bumping into Will Watson. When Tiffany's heavy steps tread the floorboards above, she back-steps to the console. Quietly, she searches through the keys in the dish. There must be a spare set in here. The keys clink and scrape against the side as she moves them around. She pauses, wondering how loud she's being. A cupboard door bangs upstairs. The search continues until she finds a single key that is identical to the front door key attached to Tiffany's set of keys. She double-checks before popping it in her pocket.

Leo is playing with his train track when she enters the kitchen. He stares at her. If she's not mistaken, there's a wariness to his expression. But what does she know about kids? She has no experience with children. And never wants to. Mum's voice whispers in her ear, *It's worth befriending this little fella. You never know when he might come in handy.*

'I like your trains.'

He ignores her.

She sits at the same stool where Tiffany sat the other night, talking to Will. She's an arm's length from where he was chopping vegetables. Her whole body starts shaking. She places her hands on the marble surface to steady herself, taking large, deep breaths. Keeping calm is a must. She could ruin everything if she starts showing her nerves now.

She sips her coffee, trying to calm her racing heart. It's too much of a risk her being here. She's playing with fire. Will could turn up at any minute, and all her plans will go up in smoke. Berating herself, she shakes her head. She's panicking unnecessarily. Tiff has already said that Will won't be home before six, and it's not even lunchtime.

She takes deep breaths and looks around. The opulence from the hallway flows into this room featuring high-gloss units and state-of-the-art appliances.

Tiffany appears, her hair now tied pineapple style on top of her head, showing more of her glowing skin. It suits her. 'Here we go.' Three pairs of maternity jeans appear on the worktop. 'I found these jumpers, too.' She digs a handful of tops from a plastic bag. 'I have so many. If you like them, feel free to take them.'

This is handy. Very handy. It'll stop her having to take

Prunella's clothes. And that means she doesn't have to go and clean for her anymore.

Her fingers run along a taupe-coloured knitted jumper, the fabric smooth and silky. 'That's so kind of you.' She swallows hard. Tiffany's kindness is overwhelming. She didn't expect her to be such a lovely person. 'Your house is beautiful. How long have you lived here?'

'Three years. We used to live in a small flat, but Will's business started doing really well, so we decided to invest in a family home.'

'Nice neighbours?'

'Great.' Tiffany nods to the left. 'An older couple live that side. Their children have all left home, and they're thinking of downsizing.' She nods to the right. 'That side is a family with teenage kids.' She points to the clothes. 'Do you want to try them on? You can go into the living room if you want.'

Violet grabs the opportunity to see another room. 'Sure.'

Tiffany points to the hallway. 'First door on the right. Would you like a quick bite to eat while you're here? You must be hungry. You didn't eat in the café, and you said you were peckish earlier on.'

This woman doesn't miss much. Violet needs to be mindful of this.

'I could rustle up a sandwich. I've got some lovely sourdough bread I bought fresh from the bakery yesterday. I always find it better on the second day.'

'I'm fine, thanks, but I should get going after I've tried these on.' Grabbing her bag and the clothes, Violet heads to the living room and closes the door. But she doesn't try any of them on. Instead, she takes in the luxurious velvet sofa, gold coffee table and marble mantelpiece. The curtains match the cushions on the sofa. Wait until she describes all this to Mum.

She picks up a shiny gold-coloured placemat from the coffee table. Grinning, she shoves it into her bag. A rush of adrenaline pulses through her. She never took herself for a thief. She'd never stolen anything before she took those clothes from Prunella's wardrobe and the makeup from her dressing table. But the temporary sense of power she has over this family is like an addictive drug. She can't keep away from it.

From the mantlepiece, she swipes a photo of the three of them – Will, Tiffany and Leo – sitting pretty in an expensive golden frame. They won't miss it. There are about a dozen photo frames here. She throws it in her bag to join the placemat, towel and remote control. It's all petty, apart from the key. But it'll cause a stir when they notice things are missing.

She gives it a couple of minutes before returning to Tiffany.

'Did they fit?' Tiffany asks.

'Like a glove. Thank you. How much do I owe you?'

Tiffany's eyes narrow as if she's offended Violet has introduced money into their new-formed friendship. 'I wouldn't take a penny. There're all yours.' She reaches into a cupboard below the large white butler sink and produces a carrier bag. 'Here you go. Chuck them in there.'

Violet folds the clothes and places them in the plastic bag. The desire to find out more about this woman's husband consumes her. 'Where did you and Will meet?'

She loves him, Violet can tell from the way she smiles every time she mentions his name or talks about him. 'I worked for him,' Tiffany says.

'You slept with the boss?' Violet laughs for effect.

Tiffany raises her eyebrows and nods, suppressing the smile that looks as if it wants to burst from her lips. 'I sure did. I was his PA...' She giggles. 'In more ways than one.' She peers across at Leo playing with his train track and pats her belly. 'I did bear his children, though.'

'How long did you work for him?'

'Not long. Shortly after we got together, I left.'

'Why?'

'Between you and me, I couldn't stand his brother, Lewis, who worked for him back then.'

'He doesn't anymore, then?' Violet asks.

Tiffany shakes her head. 'They had a bust-up shortly after I left and went their separate ways.'

'What was the bust-up about?'

She pauses.

That was one step too far. Violet needs to watch it. She's being too intrusive. But she's inquisitive.

Tiffany continues. 'Let's just say, he's a bit of a loose cannon, is our Lewis. Funnily enough, the business went from strength to strength after that.'

'Do they not speak anymore?'

'They do. It tore the family apart at first, so Will gave in and patched things up with him. He couldn't bear to see his mum so upset. I get on well with his wife, Jacqui, so that made things difficult as well.' She shrugs. 'Families, eh?'

Violet nods.

Families, indeed.

Before Tiffany can ask her any more about her family, Violet downs her drink. 'I must get going. Thanks so much for the clothes.' She turns to Leo who is playing contentedly on the floor. 'Bye, Leo.'

He ignores her and rams a train along the track.

Tiffany rolls her eyes. 'Say goodbye, Leo.'

The boy grunts.

'Sorry,' she says. 'He's tired.'

Violet follows her to the front door. 'Thanks for the coffee.'

'See you at the gym, tomorrow perhaps?' Tiffany says.

'I'll try.'

'You've got my number. Ping me yours.' She laughs. 'And we can chat some more about the trials and tribulations of pregnancy.'

'I will do.'

Violet hurries back to her car, and googles the cheapest way to source a pay-as-you-go phone.

She's got to play the game if she's going to become Tiffany's new bestie.

35

VIOLET

'What do you think?' Violet parades up and down the kitchen in front of Mum, stretching her hands over her belly. 'Clever, eh?'

Mum's thinning eyebrows pulsate.

Violet lifts the silky knitted jumper Tiffany gave her. 'It's OK. It's only pretend.' She pats the fake bump. 'I've used it to worm my way into Tiffany Watson's life.' She throws back her head and laughs. 'And it worked a treat, Mum. Remember me telling you she's pregnant? Well, I'm now her new pregnancy buddy.'

'Very clever.' The Irish lilt in Mum's voice is strong tonight. It goes like that. Sometimes it's as strong as a fast-paced, heavy Glaswegian accent. Other times, it's more subtle, a musical tone folded in each word.

Violet performs a fashion show, trying on each of the six tops Tiffany gave her. 'They're all on the large size, I know.

But that doesn't matter. I won't be wearing them for much longer, will I?'

Mum's eyes follow her parading along the kitchen.

'Which one do you like best? It's this one for me.' Violet rips off the pink top she's wearing and replaces it with a yellow V-neck sweater from the plastic bag. 'Not like me to go for something bright, eh, Mum?' The vibrant colours are a stark contrast to her usual black and grey. 'But Summer Smith likes colourful clothes.'

'They suit you.'

'Thanks, Mum.'

After she's modelled the last sweater, she removes it and rips the Velcro from the fake bump. It falls forward into her hands. She rolls it up into a ball. 'I don't blame you for not wanting to see Dad. Good for you for sticking to your guns, Mum. Rose thought you were being difficult. But she doesn't know what we know, does she?'

She feeds her mother a spoonful of Greek yoghurt with pureed blueberries. It's a dessert her mother usually enjoys, but she's having trouble getting her to eat today. She couldn't even get a mouthful of the scrambled eggs she made into her. Come to think of it, she's not eating at all well at the moment.

'I got into his house, Mum.'

Her mother grunts.

'I. Got. Into. Will. Watson's. House.' Violet gives her mother her biggest smile. One that sparkles with optimism. 'Aren't you proud of me?'

Mum's eyes flutter. There it is, the glint in her eyes as they fix on hers that shows she's in this with her. 'Clever girl,' she says.

'Open your mouth, Mum. You've got to eat. You've got to keep strong.'

Her mother drops her head, staring at her thumbs tapping vigorously together.

The love songs on the radio grate on her nerves. 'Let's put some of our music on, shall we?' She stands up. 'I'll never understand how Rose listens to this rubbish.' She finds the Classical FM station. 'That's better.'

She tries to tempt her mother with another spoonful of yoghurt. 'They've got so much money, Mum.'

Her mother rejects the yoghurt, sticking out her tongue like a child. The creamy mess slides down her chin, and a dollop drops into her lap.

'Sorry, Mum. You really don't want this, do you?' Violet grabs a tissue and wipes her mother's chin.

Her mother's bottom lip quivers.

'What is it? What's wrong?'

Her mother's shoulders shudder. Tears fall.

This isn't a one-off. She cries a lot. Enough tears to fill a cup some days. But only in front of Violet. Rarely in front of Rose, and never in front of Dad. When they were younger, and he returned from one of his 'work' trips, Violet would tell him how upset their mother had been, but although he never expressly stated it, he never believed her. She could tell by the way he pulled his jaw sideways and arched one eyebrow. She hated him even more for that. In the end, she stopped telling him.

'Now, now.' Violet grabs a fresh tissue and wipes her mother's eyes. 'There's no need to cry, Mum. Good things are happening. The bloke who did this to you... he's going to get his comeuppance. I'm going to get revenge for you and Bean, Mum.' She presses her hands on her mother's shoulders. 'I promise you. I won't let you both down.'

Violet lets the tears fall. Experience tells her it's for the best. It usually takes about a quarter of an hour. She hugs her. 'There, there.' She holds her tighter. Her mother's limp body shudders in her arms. Only when her eyes dry does she let her go.

'You need to be happy, Mum. Not sad. How about a cup of tea?' She leaves her and goes and switches on the kettle. She touches her belly, catching her hand on her jutting hip bone. It feels a little odd after having worn the fake bump for a large part of the day.

She makes herself a cup of black tea. After pouring tea into Mum's sippy cup, she adds a dash of milk and a spoonful of sugar. She takes it back to her mother and feeds it to her, while she continues telling the story of her day so far. 'The kid is kind of cute. But I'm not sure he likes me. Tiffany likes me, though.' She pauses for breath, realising how quickly she's talking. 'Their house is full of posh things. They've got one of those TVs that's ten times as big as ours. OK, that's a bit of an exaggeration. But it is at least three times as big. And one of those fireplaces that's built into the wall with an opening either side to stack logs.'

Mum slurps the last of her tea.

'We've only got seven days to go. Then this will all be over. Justice will be served. I'm working on the best outcome that will satisfy us the most.'

Seven days.

Her thoughts spiral.

She has to get this right. Maximise the pain, the anguish, and the hurt. Make Will Watson wish for death.

'What do you think, Mum? Who should it be first? Leo, Tiffany, or Will? Or perhaps, all three of them go together?'

36

ROSE

'Who do you think the three kids are, then?' Jamie shoves the last chunk of a Danish pastry into his mouth. We're taking a break in the staff room at work.

I return the photo to my bag. 'I can't help thinking the worst.'

'That they're his kids?'

I shrug. 'It makes sense. When we were growing up, he spent a lot of time away with work – or so he said that's where he was. I can't quite believe it, but what if he had another family? From Mum's diary entries, she thought he was having an affair.' I press my hands on my stomach. 'This is all making me feel constantly sick.'

He washes down the pastry with a swig of tea from the Spider-Man flask he brings into work every day. He is such a big kid at heart.

'I'm thinking of going to the address I found in the diary.'

He raises his eyebrows. 'Is that a good idea?' He takes another sip of tea and tells me it could open a can of worms that may well need containing right now. 'Why don't you try to coax more out of your dad?'

'He's not in a fit state. Not after his reaction. It could be the final straw.'

'Jeez, hun! Don't you think you've got enough going on without digging up the past? I'd leave well alone if I were you. You don't even know if the same people still live there. They could've moved years ago.' He screws the top on his flask. 'I'd better get back to it. See you later.'

He leaves me in the staff room: a square room with a sofa, tables, and chairs, and a small kitchenette for making drinks or heating food in the microwave. A group of chatterbox women sit at one of the tables. They always take their morning break together. Jamie passes them on the way out, stopping briefly to chat. 'Are you ladies ready for the blizzard that's coming? We could all be snowed in for Christmas.'

'Don't start spreading that around, Jamie,' one of the ladies responds. 'You'll have the patients panicking,'

'Stock up on your toilet roll.' The comment that makes them burst into laughter. One of them high-fives him.

I turn to my phone and google the address from Mum's diary. 23 Brook Street in Cadley, a town about an hour away.

I have to go there.

I ask to take a half-day's holiday, and the staff manager tells me to take it as compassionate leave. 'We've got a full team today. Go and spend time with your family. You can make up the hours another time.'

My stomach rolls like the undulating roads all the way to

Cadley, mainly because of what I could soon find out, but also because being behind the wheel is playing havoc with my nerves. I enjoyed driving before I passed my test. Then the accident happened. Now I falter at every junction and slow more than necessary at every bend. Roundabouts are worse still.

When I get to Brook Street, I turn off the engine and sit outside number 23. A tall man appears from the neighbouring house, tugging a beanie hat over his ears. A few doors down, a woman carrying two shopping bags enters a house.

My stomach turns with a mix of emotions. Jamie's words echo in my mind: 'Leave well alone.'

I stare at the picture in my hand. The same picture I've studied for hours since I found it. The woman has the same dark hair as her three children. They are definitely hers. Their eyes, a cornflower blue, give it away. And their smiles – the way one side of their lips lifts higher than the other. But none of them resemble my father. I wonder if I've got this all wrong. But I fear I haven't.

I can't do this. Jamie was right. I shouldn't be here. I switch the engine back on, only to turn it back off again. Driving away will be worse than facing it head-on.

Drawing in a deep breath of courage, I leave the car and cross the road to number 23. My pulse is racing like the wind whipping around me. Gingerly, I walk up the path. A beautiful Christmas wreath hangs from the front door, artificial evergreen stalks intertwined with bright red berries centred around a golden velvet ribbon. There's no bell, so I use the knocker. The sound echoes around the street. I turn, half-expecting people to be looking out of their windows.

After what seems like forever, I knock again, harder this

time. But still, no one comes to answer the door. Frustrated that I haven't been able to face my fears, I knock a final time when a voice from behind startles me. I turn.

'Can I help you?' a woman asks. The bottoms of her flared jeans drag along the ground. An uneven line of wetness seeps into the hem. I swallow hard.

It's her.

The woman from the photo. But her long, dark hair is now cut into a nothing style, and lines wrinkle her once-youthful face. She stops in her tracks. It's as if she recognises me, too.

We stand staring at each other. This is the woman who has mothered my father's other children – the mother of my half-brothers. I'm certain of it.

How could he? I've looked up to Dad for as long as I can remember. He's my go-to person.

She draws her tatty handbag to her chest, hugging it tightly.

My voice falters. 'I'm Rose. Rose Sapphire.'

The woman's voice is raw, imbued with vulnerability. 'You'd better come in.' She produces a set of keys from her coat pocket and opens the front door. The sharp smell of stale cigarette smoke hits me like a brick. She gestures for me to step inside. 'How about we start with a cup of tea?'

I nod. My throat is tight. I can't believe I'm here.

'I'm Karen, by the way.'

37

ROSE

Karen pushes open a door along the dark hallway.

'How did you know my name?' I ask.

'Let me get that tea. Then we can talk. Sugar?'

I nod. 'Two, please.' I step into the cold living room. An old metal-framed sofa and a large coffee table dominate the small room. A clean ashtray rests on the table, alongside a packet of cigarettes and a lighter. The same acrid smell of tobacco from the hallway permeates the fabric of the room. It's suffocating. And there's a stagnant sadness in the air, as if the room has lost its soul. Photographs of a teenage boy I recognise from the photo of her and the three boys sits on the mantlepiece, along with two burnt-out candles in ivy-patterned tins. Other than that, there are no soft furnishings or mementoes that make a place a home.

Karen returns with two cups of steaming tea and places them on the coffee table. 'You look like your father,' she says.

'People say that. Violet looks like our mum.'

She points to the sofa. 'Take a seat.'

I perch on the edge of a cushion.

She rubs her hands together. 'Chilly, eh?' She steps to the radiator below the window and fiddles with the dial. 'Does your father know you're here?' We're conversing as if we're both waiting for the other to address the monstrous elephant in the room.

I shake my head.

'So how did you find us?'

I take the photo from my coat pocket and hold it up. 'I came across this.'

'Where?'

'In one of my mum's diaries. Your address was written beside it. I thought you might've moved.'

'I... I couldn't afford to.' She stares at the photo. 'Jerry wondered what happened to that photo.' She picks up the packet of cigarettes. 'Do you mind if I smoke? I'm finding this all pretty stressful.'

I shake my head.

She takes a cigarette from the packet. 'I'm trying to give up. It's so hard.' Placing the cigarette between her lips, she lights it and takes a deep drag.

I wave the photo at her. 'Are these boys his sons?' I don't know why I'm asking. The answer is as clear as the two of us sitting here having this conversation.

She nods.

'I think you need to rewind. Start at the beginning, Karen. Please. I need to know everything.'

She sighs heavily. In resignation more than anything. 'Your dad and I were together for twenty-five years. He was leading a double life for a large part of it.'

I want to laugh. I want to cry. Everything I've ever believed in is falling apart around me and nothing I can do can hold it together. 'And you never knew?' I ask.

She shakes her head.

'How could you not have known?'

'The same as your mother. I thought he was away on business.' She shrugs. 'What can I say? Your father was a player. A clever, manipulative man. He was an addict. Addicted to the thrill of having women under his control. With hindsight, I always had a niggling doubt he was having affairs, but I had three small kids. They came first. So I buried those doubts.' She scoffs with a wry smile. 'But it all came to a head when your mother came here, and I found out about you and your sister.'

I rub my fingers along my brow, trying to iron out the creases, but they're as stubborn as my sister.

'I'm sorry, Rose.'

'Hang on. Is my father a bigamist?'

'No, we never married. We were going to. We were engaged. But he kept putting it off.' She clicks her tongue. 'There was always an excuse with Jerry. It was another huge blow, when I found out he'd actually married your mother.'

'How did my mum know where you lived?'

'She followed your dad here one evening, just before Christmas 2008.' She points to the window. 'She spied on us through there.'

My stomach is twisting and turning. 'What happened? What did she do?'

'She left it a while before coming back to have it out with me. Maybe she was plucking up the courage.' She exhales a large breath. 'Or more likely trying to calm down. Boy, she was one angry lady.' She shrugs. 'I don't know.'

'When was that?'

'At the beginning of 2009.'

'The year she was shot,' I say.

'Dreadful business. I'm terribly sorry for what you and your sister have been through. It couldn't have been easy for you all these years. I hated her when she first came here. I could've killed her. I felt she'd ruined my life. But then a friend of mine pointed out that she was as innocent as I was. Your father was the one I should be thinking the worst of. I'd never have wished what happened upon her. I guess they've never found the culprit?'

I shake my head. 'It's a cold case, as they say. We haven't heard anything from the police for years.'

'Your father couldn't help himself where women were concerned, Rose. He might have changed, but he was a self-centred, selfish prick in those days. I tried to end it with him several times. I really did, but I was weak. He promised me he was going to leave your mum.' She sucks on her cigarette and blows out a large puff of smoke. 'I believed him.'

I peer around the room. All those times I thought my father was at work, he was here with this woman and their children. It's sickening.

'But then, that summer, I discovered your mother was pregnant. He was still playing the two of us. That's when I told him I wanted nothing more to do with him. My boys also refused to see him. He begged and begged, but why would I take him back? He denied it, but he was lying again. He'd obviously still been sleeping with your mother. I didn't see him for months. Until after your mother was shot, and he came back here. The audacity of the man. He was looking for pity. But I had nothing to give him. I was better off on my own. And that's the way I've stayed.'

I can't believe I'm hearing all this about the man I've loved and respected all my life. I should hate this woman, but I don't. My father destroyed her life, just like he ruined my mother's. Violet made a comment once that she thought Dad was having an affair, but I shut her down. But she was right all along. It now makes sense why she hates him so much.

'How is your father?' Karen asks.

I search her eyes. She's battered and bruised from what he's done to her. 'He's not in a good way. He has cancer. He's in a hospice.'

She fleetingly screws her eyes shut. 'I heard.'

'How?' I ask.

'Will, my son, told me.'

I frown. 'But I thought your sons didn't have anything more to do with him?'

'Will sought out your dad at the beginning of the year. People change, Rose. My son became a father himself, and he wanted his dad in his son's life.'

'What about your other two sons?' I stop myself from saying 'half-brothers'.

She points to the photo on the mantlepiece. 'Ross, the youngest, died.' It's strange there are no photos of her other sons.

'How?' I ask.

'A motorbike accident.'

'Gosh, that must've been awful.' Life hasn't been kind to this woman. I should hate her, but some part of me wants to reach out and give her a big hug. 'How old was he?'

'Fourteen. He was on the back of his brother's bike. The weather was bad.'

'I'm so sorry.' That explains the sadness I can feel in this room. 'And your other son? Has he seen his – my – father?'

'No. He's had no contact with him since the day I kicked your father out.'

'I want to meet them.'

She sits back on the sofa, her cheeks puffed out, considering me intently. 'Are you sure about that?' Her tone has changed. She doesn't think this is a good idea.

I nod. 'I think so.'

'What about your sister?' She points to the photo. 'Does she know about us?'

I shake my head. 'V's not well.'

'What's wrong with her?'

'She has some mental health problems... she...' I bite my lip. It feels wrong talking behind my sister's back, particularly with this woman. 'I'll have to find the right time to talk to her about it first.'

'And I'll need to discuss it with my sons,' Karen says. 'This is a sensitive situation.'

38

VIOLET

The thought of returning to Radstone becomes an obsession. The Watson family are on her mind all day, every day, every waking moment. She's itching to get back to the Ridgeway to meddle in their lives, mess with their heads. The feeling is powerful, an electric force that's now sparking out of control. There's five days to go before they meet their end, but tormenting them in the meantime makes her feel more alive than since she was a nine-year-old child.

'I'm meeting a friend after work, so don't expect me back until later.'

Rose stacks their dinner plates. 'Which friend?'

Violet taps the side of her nose with her finger as she cleans Mum's mouth. 'All good, Mum.'

'Violet Sapphire, have you met a guy?' Rose asks.

What a great idea. Why didn't she think of this before? A

new man. It'll get her sister off her back asking where she's going all the time. She forges a coy smile. 'Maybe.'

'Tell me.' Her sister's face lights up. 'Who?'

Violet shrugs. 'Not much to tell at the moment.'

'What's his name? At least tell me his name.'

'Declan.' Her insides twist. She hates lying to her sister. Rose is too damn sweet to lie to.

Her sister's jaw drops. 'I knew it.'

'Knew what?'

'That something was up with you. Where did you meet him?'

'I'm not telling you any more.'

'You've got to.'

'I'll see how things go.'

Knives and forks clink as Rose drops them onto the plates. She asks Violet more questions about Declan: the fake husband turned fake boyfriend. 'What about Dad? You must go and see him,' she adds. 'You haven't been this week.'

'I'll go tomorrow.'

It's freezing when she steps outside, despite the extra layer of thermals she's put on under her jeans and jumper. She's never enjoyed the extremities of winter, but it's really got to her this year. The cold bites deep into her bones, but the warm glow in the pit of her stomach for where she's about to go soon heats her from inside out.

The gritting trucks are out in force. She gets stuck behind one spreading their load, preparing the roads for the snow forecast for the early hours of tomorrow morning. Along with the slowing traffic from the tail of the rush hour, it elongates the journey by a good twenty minutes. Her mind is buzzing.

It's as if she's come alive since her sister collided with Will Watson's car.

When she finally reaches her destination, she dodges the potholes the best she can and turns off the engine along the road at the back of the Watsons' house. The downstairs is lit up, as is one of the upstairs bedrooms. From her last visit here, when she picked up those maternity clothes, she now knows that's Leo's room. He must still be awake.

She dons Mum's old coat and her hat and creeps along the garden to number 12. Passing the trampoline and the swing, she slides along the hedged fence. Steam rises above the gurgling bubbles of the hot tub. They must've just been in there.

She steps closer. A security light clicks into action. She dodges behind the storage unit, avoiding the thorns of the overgrown blackberry bush. The bifold door swipes open.

'I can't believe you're making me do this,' Will says. There's a roughness to his voice, weathered as if he smokes. She can't remember him speaking like that after the accident. But then, she wasn't totally with it that day.

'How many times have I told you, relaxing in the hot tub is good for us,' Tiffany replies. 'Especially you, with the amount of hours you work.'

'Are you sure it's good for the baby?'

'Ten minutes is fine. You know how much it relaxes me being in here.'

Violet smiles. They haven't just been in there. They're about to get in.

This is going to be fun.

Real fun.

39

VIOLET

She shimmies around the side of the unit until she's close enough to hear every word. Who knew spying on a married couple could turn out to be five-star entertainment? Despite the intense cold, she's enjoying herself immensely. More than she can remember in fifteen years.

Tiffany slips off her ankle-length towelling bathrobe. She giggles. 'Quick. Quick. I'm freezing.' Will helps her into the water. Her belly swiftly disappears below the surface, followed by her shoulders. 'This is so relaxing.' She tips her head backwards and rests it against the padded side. 'It'll help your neck, too. How is it?'

Will discards his matching bathrobe. Violet's stomach flips to see the tattoo circling his wrist. He steps into the hot tub, quickly immersing his body into the water. He rubs his neck. 'It still hurts.'

'Perhaps you should see the physio,' Tiffany suggests.

'I'll give it a few more days.'

'Can't you claim on insurance for that kind of thing?'

'It's not that bad.'

They chat about the baby they can't wait to welcome into their family, and Leo, whom Will obviously adores as much as his wife does.

'I wish you didn't have to go away this weekend,' Tiffany says.

He's going away for the weekend? Violet's interest is well and truly piqued.

'I'll only be gone one night. I can't miss Stevie's stag do.'

'So close to Christmas, though.' Tiffany shimmies down further into the water. 'It's not that I mind you going. I know how much you've been looking forward to it. I don't want to be stuck with Lewis.'

'Oh, come on. He's trying.'

'I know.' She sighs deeply.

'Give him a break. He loves Leo. I know what he can be like, but he's been a good uncle. You can't fault him for that.'

'I know. I'm sorry. I'd rather you were with us when we go to Winter Wonderland. We always go together.'

'I know, darling, I feel bad. But I'll be back early Sunday afternoon.'

Violet smiles. So Tiffany is going to be here all alone on Saturday night.

'Lewis said he'll pick you up at noon on Saturday.'

She relents with a sigh. 'OK.'

'Did you find the spare key, by the way?'

'No.'

'Honestly, Tiff, you must be more careful. Things are going missing all over the place. It's irritating.'

'Why are you accusing me?' Tiff looks crestfallen, like a berated schoolchild.

'Losing a front door key is serious. Anyone could get in.'

Violet stifles a giggle.

The water sloshes. 'Did you hear that?' Will looks towards the storage unit.

Violet edges away from the side of the unit, her heart beating louder and louder in her ears.

'Hear what?' Tiffany says.

'I thought I heard a noise from behind the storage unit,' Will says.

'That happened to me the other day. I thought I heard something out here,' Tiffany says.

'It's probably a fox,' Will says.

'This place gives me the creeps sometimes.'

'Don't be silly,' Will says. 'It's just animals.'

'Let's get a dog,' Tiffany says.

'Where did that come from?'

'You know how much I've always wanted a dog. I'd feel safer with one around.'

Will sighs. 'We've talked about this. It's such a big commitment. Who's going to look after it when we go away? And, anyway, we've got a new baby on the way. It's not a good time.'

Violet peers around the side of the unit, enough to continue watching them.

'It's the best time to get a dog. I'm at home more, so I can train it. And it can get used to us all before she arrives. It'll be better than getting it after she's born. Jacqui's friend's dog has had a litter of Labradors. Ten weeks ago. They're the cutest. There's one left. The person who was meant to buy him backed out. Please. Please, Will. I really want this.'

Will sighs as if he's already resigned himself to the non-human addition that's about to join the Watson family. 'Who's going to look after it when we go to Thailand?'

'Jacqui said she and Lewis will.'

'Got it all planned, haven't you?' The roughness in his voice turns to a loving chuckle.

A shiver of cold rips through Violet.

Will's head turns towards her. 'There it is again,' he says. 'Did you hear that?' The water sloshes and splashes as he clambers out of the tub.

It's time for her to get the hell out of here.

As nimbly as her legs allow, she edges along the side of the storage unit.

He's coming after her.

Her stomach is in her throat. He can't catch her here. It'll ruin everything she has planned. A blackberry thorn rips her coat, attacking her as if punishing her for being here. Lengthening her stride, she slips along the hedge until she reaches the road.

She glances over her shoulder. He's nowhere to be seen. But she can't chance it. She crosses to the other side of the road and loses herself in the woods. It's dark and frightening, but she has no choice. She sneaks behind a tree and rests her head against the trunk to regain her breath.

After about a minute, she dares to peep around the tree trunk. He's standing in the middle of the road in his bathrobe, glancing from side to side. Despite the terror bolting through her, she can't help but stifle another giggle. She wills him to go back inside. As much as the excitement is exhilarating, she's bitterly cold and needs to get back to the car. She's going to freeze alive out here.

He steps towards the woods.

He's coming in here.

She whips her head behind the tree trunk and leans it against the rough, cold bark, holding her breath.

'Who's there?' he shouts.

Fear paralyses her. The only part of her moving is the beat of her heart, pulsing in her ears so loud she fears he'll hear it.

Footsteps crack on twigs and fallen branches from the inclement weather back in October. He's getting closer. 'Who is it?' he shouts. 'Who's there?'

She clenches her jaw to stop her teeth from chattering, and she hangs tight. This is a waiting game. He's in a bathrobe. She's in a padded winter coat. It's a game she's going to win. She doesn't have to wait for long. A couple of minutes pass before his footsteps tread along the ground again. She edges her head to the side of the tree until one eye sees him making his way back to his house.

She's unnerved him.

The thought fills her with immense pleasure.

It's the delicious start of what's to come.

40

ROSE

Since meeting Karen, the thought of my half-brothers plays on my muddled mind. I've tried to broach the subject with V, but the right time never seems to arise.

'Over here, Rose.' Auntie Audrey waves from beside the entrance to the church. She's wearing knee-high black boots shined to a high gloss, and her best coat, a double-breasted wool peacoat with a fur trim.

I hated going to church when I was a kid. Mum and Auntie Audrey always sat me and V between them, squashed up like commuters on a packed train. I don't attend church often these days, but I always come to this late evening candlelit service with Auntie Audrey every Christmas. I look forward to it. V refuses to set foot inside a church, so she stays at home with Mum. Auntie Audrey and I usually go to dinner first, but V was late back from work this evening, so I had to cancel and come straight here. I kiss her cheek. 'I need to talk to you.'

'We haven't time now. After the service, there'll be time to chat.'

The church is still and peaceful when we walk inside to the scent of pine from the full and rounded Christmas tree. Shadows dance around the congregation from the golden flicker of candlelight, and the altar gleams from fairy lights threaded through sprigs of holly.

A young boy with the voice of an angel begins singing *Silent Night*. The rest of the choir slowly joins in. My thoughts are filled with Karen and my half-brothers as I wonder if they ever go to church. I have so many questions but there is no one to answer them. How much of his time away did Dad spend with them? And more importantly, are there other women and children, siblings, who we don't know about?

After the service, Auntie Audrey mingles with the congregation that's now humming with chatter and the background accompaniment of the lively organist. I tail her like a spare part, inwardly trying to hurry her along. I'm conscious of getting home. V was in a strange mood again when she got home from work, and I'm anxious to get back to her. But Auntie Audrey is in her element, hobnobbing with her church friends, until an auburn-haired woman approaches us. 'Audrey,' she says. 'How wonderful to see you.'

Auntie Audrey does a double-take. 'Nicolette.' Her eyes open wide.

'It's been too long,' Nicolette says. 'How's your sister?'

Auntie Audrey pauses, her eyes flitting around nervously. 'She's getting there. What are you doing here?' She crosses her arms tightly across her chest. I've never seen her so uptight.

'We were visiting Charles's mum, and she insisted on coming to this service tonight. She lost her husband last year, and they used to come together. Pamela Hales, you probably know her. Oh, there he is.' Nicolette waves. 'Charles, over here.'

A distinguished-looking man with thick, dark curly hair approaches us. 'Hello, Audrey.' He sweeps a wad of curls out of his eyes. He's got a heck of a lot of hair for an older guy.

Auntie Audrey nods curtly. 'Hello, Charles.' She turns to Nicolette. 'I'm sorry, but we have to go.' She grabs my arm. 'We've left my niece with my sister, and she's not been too well. Have a wonderful Christmas. Please give your mother my kind regards.'

'Who was that?' I ask as we leave the church for the cold night air.

'Some people I used to know.' She's hurrying me along faster than is safe for the icy path.

'Slow down, we'll slip.'

'Sorry, love. I'm tired. I want to get home.'

'You didn't seem comfortable with them.'

She shrugs. 'What did you want to talk to me about?'

I glance around, ensuring no one is around. 'Just after the accident, when Dad could still speak, he seemed to think he had a gun in the house.'

She looks at me in horror. 'A gun? Where?'

'In the junk room. And what's more, he wanted me to get rid of it.'

'He asked you to do what?'

'Get rid of it,' I repeat. 'But I can't find it anywhere.'

Her face is full of concern, her eyebrows drawn together.

She steers me out of the church gates and towards her car parked at the end of the street. 'Does he mean the one from when he used to belong to that gun club? Your mother hated him going there.'

I shrug.

She twists her lips and shakes her head. 'It was probably the drugs talking. They can make you do that, you know.'

We reach her car and she clicks it open with her key fob. 'Don't worry about it. Your mother would never have let him keep a gun in the house.' She yawns. 'I must get home, love. I hope you don't mind. I'm tired tonight.' She presses her hand against my shoulder as if she's pushing me away. 'I'll see you tomorrow.' She gets into the car.

Unless I'm mistaken, for the first time in my life, she can't wait to get away from me.

41

VIOLET

Violet couldn't put it off any longer. She's had to come and see her father. When her sister got home from church with Auntie Audrey, she practically pushed her out of the front door.

She doesn't mind. She's overdue a chat with him.

'What are you doing here?' His voice is barely audible.

Mingling with the waft of death is the smell of him in here... lies, deceit and deadly secrets.

He continues, but she struggles to make out what he's saying. He's deteriorated since she last saw him. Rose said he was bad, but his emaciated body now looks like a shell of his former self. It can't be long now.

She moves the chair by his bed and perches on the side. 'Aren't you pleased to see me, Dad?'

Silence.

'So, how are you? You're not looking great, if I'm honest. What would all your other women make of you now?' She's being spiteful, but she can't help herself. Years of pent-up anger, hurt, and frustration are seeping out of her, and there's nothing she can do to stem the flow.

Her father turns his head labouredly, as if he can't bear to look at her.

'That's right, Dad. Turn away from me. Do what you've done all my life. I always have been a disappointment to you.'

She has no wish to be here a moment longer than she needs to be. She's sure he feels the same, so she cuts to the chase. 'I see you've been sending your darling daughter on some errands for you.'

His glassy eyes meet hers.

'Guess what?' She stands and lowers her head until it's a breath away from his ear. 'I have the gun.' She sits back in the chair. 'I've had it for a while.'

His eyes widen. 'No,' he mumbles.

'Oh yes. When you first fell ill, I was drawn to the attic room, wondering why you kept that cupboard locked and forbade us from going in there. Naturally, I was inquisitive. It didn't take long to find the key in your desk drawer. You really should've been more imaginative. But that's the way you've always been with me, Dad, hasn't it? You've always underestimated me.'

He turns his head away, as if he's willing the conversation to end. He's powerless, and he knows it.

'All my life, I've refrained from facing you for Rose's and Mum's sake, but no more. I'm the one in control now. And it feels good. Payback. I'm getting even for the pathetic excuse of the father you've been to me and Rose and the rotten husband you've been to Mum.'

She continues with her well-prepared speech. A speech she's tinkered with over the years, waiting for the right moment. 'You know, Dad, when I found the gun, it provoked a childhood memory. It was the missing piece from the night Mum was shot that for some reason I'd blocked out. It was there, in the depths of my mind all along, but I couldn't draw it out. But then, boom. It came flooding back.'

He starts coughing as if he wants sympathy. But she's none to give him. She's used every ounce she's had on her mother.

'That monster you got to shoot Mum – he dropped the gun and fled.' She sits on her hands. If she loses control now, she doesn't trust what she might do. 'You came running down the stairs, where Mum was bleeding out on the floor. And what did you do?'

He reaches for the control panel to call a nurse. She pushes it out of the way.

'You picked up the gun and ran back upstairs on the pretence you needed to get your phone. But really it was to hide it. Because it was your gun the murderer got out of the safe. You knew you'd get into trouble.'

She presses her fingertips to the inner corners of her eyes and keeps them there for a while. She refuses to let him witness her tears.

Her voice wavers. 'If you'd acted quicker, not worried about yourself, you selfish prick, you could've got Mum the help she needed much quicker, and she'd be OK now.'

'No, Violet,' he says between outbursts of coughing and spluttering. 'Not true.'

'What was it, Dad? Were you just fed up with her? More content playing away with all your bits on the side? So you decided to get her shot. You are pathetic.'

'No.' His voice is barely a whisper. 'You've got it all wrong.'

'What I don't understand is why you didn't get rid of the gun – destroy the evidence?'

'I should've...' Another cough. 'Ages. Ago.' Another splutter.

There's little fuel left in his tank. He dips in and out of consciousness. She nudges him. She won't let him go. Not before she's finished with him. 'Dad.' She raises her voice. She will have her say. 'Dad!'

He's back with her.

'So come on, Dad, why didn't you get rid of the gun?'

'I was stupid. I should've... ages ago.'

'You can do better than that.'

'Time never seemed right.' He gasps for breath. 'I was scared. Willing it all to go away.'

'As always, only thinking about yourself. So how much did you pay the guy to fake the break-in and shoot Mum?'

'No. No. You've got it all wrong.'

She closes in on him once more, her breath in his ear. 'Well, guess what, Dad. I've found him.'

'Who?'

'The person you got to shoot Mum, of course.'

'I don't understand.' He's struggling to keep his eyes open.

'Let me spell it out to you.' She gives him a shove. 'Dad! Open your eyes.' He's back with her. 'I've found him, and I'm going to use your gun – yes, your gun – to get revenge for Mum and Bean.'

She stares at the tube leading to the bag of medication extending her father's life. It would be so easy to switch the whole lot off and see him float away in front of her.

But no. That would ruin her plan. She wants him to

suffer, like Mum has all these years. Like Rose and she have. Like her baby sister did. She wants the knowledge that his daughter is going to carry out an abhorrent act of revenge to fuel his dying moments.

42

VIOLET

'Please come along, Summer,' Tiffany says. 'I've asked a few of my other friends, but they're all busy.'

They are walking side by side on treadmills set to a gentle incline. The machines overlook the entrance to the building and a line of bare-branched trees. After she obtained a pay-as-you-go phone and gave Tiffany her number, they've exchanged many texts discussing the ins and outs of pregnancy life. She has learnt so much.

'Even if it's only for an hour,' Tiffany adds. 'Please.'

Tiffany is begging her to join her, Leo, and her brother-in-law on Saturday at the local town's version of London's Winter Wonderland. But Violet needs to show some restraint here. She can't come across as too eager. 'I'll have to see. We're meant to go and see my in-laws at some point over the weekend, but I'm not sure if we're going tomorrow or Sunday. I'll ask my husband and text you.'

Since forming this fake friendship with her, she's found it weird talking about her pretend husband, nearly as much as her pretend baby. It's like she's living out this whole other life that she would've quite liked once upon a time. But that was before a group of girls at school repeatedly told her that no one would ever have her. Their cackling still torments her.

You're a dead thing, Violet Sapphire. Undatable.

You make boys want to vomit.

You're going to grow up a lonely old woman.

'Hey, Summer. Are you OK? You're miles away.' A tap on her arm returns her thoughts to the present. Tiffany is not letting up. 'You'll be doing me a favour if you come along.'

'You sound as if you don't like your brother-in-law,' Violet says.

Tiffany smiles coyly. 'What gave you that impression?' She sighs. 'Like I said, Will and Lewis have a complicated relationship.'

'Yes, I remember you saying there was some sort of bust-up associated with the business.'

She's enjoying learning so much more about Will Watson. Every time she picks up another snippet of information, she adds it to her investigation wall. She now knows that Will's brother, Lewis, his wife, Jacqui, and Will and Lewis's mum, Karen, are spending Christmas Eve at Will and Tiffany's house. This will challenge her plans, but she refuses to let it ruin them. Tiffany mentioned that Karen might stay the night, although she hopes not, because Karen smokes like a chimney, and she can't stand the smell that lingers on her mother-in-law's breath.

'I'm sure it all stems from their difficult childhood. Their mum kicked their dad out for having an affair. Their brother Ross was killed in a motorcycle accident.' Tiffany rolls her eyes and shakes her head. 'Terrible, terrible affair. Lewis was driving. It wasn't his fault. The weather was bad. The bike lost the road. It affected him badly, which is understandable. He's never got over it. Will maintains Lewis has always been a bit jealous of him because he has made something of his life. Will tried to include him, he really did, but Lewis messed up. He always does.'

How Violet wants to tell her that her husband made something of his life because of the money and the jewellery he stole from her parents. A small fortune that steered his life onto a better path. Her insides twist with how much she wants to see Will Watson dead.

But patience, Violet. She stares at her trainers pacing the belt of the treadmill. Another four days and his end will come. But first, he needs to suffer more. 'It's hard when your parents split up, I guess,' she says.

'Lewis started mixing with the wrong crowd – drugs, shoplifting.' Tiffany rolls her eyes. 'You get the picture. Will felt sorry for him, so he gave him a job in his business to help him when he was really down. As I said before, Lewis messed up. The rest is history. I have to admit, he is a good uncle to Leo. But, if I'm honest, I don't like leaving Leo with him. That's why I'm going to Winter Wonderland with them. My sister-in-law, Jacqui, was going, but she's had to work, so he wanted to take Leo on his own, but I wouldn't feel comfortable.'

She lowers the incline on her treadmill and slows the pace. 'I think I'm done for today.' She takes her towel from the arm of the treadmill and wipes the film of sweat from her forehead and chest. 'Guess where I'm going now?'

Violet sets her treadmill to cooldown mode. 'Where?'

'Will's finally given in. We're getting a puppy. I'm so excited.' She whips out her phone from the pocket of her leggings and swipes the screen. 'Look at this beauty.' She turns the screen to face Violet.

It's a picture of her holding a black, fluffy Labrador.

'He's cute,' Violet says.

She sparkles her white teeth in a big smile. 'Ozzy.'

Rose has always wanted a dog. When they were kids, she begged and begged Dad to get them one, but Violet sided with Dad. They had enough to look after with Mum. She shakes her head to clear her thoughts. She can't think about Rose. Not when she's in Summer Smith mode. It feels wrong, as if she's cheating at a game they're playing.

Tiffany takes back her phone. 'Will's meeting us here and then we're going to pick him up.'

Violet's stomach turns. 'He's coming here?'

She nods. 'Hey, you can meet him. We're going to have lunch first. You can join us. I've told him all about you.'

43

VIOLET

'Sure,' Violet blurts out before she has time to think this through.

Tiffany continues. 'I think he's worried about me at the moment.'

Violet's insides twist with dread. Will Watson is coming here. He'll recognise her from the accident. She racks her brains as to how she's going to get out of this one. 'Worried? Why?'

Tiffany shrugs. 'It's strange, and I can't explain it, but a few things have gone missing in our house.'

'What kind of things?' Violet asks.

'Small things – the TV remote control and a coaster from our living room. He thinks it's me, but I swear I never touched that frickin' remote control. And a spare front door key, would you believe? I never touched that either! And he said he didn't. It caused a massive argument.'

'The same thing happened to me. Declan couldn't find the can opener and blamed me. But he was right. I'd put it in the fridge. It'll all turn up.' She rolls her eyes. 'Pregnancy brain, eh?'

Tiffany stops her treadmill. 'Please come on Saturday. There's a great Christmas market there. You can pick up some great presents. Last year, I bought Will's mum and sister some beautiful wreaths. They loved them.' She steps off the treadmill. 'I'll see you in the café. How long are you going to be? I can order for you.'

Violet's reply is slow as her mind works at triple speed. 'It's fine. I'm going to do some weights. I'll order when I get down there.'

She raises the incline of the treadmill. Her heart is racing as she tries to work out a way to get out of this one. The café is next to the entrance of the building. They will notice her if she tries to leave without saying hello.

She could stay here until they've gone, but she needs to go now. This is her chance. The opportunity to get to their house while they're not there and do what she needs to do.

The desire to increase the speed to twelve kilometres per hour is compelling. If she weren't in disguise, that's what she'd do to calm herself down. Instead, she clenches her jaw, willing herself to stay calm. She's going to have to chance slipping out without them seeing her.

But she can't stay calm. The light in here has got too bright. And the music too loud as if a member of staff has turned up the speakers to full volume. She cradles her head in her hands. She can't stand it. She stabs the stop button. Drink. Her throat is chalk dry. She's gasping for water. She hurries to the water station and drinks cup after cup of water.

She bumps into Tiffany as she enters the changing room.

Tiffany's cheeks are flushed, her hair shining in the fluorescent lighting. She looks a glowing natural picture of health. 'Hi, again. Will's just texted. He's picked up Leo and is waiting in the café. I'll see you down there when you're done.'

'Sure.' Violet rushes past her and marches to her locker. The changing room is busy. Voices merge into a solitary howl. She finds an empty cubicle and removes her leggings and T-shirt. Her armpits are damp and not because of the workout. She slips into a pair of Tiffany's jeans. Locker doors slam closed. She flinches. The room is closing in on her. She has to get out of here.

She hurries down the stairs until the edge of the café comes into view. Sweat runs down her back. She can't see them. She takes each step slowly, cautiously scanning each table and its customers. As she reaches the bottom step, she stops. There they are. She bends her body out of view. Will is sitting next to Leo, their backs to her, but Tiffany will see her if she tries to pass. She can't risk it.

She turns left and marches to the back of the building. She has to leave from a fire exit. It will set off the fire alarm, but it's her only option. She reaches the fire door and dithers, staring at the notice that says *Push hard in case of fire* above the horizontal bar. CCTV will catch her leaving from this door. How will she explain that away? She's got no choice.

Her heart is about to explode. She shoves the bar. The door bursts open. A rush of cold air hits her. She waits for it, but the shrill of the alarm doesn't come. They must have forgotten to set it. She's always considered herself an unlucky person, but today she must've lucked out. The door clangs shut behind her. She doesn't wait for any delay. She races to her car.

Once inside, she texts Tiffany.

. . .

I hope you don't mind, but I won't stop for lunch. I'm suddenly exhausted and need to lie down. See you soon. Saturday, hopefully, if I can make it work. Sx

She starts the car and drives to number 12 the Ridgeway. Another ten minutes, and she's letting herself into the front door with the key she had cut from the one she borrowed from the ceramic bowl in their hallway. Thankfully, they don't have one of those video doorbells Dad had fitted a while back. Adrenaline races through her, replacing the feelings of unease from earlier. It's an electric sensation she's come to enjoy since Will Watson collided with her father's car. She's hot, buzzing, unstoppable. And more alive than she's ever felt.

She disables the alarm using the code she saw Tiffany punch into the keypad before. With no time to waste, she drops the original key into the bowl and rushes to the living room, where she replaces the photo she took while she was trying on Tiffany's old maternity clothes. It's no longer of use. The copy she made is now on her investigation wall.

From her bag, she produces the gold coaster and places it in the crack between the sofa, leaving a fraction of the edge on show. She then rushes upstairs to their bedroom and wedges their TV remote control between the mattress and headboard of the bed.

Back downstairs in the kitchen, she scans the room, noting the number of steps from the bifold doors to the centre island and then to the kitchen door. Leo's toys in the corner catch her attention. She looks away. There's no room for sentiment now.

She spends five minutes wandering around the downstairs rooms, confirming her plans for Christmas Eve. Learning they are holding a family gathering here has kicked an obstacle in her way. An obstacle she really doesn't want. Having to deal with other people wasn't in her plan.

But it's OK. She's got this.

44

ROSE

Jamie squeezes my forearm as we wait at a set of traffic lights. 'What a shitshow!' he says.

'I still can't believe my father has another family. It's sickening.' I glance sideways. 'I want to tell V, but I can't seem to find the right moment.'

'She deserves to know, don't you think?'

'It'll trigger her. Anything stressful like this always does.' I shake my head with worry. 'She's already spiralling.'

'What do you mean?'

'I keep waking to her pacing up and down her room in the middle of the night.' I sigh heavily. 'I hear her talking to herself – have done for years. but I can't challenge her on it because she only denies it. She stopped doing it for a while, because she gave up on finding the person who shot Mum, but it's all started again. And she's hardly eating.'

'I didn't want to say anything. It's not my place, but now you mention it, she is painfully thin.'

'She's got an eating problem – has done so since I can remember. It comes and goes according to her anxiety levels. They thought it was anorexia when she was a teenager, but she was never officially diagnosed with that. They believe it's related to the trauma she suffered as a child. She was hospitalised and got better. Only because she couldn't bear to be away from Mum. But now it seems she's gone backwards again.'

'That's sad,' Jamie says. 'She's such a pretty girl.'

'She is, but you can't tell her that. I've tried and tried over the years. She thinks she looks like a witch.'

Jamie's mouth opens. He frowns. 'Really? That's a pretty distorted view of herself.'

I give him a straight-lipped smile. 'When she went into therapy, that's what she said she told the therapist.' I bite my lip. 'The therapy did her some good at first. She gained two stone. She looked so much better, but it wasn't enough. Her weight has yo-yoed over the years. And now she's regressed again. And these past few weeks...' I shrug. 'I don't know if it was the accident, or what's happened to Dad, but I fear she's slipped back into her old ways. She thinks I don't notice her feeding her own dinner to Mum, then blaming Mum for not eating, but I'm not a fool.'

'It's surprising you came out of all of this so sane.'

I laugh. 'Me too. So you see why I'm finding it tricky telling her about what I've found out.' I tell him it'll tip her over the cliff she is standing so precariously close to the edge of.

'But, still, Titch. This is a big reveal to keep from her. If she'd found this out and didn't tell you, wouldn't you be a bit peeved?'

I smile briefly. 'You're always the voice of reason. She's met a guy recently.'

'That's good news, isn't it?'

I shrug.

'Who is he?'

'I don't know, other than he's called Declan. She's being secretive. But how she's been acting, I don't know if he's any good for her. She's started wearing make-up, too. Lots of it. Not all the time. Only when she's going to meet him. By the way, I told Karen I want to meet my brothers.'

He raises his eyebrows. 'Then you can't keep this from your sister.'

'Damned if I do, damned if I don't. I still can't believe our dad has done this to us.' I shake my head in disbelief. 'If they agree to meet us, then I'll tell V. If not, then I might as well wait until she's in a better place mentally.'

'Are you going to tell your dad what you've found out?' he asks.

'What's the point now? It could finish him off. I'm angry with him, but I think it's best all round to let him go in peace.' I sigh heavily. 'Some Christmas this is going to be.'

My phone rings. It's Carlos from the hospice. 'Rose, is that you?' I don't like the edge to his voice. It's laced with apprehension and an edginess I've not noticed before. 'I'm afraid I have some bad news.'

I close my eyes and shake my head.

'Your father passed away at twenty minutes to two this afternoon.'

45

VIOLET

Violet's boots crunch on the unspoilt fallen snow through the dense trees, the gun weighing down her coat pocket. Other than the muted drone of the motorway traffic and her feet beneath her, it's quiet. Peaceful. Like the calm before an almighty storm.

The smell of earth and bark from bare-branched trees fills the air. She walks with purpose, snaking around the trees, for about twenty minutes. A mile should be enough. Thankfully, she doesn't come across another soul. But that's hardly surprising. It's bloody cold, and these woods are notoriously dense. When she reaches a suitable area, where giant trees disappear into the darkening sky, she stops and listens. The faraway rumble of an aeroplane fades into silence. She stands for a few minutes, her breath fogging the air like white puffs of cloud, until she's satisfied she's alone. This feels like the ideal spot.

Violet removes a piece of chalk from her pocket, marks a cross around head height on the trunks of three neighbouring trees, and takes six long steps backwards. That's about the distance from the entrance to Will and Tiffany Watson's kitchen to their bifold doors.

She turns to a sound in the shadows. She shivers. There it is again. She waits. A red squirrel darts across her path, disappearing into the undergrowth.

With a trembling hand, she takes the gun from her pocket. This is no good. She needs to settle her nerves, or perhaps her raw excitement. When it comes to it, she can't show any signs of either emotion. Once this gun comes out on Christmas Eve, she must be on her game. She must be the master of the situation. The winner. She fumbles in her bag for a cigarette and lights it. Smoke curls from her lips into the clear air. Each inhale is grounding as she ruminates the task at hand.

Come on, Violet. Think of what that man did to Mum. Think of how he's going to react when he sees you pull a gun in his kitchen on Christmas Eve.

The thought brings a smile to her face.

She flicks the cigarette butt to the ground and extinguishes it underfoot. From her pocket, she grabs a tissue, wraps the butt inside and places it in the side pocket of her bag. She hates ruining nature.

The weight of the gun feels pleasing in her hand, heavy and commanding. She takes three deep breaths, aims at the cross on the first of the marked trees and squeezes the trigger.

Birds scatter as the gun recoils. The sound of the shot echoes around the woods and fades into an empty stillness. The bark splinters slightly above the cross. She feels the tension leave her body with a satisfactory release of breath.

That felt good. Really good. And the result wasn't too shabby for a first attempt. But she must get the shots away quicker. She's got plenty of bullets to keep trying.

Is that how Will Watson felt the night he shot her mother? Did he think it felt good? Or did he run in fear he'd done something wrong? She wants to know. She has to know.

She lets out another long, hard breath, staring at the gun in her shaking hand. For twenty minutes, she aims at the trees in quick succession. One. Two. Three. And again. One. Two. Three. It's as if the gun has become part of her.

It's going to be OK.

She's going to be OK.

46

VIOLET

Before taking the gun home, she texts Tiffany. She's studied the Winter Wonderland event's plan online and worked out a good place to rendezvous when she gets there.

> I can make it, but not until later. I'll meet you by the German sausage stall around two o'clock. Summer X

A message pings back within the minute.

That's great. I'll have to feed Leo lunch first, but perhaps we can have a drink together?
Tiff X

This is going to be such fun.

When they were kids, every December, her mother used to take Rose and her to the town's Winter Wonderland on the Saturday afternoon it opened. It was simply called the Christmas Winter Fair in those days, a low-key event with a few meagre rides and a scattering of stalls, where people dressed in Christmas jumpers sold their festive wares. However, as time has passed, it's grown to be a full-blown affair, the highlight of the town's year, featuring sprawling wooden huts and endless rides. The local committee starts planning the event in September each year, and it runs for two weeks from mid-December until New Year's Day.

After Mum was shot, Auntie Audrey used to take Rose. An offer that was open to Violet, but one she never accepted. She couldn't bear to be there without Mum, and someone needed to stay with her because Dad was rarely around at that time of year.

The afternoon sky is fading to dusk when she arrives. The bright lighting of the funfair and lines of wooden huts illuminate the greying skies. Kids scream on the bumper cars and the waltzer, and a cacophony of cheers streams from the beer tent. Music blares out from a substandard Tannoy, crackling like one of her father's scratched vinyl records.

Rose keeps trying to call her, but Violet can't face her sister at the moment. She seeks out the German sausage stall, one of the wooden huts with a long queue of people waiting to buy the bratwursts, frankfurters, pretzels, and sauerkraut on offer. The greasy smell of the sausages sizzling on the open-air grills makes her want to vomit.

She sneaks around the side of a wooden hut, where a woman is selling homemade Christmas ornaments. A range of baubles in different shapes and sizes hang from the roof on pieces of red ribbon. Pinecone snowflakes and dried pieces of lemon and orange dangle from the branches of a large artificial tree in the centre of the display.

She spots Tiffany waiting by the sausage stall, talking to a man. He must be Tiffany's brother-in-law, Lewis, because he bears a striking resemblance to Will in both tallness and facial features. Leo sits on his broad shoulders, one hand on Lewis's head, the other waving a glittery wand.

Perfect.

She removes her woolly glove, finds her pay-as-you-go phone and sends Tiffany another text.

> I'm sorry, I'm running late. I won't make it until three. Summer x

Tiffany checks her phone and says something to Lewis. He points towards the rides. She nods and follows him.

Violet tails them, moving closer, waiting for her chance.

Lewis pays to take Leo on the bumper cars. He straps him in and holds him tight as he whizzes around the track, roughly knocking into anyone and everyone he can. Squeals and screams echo around. Leo finds the ride hilarious.

Tiffany waits by the entrance laughing while trying her best to disguise her distaste.

Her lucky break arises when a loud bell rings and riders scuttle from the cars. Lewis takes Leo's hand and leads him back to Tiffany. She points to an avenue of huts, says something, and they head in Violet's direction.

Violet steps backwards, worming her way between two huts.

They pass her. Leo stops abruptly and jumps up and down. He points to an older man selling candy floss. Tiffany and Lewis converse. Lewis nods and steps aside, holding Leo's hand. He tells the kid to calm down as Tiffany stands in line to order a candy floss.

A phone rings.

And her chance arises.

It all happens so fast.

Lewis lets go of Leo's hand and answers the call on his phone. Tiffany turns her head to move along the queue at the candy floss stall. Leo is captivated by an animated pair of elves manning the entrance to Santa's grotto in a tent a few stalls from where Violet stands. The kid leaves Lewis and wanders across to the guy dressed in red, unnoticed by Lewis or Tiffany.

Violet grabs her opportunity and swoops in, firmly taking Leo's hand as if he were her own child. She skittles off, away from Tiffany and Lewis, and down a narrow gap between two huts with the kid in tow.

47

ROSE

First, I phone V. The call diverts to her voicemail. 'Damn, she's not answering.' I leave her a message and ask her to contact me as soon as she can.

I then call Auntie Audrey. She assures me she'll stay with Mum until I return, even if V gets there first. 'I won't say anything to your mother, love. It's best coming from you.'

I text Karen.

> My father passed this afternoon. Rose

We exchange messages

I'm sorry to hear that. I hope you're OK.
Karen

Please let your boys know. Rose

I will do. Take care of yourself. Karen

Jamie holds my hand when we walk into the hospice.

Carlos is waiting for us. 'Would you like to see your father?'

I nod. I've been mentally preparing for this moment for days, but it's come much quicker than expected. V said she hoped he'd wait until after Christmas before taking his final breath. This time of year is dark enough as it is.

My hand shakes as I sign us in.

'Are you sure you want to see him?' Jamie asks.

I swallow hard. 'Yes.'

Dad's room smells of soap from where staff have cleaned him. His eyes are closed, and his hands rest by his sides. I've seen dead bodies before, but nothing can prepare you for seeing someone you love dead.

The outpouring of grief I thought would come with his passing doesn't arrive. All my life I've been the child of our family, but with V's current state of mind and everything I've found out, now it's as if I need to play the adult. I need to keep strong for her.

'A doctor was here for another patient, so she issued a death certificate,' Carlos says.

'What did she put as the cause of death?' I ask.

'I'll have to check.' Carlos straightens the sheets by the base of the bed. 'Would you like me to contact the funeral director, or are you going to do that? There's no rush.'

'Would you do it, please? But hang tight. I can't get hold of my sister.' My voice falters. 'I need to ask her if she wants to see him before they take his body away.'

'Understood. I'll take care of things. Would you like me to stay or leave you alone for a while?'

I look at Jamie. He shrugs. 'It's up to you. I'll be here.'

'You go,' I tell Carlos.

'I'll be at the front desk if you need me.' Carlos steps backwards towards the door. 'Just shout.'

'Do you want me to stay?' Jamie asks.

I nod. 'Most definitely.'

I try to call V again, but she still doesn't answer.

I'm not a religious person, but I hold Dad's cold hand and say a silent prayer. I try to put aside the revelations I've discovered and talk to him about happy times, several sentences beginning with, 'Do you remember when...'

Jamie's presence is a comfort. We stay for half an hour. I've run out of stories, and it's enough. The sense of bitterness burning in my throat is leaving a bad taste in my mouth. I still love him, but my father is not the person I thought he was. I need to deal with these feelings. I stand and kiss his cold forehead. 'I'll return with V later on and pack up his things.'

'What if she doesn't want to come?' Jamie says gently.

'Good point. I'll pack them up now. Then we can get the funeral directors to take him straight away if V decides she doesn't want to see him. She can always go and see him at the funeral directors' if she wants to.' I choke on my words. It all sounds so final. I try her number again. 'Damn. Why the hell isn't she answering?'

I open the wardrobe and find the small suitcase I packed for Dad when he transferred from the hospital. It's hard to believe it was only three weeks ago that the doctor spoke those words, 'I'm afraid there's nothing more we can do for him.'

The two shirts and the pair of trousers hanging on the rail remind me of the hope I had back then that he would somehow miraculously recover, despite being told otherwise. I neatly fold them and pack them in the suitcase.

Carlos hands me a pen when we stop at the reception desk on the way out. 'Don't forget to sign out.'

I go to initial at the end of the line where I signed in earlier, but pause. The entry at the top of the page catches my interest. Violet came here to see Dad today. I gasp at the entry two lines below. Will Watson also came to visit Dad earlier today. But it's not only the name that makes me look at the entry in more detail, but the make and colour of his vehicle – a red Audi. The numberplate is vaguely familiar. It's the car I collided with that day. I flick the pages of the book backwards until I get to the day of the accident.

Will Watson – my half-brother – came to see Dad that day.

48

VIOLET

Violet squeezes Leo's hand. 'You remember me, don't you, Leo? I'm your mum's friend, Summer, from the gym.'

He nods, eyeing her warily.

'Where's your mum?' She continues leading him away from Tiffany and Lewis but keeps them in her vision.

The kid frowns. He looks behind him, but from his vantage point, there's only a sea of legs and the heads of toddlers like him.

'We'll find her, don't you worry. You know, you really shouldn't be wandering off.' She waves her phone at him. 'I'll call her. Hey, do you want to go and see Farmer Christmas? He's in that tent over there.'

Leo nods enthusiastically, his separation anxiety soon washed away with the thought of seeing the big fella in red. 'Will he give me a present?'

'I'm sure he will.'

'Can we wait for my mummy?'

'Let me call her.' She smiles reassuringly and looks at her phone. 'Oh, there's no signal,' she lies. 'I'll drop her a text.' But she doesn't. Not yet. The timing isn't right.

An undeniable deep sense of satisfaction settles inside her. It's wholly chilling to know how this is going to affect Will Watson. As soon as Tiff knows she's lost Leo, she'll be on the phone to Will. Violet smiles at the thought. He's miles away at his stag weekend. It will completely freak him out. He'll have to cut short his trip and come back.

Leo turns his attention to the elves who are handing out leaflets to passing kids. Violet's regular phone rings. It's Rose again. She ignores it.

The adrenaline racing around her body is out of control as she thinks about what to do with the boy. Her plan has been to take him for a short while to wind up Tiffany and Will.

But now that he's putty in her hands, she wonders if she could do so much more to bring his father deep pain. The pain she's experienced since she was nine years old.

'Your mum's going to join us.' She squeezes his fingers. 'Come on, let's go and see what Santa has for you.'

He skips along, his little hand tightly gripping hers.

She pays one of the elves, shocked. Ten pounds for the kid to sit on Santa's knee for a couple of minutes and receive a plastic piece of gaudy crap sounds exorbitant. But that's the price of having kids. She's glad she's never going to have any. The elf hands her a ticket. 'Wait in the queue over there. It should only take ten minutes,' she says in a shrill voice.

'Don't worry, your mum will be here soon,' Violet says to Leo as they join the queue. 'Let me see if I can see her. Don't move from here, OK?'

He nods solemnly. 'Will you be back to see Farmer Christmas with me?'

'I'll be right back.' She winks at him. 'I promise.'

She nips to the front of the tent and peeps outside. Tiffany's phone is stuck to her ear, but she appears to be shouting at Lewis. He is shouting back, arms held aloft, but Violet can't work out what they are saying. She grins. This is so much fun.

Tiffany storms off, leaving Lewis searching around the stalls. His vision meets Violet's. She freezes. But he quickly moves on as he scans the area around him.

She returns to Leo, who is waiting anxiously in line.

'So have you been a good boy this year?' Santa asks in a fake gruff voice when they finally enter his grotto. A cosy sanctuary that sparkles with the magic of Christmas – if you're a kid, that is. It's a suffocating hellhole if you ask her. The gaudy red and golden fabric draped over the inner walls of the tinsel-covered tent is another reminder of this shit time of year. She can just about make out Tiffany's screaming voice in the background.

Leo stands in front of Santa. His eyes are wide in wonder. No doubt he can't believe he is actually speaking to Santa himself. He nods and shakes his head, too in awe of his Christmas hero for words to leave his mouth.

Even in the most joyous of times, Violet can't understand why anyone would have kids. The old guy looks at her, his fake white beard sitting crooked on his face. 'Has he, Mum?'

'Sorry?'

'Has he been a good boy?'

She gives Leo another wink. 'Very good. Always such a good boy.'

She smiles for the brownie points she's earning here.

Once her final plan comes to fruition, it'll be advantageous to have this kid on her side.

Her pay-as-you-go phone buzzes. It's Tiffany. Her call rings to voicemail. It's not enough time. Will needs to suffer for much longer. Violet imagines him leaving his friends in a hurry and speeding down the motorway back home. Perhaps he'll have an accident. Crash his car and be done with. No. That wouldn't be satisfying enough. She needs to witness his reaction when she faces him with the crime he committed fifteen years ago. The crime he thought he'd got away with.

Leo takes the gift wrapped in paper printed with snowmen from Santa.

'Now you be a good boy for your mum. And next year you can come back and see me.'

Leo's eyes light up. He drops his head backwards and smiles up at Violet.

She leads him out of the grotto and scoots down the side to a quiet space away from the crowds. It borders an area of thick, tall bushes that wander off into the distance. A thought consumes her as she stares into the abyss. Now is her chance. All she has to do is pick him up and run with him.

49

VIOLET

She stalls. A mixture of feelings washes over her. It's that smile. He trusts her. He wouldn't scream.

No. She can't do it. She can't harm him. She's a bad person. She knows that. It wasn't always this way. She used to be a good girl. But whatever, she can't harm a kid. 'Open your present, and I'll call your mum again.'

She texts Tiffany, telling her she's found Leo and she's taking him to the grotto. She'll say she sent the message when she first found him. Then she calls Tiffany's number.

Tiffany is frantic. 'Something dreadful has happened,' she cries. 'I've lost Leo.'

'Calm down. Didn't you get my text? I found him. He's with me.'

'Oh, my God, please tell me you're serious.' Tiffany's raw cries of pain cut through her. 'I'm going out of my mind. So is Will.'

Violet sucks the grin forming on her face into her cheeks. 'Where are you?' she says. 'I'll bring him straight to you.'

They meet back at the sausage stall. Tiffany grabs her son. He yelps like a puppy. She holds him tightly as if she'll never let him go. Tears stream down her pale face.

Violet wells up. And it's not fake. This isn't good. She can't afford to get all sentimental now.

Leo drops his gift from Santa to the floor.

Lewis ruffles Leo's hair. 'Don't ever wander off again, kiddo.'

'I found him at Santa's grotto,' Violet says. 'I tried to call you, but I had no signal. I did send you a message.'

Tiffany wipes her mascara-smudged eyes. 'Yes, yes. It's poor in places.'

Lewis eyes me suspiciously. 'Mine's been fine.'

'I only let him out of my sight for a second,' Tiffany says.

'It only takes a second,' Violet says.

A phone rings. It's Violet's regular phone, but she's set the ring tone to the same as the pay-as-you-go phone. 'Seems your signal's OK now,' Lewis says.

'Lewis!' Tiffany barks. 'I need to call Will. He'll be going out of his mind. He's on his way home from his weekend away.'

'Can we get a sausage, Mum?' Leo says.

Violet turns her back and glances at the screen of her phone. It's Rose again. She answers it this time, smiling as her sister delivers her message: Dad has finally gone.

She turns back to Tiffany, Lewis and Leo at the sausage stall. 'I need to get going,' she says. 'My father has passed away.'

'Oh, my goodness. That's dreadful. I'm so sorry,' Tiffany says.

'I'll catch you soon,' Violet says.

Tiffany gives her a sympathetic look. 'I hope your Christmas goes OK.'

Another smile forms on Violet's face as she turns and hurries back to her car.

50

ROSE

'What are you saying?' Jamie steers the car out of the hospice driveway.

'The guy who ran into me that day, Will Watson, was... is... my half-brother. Karen said one of her sons had been in touch with Dad recently. He'd been to see Dad the day of the accident. So I guess it wasn't so much of a coincidence that he was on that roundabout that day. He went to see him again earlier today.'

The inside of the windscreen steams up. Jamie turns on the heater, blowing hot air to clear the condensation. 'Talk about being in the wrong place at the wrong time.'

'I can't believe it. I was standing after the accident talking with my half-brother, exchanging personal details and neither of us knew.'

'That's not surprising. I saw him briefly at the hospital. You look nothing alike, and you have different surnames.'

'I guess so. Would you mind stopping at Tesco Express before you drop me off, please? I need to pick up a couple of things.'

'No problem.'

I stare at him. Butterflies I've never noticed before flicker in my tummy. Nothing is ever a problem for him.

In the supermarket, I pick up a carton of milk and a block of butter. When I head to the self-service checkouts, a lady approaches me. 'Hello. It's Rose, isn't it? Audrey's niece, Violet's sister?'

I stare blankly at the woman who wears a quilted coat with a fur-rimmed hood. 'Yes.' I do recognise her, but I can't think from where.

A couple of over-excited kids barge in front of me to pay for bars of chocolate and bottles of Fanta.

'I'm Cressida,' the woman says. 'Your sister, Violet, cleans for me every week. We met in town once, briefly. Violet was waiting outside the pharmacy for you.' She speaks with a plummy accent as if she's related to royalty.

'Yes.' I nod. 'I remember now.'

'How is she?'

'Fine.'

'Tell her I miss her and to let me know when she's coming back to work. Two weeks without her magic touch, and my house is a ghastly mess.'

'Two weeks,' I whisper. The hairs on the back of my neck stand on end.

'How is your father, by the way?' she asks.

'He passed away.'

'That's so sad. Please send Violet my fondest regards.'

'I must dash.' I pay for my items and run back to the car.

. . .

'She hasn't been to clean that woman's house for two weeks,' I say to Jamie when I tell him about my encounter with V's client. 'So where has she been going?'

'Perhaps she's been with her new boyfriend.'

I screw up my face. 'No. Something else is going on. She hasn't mentioned cancelling any clients to me. You know, she's always had something against Dad.' I wave my hands about theatrically. 'As if she blamed him in some way for what happened to Mum. I wonder if she knows something I don't. I need to talk to her. Sit her down and have a frank conversation with her.'

'You probably need to let her process his death first.'

I drop my hands into my lap in frustration.

He takes one of my hands and squeezes it. 'I'm sorry for what you're going through.'

Mum is asleep when he drops me home. Auntie Audrey is washing up in the kitchen. She turns from the sink. 'I'm sorry, love.' She removes her rubber gloves and wipes her hands on a tea towel. 'Come here.' She opens her arms.

Auntie Audrey has always been good for a cuddle. She replaced Mum in so many ways while V and I were growing up. She always said we were the children she never had.

She makes tea. 'I'll come back tomorrow morning before church, and we can tell your mum together when Violet is here if you want.'

'That's a good idea.'

I take a sip of tea. 'You know I asked you the other day about Mum and Dad's relationship? Well, I found something out.'

She lifts her cup of tea but stops it inches from her mouth.

'Did you know Dad was having affairs before Mum was shot?'

Her face pales. She places her cup on the table and sucks her lips into her mouth.

'Well, did you?'

She doesn't reply, but the look on her face answers my question.

'Tell me what you know, Auntie. Just tell me.'

If I'm not mistaken, there's a glint of fear in her eyes.

I fill the silence. 'I found Mum's old diaries. Dad had another family. V and I have two half-brothers. Three actually, but one died.'

She drops her chin to her chest like a scolded schoolchild.

'You knew, didn't you?' I'm stunned. 'Did Mum tell you before she was shot?'

She slowly lifts her head and gives a faint nod.

I grab her hand. 'What aren't you telling me, Auntie? You're keeping something from me. I know you are.'

'I'm not sure what good it will do to dig up the past.'

'But I want the truth. I *need* the truth. You've always preached to us about never lying.'

'Once you know this stuff, there's no going back. Besides, you've just lost your father.'

I raise my voice. 'Tell me.'

51

ROSE

Auntie Audrey sighs in resignation. 'Your mother suspected your father of being a serial womaniser. It was affecting her mental health. Then, one day, she asked me to look after you two girls, and she followed him. I remember it vividly. It was around this time of year, just before Christmas. She came back in pieces.' She slowly shakes her head. 'Absolute pieces.'

'Go on.' She hasn't told me anything I don't already know.

'She caught your dad with another woman.'

'Karen,' I whisper, too low for her to hear.

'Her torment turned to anger. She said she wanted him dead. I'd seen your mum worked up before, but I'd never seen her so venomous. I managed to calm her down and persuade her to wait until the new year to deal with it. There was nothing to be gained by ruining Christmas for you girls. She listened to that. She'd always do anything for you two.'

'Then what happened?' My voice cracks. I'm close to

tears. After the day I've had, it's difficult to process all this. But I have to know. 'Tell me everything, Auntie. Don't hold back. Please don't.'

'The new year came and went. Every time I tried to bring it up, she didn't want to talk about it. I thought perhaps it might settle down. Typical of me in those days – sticking my head in the sand, hoping it would all go away. I was good at that. Eventually, she told me she had confronted this Karen woman and found out your dad was leading a double life and that they had kids together.' She puffs out her cheeks, her eyes wide. 'If she wanted him dead before... well, you can imagine.' Her face is ashen. This all can't have been easy for her – a God-fearing woman confronted with such wrongness.

'And then what happened?' I ask.

'I told her to give him an ultimatum. She wanted to leave him. She even wished him dead.'

I can't imagine Mum saying that, but then what do I really know about her? Only what V has told me. I only remember snippets about life before the shooting.

'Don't think bad of her. She was a troubled woman. She became more and more depressed. She simply wanted him out of the way.'

'So why didn't she leave him?'

'Easier said than done when you have no money and two young girls to bring up, Rose. She gave him the ultimatum. Things seemed to settle down. She seemed happier, more content. Then, around the middle of the year, she announced she was pregnant. I remember being shocked. It was totally out of the blue.'

I press her some more about what happened after that, but she says there's nothing more to tell. 'The diaries that she kept – the one from 2009 is missing. It's not with the others. It seems strange that all the other diaries have been meticulously completed, but that one is missing. Or did she not write one that year?'

'I really can't say.'

Can't say or won't say? I eye her suspiciously. It's almost as if what she has just told me was well-scripted, as if she's always worried it all might have to come out one day.

'Then what happened?' I ask.

Her eyes glass over. 'Life carried on. And then Christmas came. And then... well, you know.' She shrugs.

'You're not telling me everything. I know you're not.'

She looks to the ceiling. 'OK.' She sighs heavily. 'After the accident, I found the missing diary.'

'The one from the year of the shooting?'

She nods.

'Where is it?'

'I destroyed it.'

'Why?' I ask in exasperation.

She plonks her elbows on the table and gently clasps her hands together. 'Your mum never told me any of this, but I read about it in that diary.' She rests her chin on her clenched fingers.

'Read about what?'

'The baby wasn't your father's.'

My stomach turns as I digest this revelation. 'Mum had an affair? Who with?'

'The warden from the church we used to attend.'

My hand shoots to my mouth. 'The church warden? Mum had an affair with a church warden?!' I can't believe what she's telling me. It's as if I'm listening to an audiobook, not my auntie revealing the messed-up story of my family's life.

'Yes, and a married one at that. You met him the other night when we went to church.'

'Did I?' My mind wanders back to when I accompanied her to the candlelit service.

'That Charles guy, and his wife, Nicolette.'

My jaw drops. The respect I once held for both my parents is rapidly diminishing.

'Your mum discovered your father's other family and took solace in a man who should've known better. I had it out with him. Charles was planning to leave Nicolette for your mum.'

'Did Dad know this?'

She shrugs. 'I've never spoken to him about it. How could I? If he didn't already know, then what was the point of him finding out? It's why I stopped going to that church.'

I swallow hard. This is a lot to take in. 'Does V know any of this?'

'I don't see how she could.'

'There's something else, isn't there?'

Her eyes fix on mine.

'What else was in that diary, Auntie Audrey? Tell me.'

'Nothing.' She finishes her tea. 'I need to go. I'll see you in the morning.'

Something's amiss. I've always trusted Auntie Audrey. She's been the lynchpin of this family since my mother was shot. But for the first time, I fear she's lying about something.

52

VIOLET

'The big day is fast approaching, Mum. I've got everything ready. In less than twenty-four hours, it'll all be over. Justice will be served.'

Her mother gently moans. 'Clever girl. You're such a clever girl.' She looks troubled today, unhappy almost.

It upsets Violet to see her like this. 'Don't be sad, Mum. Dad is dead. These are good times. We're going to nail the monster who did this to you and Bean, and then we'll be free – free from that noose of injustice that's been hanging around our necks for the past fifteen years.'

When she and Rose told her of Dad's passing yesterday, their mother's face remained expressionless. To Rose anyway – her sister couldn't see the glint of joy in Mum's eyes that was so evident to Violet.

She lifts a small chunk of yule log to her mother's lips. 'Come on, eat. You love Auntie's yule log.'

Mum pokes out her tongue.

Her resolve wavers. She can't resist it. She's been thinking about this chocolate extravaganza ever since Auntie Audrey brought it around yesterday. She places the spoon in her mouth. The velvety ganache melts on her tongue. So much butter and cream. She eats another sliver. But it's OK. She's going for a run in a bit. She'll do an extra lap to make up for the extra calories she has consumed.

'The gun's all ready.' Violet places the plate and spoon on the table and rubs her hands together in glee. 'I told you I went into the woods and tested it. I'm all set.' She mimics the shape of a gun with two fingers. 'Pop, pop, pop.' The sound of the front door opening startles her. 'Ssh... Rose is home.'

The waft of Chinese food precedes her sister's entrance into the room. She's carrying a plastic bag.

Jamie accompanies her, holding four bags of shopping. He dumps the bags on the kitchen work surface and Rose plonks the bag of takeaway food on the table. 'Our traditional Christmas Eve Eve takeaway. Oh, no! What are you doing eating that?' She points to the yule log. 'I told you I'd pick up a takeaway.'

Violet stands. The legs of the chair scrape across the floor. 'I'm sorry. I forgot.' She hadn't, but when her sister mentioned last night that she'd asked if Jamie could join them, Violet was relieved. She's got better things to do than sit watching those two lovebirds scoffing egg -fried rice and chicken chow mein. Because that's what they are. He fancies the pants off her. She sees it, but her baby sister is far too innocent. 'I'm going for a run.'

Rose stares at her. 'We always have Chinese the night before Christmas Eve. Besides, it's like the Arctic out there.

And it's started snowing. You won't see the ice. You could have an accident.'

'I'll be fine.'

Rose hesitates. 'I meant to ask you something. I bumped into a woman you clean for in Tesco. Cressida. She said you haven't been there for the past two weeks. Why?'

Violet's stomach tightens as her mind goes into overdrive trying to think of how to answer her sister. 'No. I've taken time off from a couple of morning clients.'

'Why?'

'I've had stuff I needed to get on with.'

Her sister's eyebrows rise and pull together. She doesn't believe her. But it doesn't matter. She's only got one more day to get through.

'Stay and have some food with us,' Rose insists. 'I've bought a bottle of wine.'

'I can't, but you two enjoy it.'

Her sister sighs in resignation. 'I've got a film sorted for tomorrow.' She asks Jamie to unpack the cartons of food from the plastic bag while she reaches into a cupboard for plates. 'One of the women at work really recommends *Our Little Secret*.'

How apt.

'She saw it last week.' Her sister points to the bags of shopping on the work surface. 'I've got all the food in for our Christmas Eve meal tomorrow. Four o'clock. Don't forget.'

'Oh, no. Sorry, Rose. I won't be able to make it,' Violet says.

'Why?'

'I'm busy.'

'But it's Christmas, V!' An 'Are-you-for-real?' expression forms on her sister's face. Violet can't blame her. Since when did she ever have anything to do other than be here with her sister and their mother? Rose tries to play on her heart-strings. A tune Violet refuses to listen to. 'Come on, I thought with Dad's passing we should be together.'

'Declan's taking me out to dinner.'

Her sister is getting more and more worked up. 'Invite him here,' she virtually shouts, exasperated.

'Maybe some other time, but not tomorrow.' Violet winks at Mum. 'I've got other plans.'

Flakes of snow melt into her face. The snow isn't settling, so the pavements are covered in a mucky slush, which flicks up the back of her leggings. Rose was right. Odd patches of ice hamper her progress. Her breath puffs into the air like clouds of smoke. She focuses on each step, releasing the tension that's been building inside of her for days for the mission she must take tomorrow. The heavy weight on her shoulders lightens, but only slightly. This time tomorrow, however, it'll be gone entirely.

Stay calm, Violet. You're nearly there.

53

VIOLET

One day to go. The anticipation is making her giddy.

Everyone is in bed. The house is quiet. With a thick charcoal pencil, she works quickly, frantically, sketching the Grim Reaper beside the photo of Will and Tiffany on her bedroom wall. She adds a scythe in one hand, and a gun in the other, wielding the weapons in their faces. She moves her pencil to the top of the wall, a slow, deliberate movement now, and draws an hourglass. But she only adds a few grains of sand.

Their time is almost up.

Mum used to take her and Rose to church every Sunday when they were small. They'd meet Auntie Audrey there. She can picture the four of them, sitting in a line on the hard wooden bench, her and Rose side by side in their pretty dresses between their two favourite people. And their best shoes they were only allowed to wear on a Sunday or special occasions. She would listen intently as the vicar encouraged patience and faith.

Her obsession with the graveyard at the back of that church started the year after Mum was shot. For years, she slipped out of school every lunchtime and sat on the bench among the graves, where she etched the inscriptions on the headstones in a notebook. It was her solace from the crazy, mixed-up world of school dinners she couldn't stand. No one missed her. And then one day, they did. After that, they tried to keep an eye on her, but she was too slick for them. She always managed to escape back to that churchyard.

They called Dad into school, but he couldn't attend because he was away, supposedly with work, so Auntie Audrey came. It was around the time she first found out about Dad's other women. He'd been texting during a film he was meant to be watching with her, Mum and Rose and left his phone on the arm of the sofa to go to the toilet. She was aghast to read the text exchange between him and a woman called Lily-May. The rage that boiled inside of her that day for him betraying her mother, betraying them all, still bubbles away today. She lived in constant anxiety that he was going to leave Mum, leave them. And she thought for a while that would kill their mother.

She paces up and down her room reading a message on her phone. Her nerves are taut. Rose has always been sentimental, but she is more upset than she thought she'd be that Violet won't be around tomorrow. Her sister is asking her to reconsider. She wants them together like they normally are on Christmas Eve. But there's nothing normal about this Christmas.

She grabs her ruler from the desk drawer, taps it on the wall and turns to the faces blurring in front of her. 'Listen up, all. I've got an update on the Melanie Sapphire case. As many of you know, tomorrow is the anniversary of the shooting of Melanie in her home on Christmas Eve, 2009. Fifteen years ago.' She raises her voice for effect. 'Fifteen.' She nods her head with purpose. 'The family, understandably, are desperate for us to resolve this case. I've been tracking the target and his wife for the past two weeks and had the house under surveillance. We're almost ready for a forced entry under a section seventeen. Be ready tomorrow evening to support. Yes, yes, I know it's Christmas Eve, but we're professionals.'

She pushes her back against the wall and slides down to the floor until her knees are level with her head. She rests her chin on her knees. She should get some sleep, but there's no way that's going to happen. She's far too wired, running on the adrenaline of anticipating how tomorrow is going to play out.

She crawls over to the bed, pushes it aside and lifts the floorboards. One crashes to the floor.

Her sister's bedroom door opens. Footsteps thump up the stairs. She waits for the knock. There it is. 'V, are you OK?'

'I'm fine.'

'What was that noise?'

'I knocked a glass of water off my bedside table.'

'Can I come in?'

'Go back to bed, Rose.'

'I'm scared.' She's playing that game again. The one she played when they were young to get Violet's attention. The one she always won. Violet lost count of the nights she slept in her sister's bed with her.

'I'm tired, Rose. Really tired. Go to sleep.' It's not a lie. Her head is pounding, and she feels constantly sick. 'We can talk in the morning.'

She removes the gun from the gap in the floorboards. It's all ready, loaded for the task ahead. Ensuring the safety catch is on, she holds the weapon in her hands, reliving the moment she shot those trees in the woods, pretending they were human heads. The Watsons' heads.

She replays the look on Will Watson's face that she's conjured in her mind.

The moment when he sees his beautiful wife's body drop to the floor.

Before he finally gets what's coming to him.

A bullet between the eyes.

54

ROSE

'You should've heard her last night. She was still up at four o'clock, muttering away. At one point, she must've dropped something because she woke me up.'

I cough. I've come down with a cold. My throat is sore, making my voice raspy. 'There was a right old bang. I went up there to see if she was alright, but she wouldn't even answer the door. Just shouted at me to go back to bed.' I peel a potato and place it in the saucepan of cold water with the others. The smell of fish rises from the oven. Every Christmas Eve, I cook a fish pie. It's a dish Mum finds easy to swallow.

Jamie takes sips from his can of lager, between preparing the Brussels sprouts. 'Maybe you've got to let her be. Reassess the situation after Christmas. There's been a lot going on, what with your dad.'

I scoff. 'She doesn't even seem upset about Dad. Something's not right. I'm sorry to sound like a broken record, but it's not.' I take another potato from the bag and scrape the peeler along the skin faster and faster. 'You don't know her like I do.' I let out an exhausted breath. 'And then—' I bite my lip.

Jamie snacks on a handful of peanuts. 'Then what?'

'I overheard her talking to Mum before she went out. She often has these conversations with Mum that—'

He reaches across to the small bowl, grabs another handful of peanuts and tosses one into the air. Grinning like a schoolboy, he tilts his head backwards, steps forwards, and catches it in his mouth. 'Carry on.'

The hand of guilt raps me on the shoulder for going behind my sister's back. I'm betraying her, but I have to talk to someone. 'When she thinks they're on their own, she talks to Mum, then imitates Mum's voice replying to her.' I wipe my hands on a cloth and split open a bag of carrots. 'At first, I thought I was imagining it. But my auntie caught her doing it a few years ago as well. So it's not just me. I've overheard her several times over the past few weeks – ever since the accident. It's as if she's become more careless at being overheard.'

He grunts, perplexed. 'So what were they talking about?'

'V said, "The time has come, Mum." And then she replied in Mum's voice, "About time, too. We've waited far too long." And then V said, "I promised you and Bean I'd never let you down."'

Jamie picks up yet another handful of peanuts. 'Bean?'

'That's what we called our baby sister.'

'It sounds as if V needs to get some help.'

'I'm worried she might be suffering from post-concussion syndrome.'

'What's that?'

'I looked it up. It's like a mild traumatic brain injury. It can happen to people weeks, months even, after a concussion, especially those with anxiety issues, which my sister definitely has.'

'Can you encourage her to go back to the hospital?'

'I think I need to.'

'I'd see how she gets on over Christmas.'

'I'm worried she needs help now. You should've seen her when she went out just before you arrived. Her eyes were all strange, her pupils dilated. And her neck kept twitching. She looked... I don't know... deranged. I'm not sure this new Declan guy is good for her.'

The doorbell rings. I flinch. 'Has she forgotten her key?' I stab the knife into the chopping board and leave him to answer it.

A guy stands at the door, holding a small Christmas basket wrapped in cellophane. On top sits a bouquet of flowers. 'Hi, is Violet in?' he asks.

'I'm sorry, she's not here.'

This must be Declan. He's older than I thought he'd be – mid-thirties. I'm surprised V has gone for an older man. But perhaps, subconsciously, she needs a father figure. But then the guy introduces himself. 'I'm Pete from Shiny Surfaces – the cleaning company Violet works for.' He hands me the hamper and flowers. 'We didn't want her to miss out on the staff Christmas present, so I thought I'd drop it off.'

'That's kind of you. I'll make sure she gets it.'

'Tell her we've missed her these past few weeks. Do you know when she'll be back at work?'

The deep sense of unease that's been gripping my stomach for days tugs a little tighter. I look from the Christmas bouquet to him. 'Probably not until the new year. When did you last see her?'

He scratches his head. 'About two weeks ago now, love. Wish her happy Christmas from us. And to you and your family.' He waves and leaves.

I return to Jamie.

He folds his arms across his chest. 'Are they for you?'

I shake my head. 'No. They're for V. They're from the guy she works for. Apparently, she hasn't been in work for the past two weeks.' I pause. 'She told me she'd taken time off from her morning clients to spend time with Dad. But she hasn't been to her evening job either. So where has she been going when she says she's going to work?' I bite my lip. 'I need to get into her room – see what's going on up there. What's the best way to do it without a key?'

Jamie pulls a face. 'Think about what you're saying, Rose. You could cause irreparable damage to your relationship. She'll never trust you again.'

'I've thought about it. Believe me. But I need to do it. She needs my help.'

55

ROSE

'Are you really sure about this?' Jamie asks.

I nod.

'What type of lock is it?' he asks.

I shrug. 'One with a key.'

He looks at me, expressionless.

'Well, will you help?'

'Of course I will if you want me to.'

I check on Mum. She's staring at the TV in the living room. 'I'm going upstairs, Mum. I'll be back in a bit.'

Jamie follows me to the top of the house.

My chest is on fire.

Jamie crouches down and studies the lock on V's bedroom door. He turns his head and looks up at me, his eyebrows raised. 'It'll probably make a mess.'

'It doesn't matter.'

'What if you find nothing out of the ordinary inside?

There's no coming back from this.'

'Just do it.'

Standing, he faces the door square on. With his hands either side of the doorframe, he steps backwards. He lifts one knee, kicks his leg forward and strikes the lock with the sole of his heavy boot.

'Careful, you'll hurt yourself.'

'It's only a cheap lock. It won't take long.' Two more blows and the lock gives way. The wooden frame splinters as the door buckles and swings open with a creak.

I rush into the room and abruptly stop. Every hair on my arms and the back of my neck stands on end. 'Oh, hell.' I peer around the mess. My hand covers my mouth. 'What has she been up to?'

Jamie stands behind me. He rests his hands on my shoulders, squeezing them as if trying to reassure me that everything will be OK.

But it won't.

This is far worse than I bargained for.

'Jeez,' I say. 'It looks like a police suspect board.' I turn, and we exchange looks of horror. 'What the hell?' I step to the wall, incredulous. Sketches of Mum, V and me when we were kids, before Mum was shot, border a mass of photos and V's artistic flair.

'It's as if she's been trying to solve who shot your mum. These sketches are macabre.' Jamie points to a drawing of the Grim Reaper surrounded by what looks like a friendship bracelet Violet has intricately drawn. 'This is some kind of timeline.' He gestures to a straight line, sprinkled with dates, that runs the length of the wall and is surrounded by scribbles, photos and etchings.

'You're right.' I stab my finger on the start of the line. 'That's the date Mum was shot.'

He points to the other end of the line. 'And this is today's date. And look at this.' His finger moves to a drawing of a gun pointing towards a woman and a man with a kid on his shoulders. Alongside them is an etching of a skull and crossbones. 'Do you know these people?'

I take a closer look at the photo. 'I know them from somewhere. I'm sure I do.'

'Who are they?'

The image rattles around my brain like loose change before the penny drops. I thump my head with the palm of my hand. My stomach turns like never before. Am I confused, or is this for real? The fear is crippling. 'That's Will Watson. The guy from the accident. Our half-brother.'

'She must think he's got something to do with your mum's shooting,' Jamie says.

I clasp Jamie's arm. 'I need to call my auntie.'

56

VIOLET

The anticipation of finally facing the Watsons is tantalising. It's like a tornado has been brewing inside of her these past two weeks, and now it's time to wreak havoc.

Every heartbeat of the drive to Radstone feels like a minute, every minute like an hour. Her muscles are tense and small beads of sweat have formed on her temples despite the arctic conditions outside.

She blasts a Christmas tune, a modern version of *Hallelujah*. It's the first time she's willingly listened to Christmas music since she was a child. It's both chilling and reassuring, allowing her to mentally prepare for the task ahead. She's nearly there. So very nearly there. She sings along with her own lyrics. 'I told you, Mum. I told you I'd never let you down.'

The gun in the shoebox now wrapped in Christmas paper rests in the footwell of the passenger seat. It serves as a constant reminder to drive carefully. Getting stopped by police will only heighten her anxiety and could ruin her plans completely. That can't happen.

Her heart thumps in her chest, every rapid beat a reminder of what's about to happen.

Justice. That's what's going to happen.

Snow continues to fall. The same weather as the year Mum was shot. She remembers it vividly. Her mother took her and Rose to the shops because she was running low on flour and didn't have enough to make her magic mince pies. She'd been crying. She wouldn't admit it, but Violet knew. She said she'd been chopping onions. But Violet wasn't stupid. Her mother and father had argued. Violet had eavesdropped on their conversation. He'd said he had to work on Boxing Day, so would be leaving Christmas Day evening. Looking back, she doesn't believe her mother gave two hoots if her dad was there or not. She was just upset for her and Rose. And Violet was upset for her.

When she reaches the dirt track leading to the back of Tiffany and Will's place, it's dark, save for the back of their house, which is lit up like the proverbial Christmas tree. The upstairs is in darkness. Leo must be in bed. Just as Rose was fifteen years ago, soundly asleep, oblivious to the drama playing out downstairs.

She slows to ten miles per hour and slots into a parking space up the road as she has on all the occasions she's been here. But this time is different.

This is the last time she'll come here.

She sits for a little while, preparing herself. The headaches she's been experiencing over the past few weeks have subsided, and her vision is now crystal clear. Silent chants ride on the waves of her deep breaths: 'I've got this. I've got this. I've got this.'

Placing the box under her arm, she leaves the car and quietly closes the door. The *Hallelujah* song refuses to leave her head. She creeps along the dirt track until she reaches the back of Tiffany and Will's house. Bodies mingle in the kitchen. She can't make out who is who until she slides along the hedge and slips to the side of the storage unit by the hot tub.

Will, Tiffany, Lewis, and his wife Jacqui, whom she recognises from the changing rooms at the gym the first day she went there, are standing in a circle celebrating Christmas as a family, heedless that their lives are about to change forever. Their new puppy darts between their legs with boundless energy. Another woman appears. It's Karen, Will's mum. Another person she recognises from the gym when she stopped to talk to Tiffany. Unfortunate witnesses, but she has it covered. If it gets too difficult, there will have to be more collateral damage.

The bifold doors open. Tiffany steps outside with the puppy on a lead. 'Wee-wee, Ozzy,' she says. The puppy immediately obliges, opening his bladder on the ground.

Violet swallows hard. Memories of that night fifteen years ago return, when she peed all over the living room floor.

'There's a good boy.' Tiffany tugs at the dog's lead as he tries to sniff the ground. 'Let's get back inside,' she says. 'It's freezing out here.'

Violet takes the box from under her arm, removes the lid and picks up the gun.

She smiles.

Soon, it will all be over.

She clenches the heavy piece of lethal metal tighter and

tighter until her fingers ache. Fear mixed with anticipation, a cocktail of revenge, rushes through her. It's terrifying, yet utterly thrilling. She thinks about all the nights she's sat with Mum, feeding her dinner, chatting with her because no one else can get a word out of her. She releases the safety catch.

She needs to work out a way to ensure Tiffany answers the door.

And she needs to get that dog out of the way. He can't come to any harm.

Leo suddenly bounces into the kitchen like a rubber ball. Will swoops him up, his hands around his middle, and holds him in the air, smiling, yet shaking his head with a stern look on his face. He says a few words before putting him down. Leo runs from person to person, throwing his arms around their legs. They ruffle his hair and speak as if bidding him goodnight.

Tiffany takes his hand and leads him out of the room. She must be taking him back to bed. This could work to Violet's advantage. But she doesn't want to wait. Who knows how long she's going to be up there with him.

Violet is all revved up.

She's ready to go.

Now.

57

ROSE

I call my sister first, swearing when the call goes straight to voicemail. 'Damn you, V!' I call Auntie Audrey. She answers straight away. 'I need to see you,' I say.

'I'm on my way to church, Rose. Can I stop by afterwards?'

'No. I need you to come straight here.' There's no mistaking the desperation in my voice. 'Now.'

Jamie places a hand of reassurance on my shoulder.

'Whatever's happened?' Auntie Audrey asks anxiously. She must've picked up on the panic in my voice. 'Is it your mum?'

'No, no. Mum's fine. I'll explain when you get here.' I end the call. 'She's on her way.'

We stand staring at the wall, Jamie's arm around my shoulders like a cape of comfort. He squeezes my upper arm with pulsing movements.

I throw out a hand, my forefinger pointing to the floorboard leaning against the wall. 'I wouldn't mind betting that's where Dad's gun has been all this time. She's had it.' I leave his clasp and step over to the gap in the floorboards. Dropping to my knees, I peer inside, but it's too dark to see properly. I shove my hand inside and feel around. 'There's nothing here.' I stand and return to the wall. 'Will you come with me?' I say.

'Where?'

I point to the wall. 'To that address in Radstone.'

He places his hands on his hips. A deep frown forms on his face.

'I think she's gone there.'

'Rose, hun, this is for the police to deal with. What if she does have the gun your dad was talking about?'

I stand in front of him. 'No way am I calling the police. She's my sister, Jamie. She might not even be there. If she is, I need to talk some sense into her. I know I can.'

'So what are you planning on doing? If she's on her way to shoot someone... perhaps she already has! Come on, think this through.'

'I have to try to save her. Please. I know my sister. I can stop whatever she plans to do.'

Jamie places his hands on my shoulders. 'You could end up getting hurt... or worse. No, I can't let you do that. You know how much you mean to me.'

An inexplicable, irresistible urge overcomes me.

I lean into him and kiss him full on the mouth.

We stare at each other in a moment of silence. 'That's not fighting fair,' he murmurs.

I touch his beard with my fingers. 'I should get downstairs, check on Mum and wait for my auntie to get here.'

The front door bursts open as we reach the bottom of the

stairs. Auntie Audrey thunders in, slamming the door shut. She's out of breath. 'Whatever's going on?' She wipes her boots on the mat and brushes snowflakes from her coat.

'You need to come upstairs.' I turn to Jamie. 'Would you stay with Mum?'

He nods, his face deadpan. 'Think about what I said.'

I climb two stairs, pausing to look back while Auntie hurriedly struggles out of her coat.

She throws me a questioning look. 'I don't like the sound of this.' She bends down to unzip her boots, takes them off, then follows me, her breathing laboured.

I wait for her to catch her breath. She's going to need it. I take her hand and enter V's room.

Her shocked face turns to me. 'Heavens above.' She steps to the wall. 'Oh, no.' Her hand reaches for the silver cross on the chain around her neck, and she lets out a loud cry.

I point to the photo of Will holding the kid on his shoulders. 'That's Will Watson, our half-brother,' I say. 'I think V believes she has found the guy who shot Mum, and I fear she may have gone to seek revenge. It's the fifteen-year anniversary today. Fifteen years since Mum was shot.' I pause, squinting at her. 'You look as if you know him.'

'I've never met him.' The look of fear on her face unsettles me even more. 'But I've met his brother, Lewis.' She vigorously shakes her head and points to the bracelet surrounding the etching of the Grim Reaper. 'If she's going for Will, I think she's going for the wrong brother.'

58

ROSE

'You haven't been telling me the whole truth,' I say. 'You need to explain, and quickly.'

Auntie Audrey sits on V's unmade bed. She drops her face into her hands.

I sit beside her and call my sister again. 'What do you mean, she's got the wrong brother?' I nudge her. 'Look at me, Auntie Audrey.' The call to my sister takes another frustrating trip to her voicemail. 'You have to tell me everything. We could help V. Stop her from doing anything stupid.'

She rubs her pudgy hands together. Anxiety is written all over her face, seeping out from between the creases on her forehead to the lines around her eyes and lips.

I raise my voice. It startles her. 'Tell me what you know!'

'I did something terrible.'

'What?'

She draws a long breath and slowly puffs it out. 'I'm sorry. You're right. I haven't told you the whole truth.'

'Well, tell me now.'

Her eyes flicker. She fiddles with her cross, twiddling it between her forefinger and thumb.

'We haven't got time to waste.' My voice is strained.

'When your mum found out about your dad's other family, she wanted to leave him. I told you that already. But she had no money, so she planned to rob him. And she asked me to help her.'

'What? How?'

'We concocted this plan to fake a break-in and empty the safe so she could take everything. She knew he kept bundles of cash in there and his mother's jewellery, which was worth a fortune. It was a stupid idea, but I agreed to provide an alibi and say your mum was with me when it happened.'

My mouth opens, but no words come out. My auntie Audrey is as pure as the driven snow.

Or so I thought.

'She was desperate. I don't like speaking ill of the dead, but your dad deserved it. He cheated on your mum for years, Rose. I saw how it tore her apart. Every day, she lost another layer of her beautiful self in the hope that man would mend his ways. Mercifully, she changed her mind about the robbery, but I never fully got to the bottom of why until I found her diary the year after she was shot.'

'The one you destroyed?'

She nods. 'That's right. I didn't know there were others stashed away in the attic, though. I was surprised when you mentioned you'd found them.'

My chest is getting tighter and tighter.

'When your mum fell pregnant, I was so happy for her, so

full of hope that she and your dad could make things work. But I was wrong. She told me she still wanted to leave him. He was still seeing other women, she said. I was shocked. I tried to convince her to wait until after the baby was born. I thought she'd change her mind. I mean, how was she going to cope on her own with two young children and a newborn? She finally agreed to stay put, and I honestly thought things were settling down.'

'So?'

She sighs heavily. 'The diary painted a different, sordid picture.' She looks me squarely in my eyes.

'There's something else, isn't there?'

Her eyes fix on the wall.

'What else was in that diary, Auntie Audrey? Tell me, please, we haven't much time! Explain what you meant about V going for the wrong brother.'

'Before your mum fell pregnant, from the conversations she had with Karen, it appears she crossed paths with Lewis. He was only nineteen at the time, but from what she'd written in the diary, I got the impression Karen had let it slip to him how venomous your mum was towards your dad – his dad, too, of course. Lewis approached your mum and found out how much hatred she harboured for your dad.'

The knot in my stomach turns painfully tighter and tighter.

'This reignited the whole robbery scenario. She wrote in that diary that she didn't need me anymore. So, where I thought she'd given up on the idea, she hadn't.'

'So, what happened? This is really important. Look at the wall again. Has Violet got this all wrong? Was the night of the shooting a random robbery that went wrong, or was my dad the target?'

'That's the thing. A while after your mother fell pregnant, there was no more mention of the robbery in the diaries. I assumed she'd called the whole thing off. There was a complication with the pregnancy. She wrote about that at length. She was scared of losing the baby due to the stress her plans would bring. She was going to leave your father. Charles, the guy she was having an affair with, planned to leave his wife, Nicolette, and your mum was going to go through the courts to take your dad to the cleaners. You know, do it all properly, take the legal route.'

'You shouldn't have destroyed that diary, Auntie. You should've taken it to the police.'

'Think about it. I didn't know whether your mum – my sister – was going to get better or not. In the early days, the first eighteen months at least, we hoped she'd make some sort of recovery. It wasn't exactly clear what your mum was planning at the time. And my name was all over it as well, Rose. How I was going to give her an alibi. Plus everything about Charles, who repented and has lived a happy life with Nicolette and their kids. That diary was toxic.'

'Even more reason the police should've seen it.'

'What if your mum had arranged with Lewis to have your dad shot, but it was dark and he got the wrong person? And then your mum made a full recovery. Then what? I found the diary about three months after the shooting. The police had made no progress in that time. They'd given up. I thought the best thing to do was to burn it.'

'And stick your head in the sand. What about Lewis? V could be in real danger now.'

'I tracked him down and confronted him. He assured me yes, he'd had contact with your mum. They shared a common hatred. But that was as far as it went. I believed him.'

'You should've given the diary to the police! They could've followed up with him through the correct channels.'

Her voice wavers. 'For ages, I did consider going to the police. Honestly, I did, but I would've ended up in trouble. Then who would've been around to look after you girls? Because your father certainly wasn't. He was having affairs right up until his cancer diagnosis.'

I point to the wall. 'So what did you mean when you said V has got the wrong brother?'

'Lewis had a tattoo.' She stands and points to V's drawing of the friendship bracelet that circles the drawing of the Grim Reaper. 'After the shooting, V maintained that the man who shot your mum was wearing a bracelet.'

She places her hands on her head. 'When I met Lewis, I saw his tattoo. I remember it because it was so unique. But I never thought for one second it was what V had mistaken for a bracelet. But in the eyes of a young girl, experiencing immense trauma, I guess she could've been mistaken.'

'So Violet always thought the tattoo was a bracelet,' I say. 'I wonder if Will and Lewis have the same tattoo? And she saw the tattoo on Will's wrist after the accident. I see what you mean. That's how she's got herself confused!'

I head to the door. 'Jamie and I need to go. You stay here with Mum. Let's hope we get to V before it's too late.'

59

VIOLET

Her timing needs to be spot on. She needs to catch Tiffany at the right moment.

She glances at Will through the bifold doors a final time. At one point, he peers outside as if he senses she's here. He stares directly at her. She remains stock-still, scared that movement will attract his attention even more. She's being irrational. He couldn't possibly see her in the darkness out here.

She scoots around to the front of the house. Crouching behind a thick bush in the front garden, she waits. She's going out of her mind. An agonising ten minutes or so pass before the upstairs lights go out.

It's time.

She sneaks out of hiding and creeps to the front door. A wooden sign saying *Santa Stop Here!* sticks out from a large container housing a bay tree draped with miniature multi-coloured baubles.

She has thought through this plan so many times, she could perform the next stage with one eye closed. She glances through the frosted pane of glass. A figure descends the stairs. 'Here we go, Mum,' she mutters. 'This is all for you. And you, Bean.'

She knocks on the door.

Tiffany appears wearing a tight-fitting little black dress, making her bump appear even bigger. Her blonde hair is brushed tight against her scalp and tied into a bun on top of her head. 'Summer! Whatever are you doing here?' She glances at the box in Violet's hands.

'I've brought you a little gift. I'd planned to give it to you at Winter Wonderland, but it was late arriving.'

'That's so kind of you.' She opens the door wide. 'Come in. Come in.'

'I can't stop,' she says, knowing full well Tiffany won't let her go without at least introducing her to Will.

'I insist. Even if it's to taste the lovely Christmas snowball cocktail I've made – non-alcoholic, of course. And you can meet Will and my family. Come on.' She beckons her with a wave of her hand. 'A quick toast to Christmas.'

Violet steps into the house. Her senses are in overdrive, every sound amplified, and her eyes feel massive, saucer-sized. Her heart is racing and she feels slightly faint. She needs to get a grip. She's shaking so much, she's going to give her game away too soon if she's not careful.

Tiffany closes the front door. 'Come on through.'

Violet follows her along the now-familiar hallway and into the kitchen. Each step feels like a thousand.

'Hey, this is my friend Summer. She's due three days after me.'

Violet prepares to take the gun out of the box, but only the two women are there, standing by the glowing wood-burning stove that's chucking out intense heat. Damn. This wasn't in her plan. The men should be here.

Tiffany grabs a glass. 'Summer's joining us for a snowball. Where have Will and Lewis gone?'

'Will wanted to show Lewis something in the living room. Boys' stuff, you know.' Jacqui waves at Violet. 'Hi, Summer. I'm Jacqui, Tiff's sister-in-law.' Jacqui gestures to the woman beside her. 'And this is Karen, our mother-in-law.'

Karen nods and smiles. 'Yes, we've already met. Hello, Summer. Nice to see you again. You know, I was thinking after we met that day in the gym that I recognised you from somewhere, but I couldn't place where.'

Violet shrugs. 'I don't think so.' Her voice wobbles. She needs to hold it together. She's very nearly there.

They gravitate towards the Christmas tree. She can't believe she's standing here. After all these years, all these days of planning, she really is finally standing here.

Tiffany reaches out her arm. 'Let me take your coat.'

Violet smiles. 'It's fine. I'm not stopping long. I need to get back to Declan and my family.'

'What are you planning tonight, Summer?' Jacqui asks. 'Any family traditions?'

'Fish pie,' Violet replies. 'My sister always makes a fish pie on Christmas Eve.'

'You never told me you had a sister.' Tiffany pours a yellow mixture from a jug into the glass that she's filled with ice. 'What's her name?' She places a cherry on a stalk on top of the drink.

'Autumn,' Violet replies. Too many questions. Too many.

Tiffany chuckles. 'Summer and Autumn, that's so cool.' She hands Violet the drink. 'Has she got any children?'

Violet shakes her head and wets her lips with the fizzy custardy drink. It tastes as sweet as revenge. The need for sugar consumes her. She takes a large sip, then another until the glass is half empty. It's fine. All the adrenaline surging through her will burn the extra calories. 'Delicious,' she says. 'Thank you.'

The sound of the men chatting approaches. Will and his brother are heading for the kitchen.

Here we go.

She tells herself not to look around. Timing is crucial at this final stage. She hands the shoebox to Tiffany. 'Open it,' she says.

Tiffany smiles. 'Are you sure?'

'Most definitely.' Violet takes a deep breath. 'You know, I think I will take my coat off.'

It all happens simultaneously with military precision – exactly as planned.

Tiffany lifts the lid to the shoebox. But she doesn't look inside. She's too distracted by Violet having removed her coat and noticing her belly, or lack of. Confusion seeps into her pretty face. 'Summer! I don't understand.' She points halfway down her body. 'What happened?' She frowns. Her hand covers her mouth. 'Oh, no, Summer. No! You didn't lose...'

Violet forges a jolly voice. 'Look at your present.'

Tiffany peers inside the box. Her jaw drops. Confusion is painted all over her pretty face in shades of grey and green. 'What... is this?'

Violet grabs the gun from the box and steps backwards as

she trains the weapon on Tiffany. The adrenaline disorientates her for a split second.

'Will!' Tiffany's raw scream echoes around the room as she backs away.

Jacqui and Karen grab each other, standing beside the Christmas tree, screeching like children.

'What the fuck?' Will lunges in Violet's direction. He's holding the puppy.

Violet trains the gun on him. Her nerves are stretched to the limit, and they're about to snap. 'Keep away from me.' Her voice is a raw growl, animal-like. She panics. The dog needs to stay safe. 'Put the dog outside. Now.'

Karen shouts, 'Do what she says! All of you. Just do what she says.'

Will backsteps to the bifold doors, opens them and releases the puppy from his arms.

Violet scans the gun around the room. 'Everyone, stay where you are.'

Will looks as confused as his wife. 'Wait. I know you.' His voice squeaks with unease. 'You're Violet.'

'No, this is Summer.' Tiffany holds up her hands submissively. 'The girl I told you about from the gym.' Her voice dips, but the fear is still apparent. 'The one who was supposedly pregnant. I've been such a fool.' She grabs her head with her hands, her fingers splaying. 'What do you want with us, Summer?'

'No, it's not Summer,' Will says. 'You're Violet, aren't you? From the accident. Is this what this is about? If it's money you want, I can pay you.' Will flaps his hands as if trying to placate the situation. 'How much do you want?'

Violet glares at the tattoo on his wrist. 'I want more than your money, Will Watson.'

'No, Summer!' Tiffany steps towards her. 'Please don't do anything stupid.'

Violet turns the gun on her.

60

ROSE

I update Jamie on Auntie Audrey's revelations. 'I have to go to that house in Radstone and check she's not there.'

'I can't drive you. I've had a beer,' Jamie groans.

'I'll drive.' The last thing I want to do in this crappy weather is to get behind the wheel of a car, but I have to do this. I pick up my car keys from the hallway table.

Jamie covers my hand with his. 'I really think this is a matter for the police, Rose.'

'I can't. I won't.' My voice is full of despair. 'You don't know what my sister's been through all these years. Can you imagine being a nine-year-old child, petrified because you caught an intruder in your home? And then said intruder shoots your mother. It's no wonder she's a little screwed up.'

'She's more than a little screwed up,' he says, gently. 'And she's got a gun.'

'We don't know that for sure. If I can get to her before she does anything stupid, it'll be fine.'

Jamie sighs heavily.

I shuffle into my coat. 'I can talk reason into her. I know I can.'

As we rush to the car, I try V's number again. When I reach her voicemail, I leave a message this time. 'V, you have to call me. Now. Please. I need to speak to you urgently.' I pause, before going for it. I hate lying to her but needs must. 'Something has happened to Mum, and I need to speak to you now.' If anything is going to make her call me, it's Mum.

I start the engine. 'Can you google the address, please?' I reverse out of the driveway.

'It's going to take twenty-five minutes,' Jamie says.

I whack the steering wheel. 'We could be too late.'

'Rose, please. Please let me call the police.'

'No, I've already told you. I can't do that to my sister.'

Snow begins to fall. 'I hope that blizzard isn't on its way,' I say. 'The weather forecast said it isn't going to hit until later on tomorrow.'

'That's what I thought,' he says. 'Just take it easy.'

The journey seems to take forever. I still haven't overcome my fear of driving since the accident. My stomach is in my throat. With every passing minute, I feel as if I'm going to throw up. 'I can't believe my auntie has kept so much from us all these years.' I shake my head. 'I thought Auntie Audrey was purer than the Virgin Mary.'

When we arrive in Radstone, Google Maps directs us to the Ridgeway. 'Here we go. Slow down.' Jamie points to a large, semi-detached house. 'There's number 12.'

I look around. 'Where's her car?'

We scout the street for the Mercedes. 'It doesn't look like she's here,' Jamie says.

My gut tells me otherwise. I turn my head, peering up and down the street as if I expect my sister to jump out at me like a jack-in-the-box. 'What about around the back of the house?'

I drive to the end of the street and turn right. At the end of the road, I stop. 'Look, there.' I point to the black Mercedes. 'That's her car.' I bang my head against the headrest. 'She's here.'

I park behind V's car and switch off the engine. I'm sweating, despite the cold. 'I'm going to find her.'

'What are you going to do? Knock on the front door? Have you thought about what you're going to say?' Jamie asks.

'No. I want to make sure she's there first.' I open the car door.

Jamie clasps my arm. 'You do know you're probably going to come face-to-face with your brothers. Have you thought about that?'

'All the way here. But there're more pressing things to worry about.' I get out of the car. Jamie doesn't move. I duck my head into the car. 'Stay here. I don't mind.'

He opens his door. 'I'm not leaving you.'

'Look.' I point to the back of the house I calculate to be number 12. 'It's the only house lit up. Other people must've gone away for Christmas.' I pull him towards the garden and throw my arm towards the glass doors. 'Oh, hell. Look! There she is. We need to get to her.'

61

VIOLET

Tiffany holds up her hands. 'You stalked me. Fooled me. Why, Summer?' She gasps as the realisation strikes. 'It was you all along. You took that stuff from our house. The remote control, the coaster.' She laces her hands across the back of her head. 'And then you returned them. Why?'

A laugh escapes Violet's lips. In the enormity of the situation, taking those items now seems so petty.

Tiffany's voice softens, but the fear remains in her eyes. 'Please don't hurt us. I never did anything bad to you, Violet.'

A shred of remorse shoots through Violet's blood. Just enough to hurt, but not enough to stop her. 'The same as my mum never did anything bad to your husband.'

Tiffany's eyes flit between her and Will. 'What on earth do you mean? What did Will ever do to you?'

'The accident wasn't my fault, Violet,' Will pleads, his shoulders shrugged and his hands angled outwards. 'Your sister was driving in the wrong lane. The weather didn't help. There was ice on the roads. Please, it was one of those things.'

She turns the gun on him. 'This has nothing to do with the accident.'

The frown on his forehead deepens. 'What then?' He gestures for Tiffany to stand back, as far away from her as possible.

She swallows hard and composes herself. The sweetness of the snowball drink has unsettled her stomach. Far, far too much sugar. She should've known better. 'Cast your mind back to Christmas Eve 2009, Will.'

'I don't know what you're talking about.' He pauses, squinting. 'I was sixteen years old. I haven't got a clue what you're on about.'

'Fifteen years ago today, you came to our house and robbed my family.' Her voice is remarkably calm for the turmoil raging inside of her. She shakes the gun at him. 'Then you used this to shoot my mother. You killed my unborn sister. You're a murderer, William Watson.'

Tiffany cries out, clutching her belly, 'What the hell?!'

'How did it feel, Will?' Her voice wavers. 'Did you run away feeling good, or in fear knowing you'd done something wrong?'

'You've got the wrong person, Violet, Summer, whatever your name is.' Will's face has turned ghostly white. 'Honestly, I don't know what the hell you're talking about.' He nods at the weapon she's pointing at him. 'I've never seen a real gun in my life until now.'

'Steady on,' Lewis interjects. He holds a palm towards her. 'Who are you exactly?'

Everything stops. Her brain scrambles as she registers the

tattoo that sits proudly above Lewis's wrist bone. Her eyes widen, frozen in alarm. 'You both have the same tattoo.'

Has she got it all wrong? All this time, she thought it was Will who came to her family home that night, when in fact, it might have been his brother. She switches her aim between the brothers, screeching, 'So which one of you was it?'

'Come on, Sum... Violet. Put the gun down,' Tiffany begs. 'Please. No good can come of you using it. Whatever happens, two wrongs don't make a right. We can talk about this. Find out what's happened here. Because there must've been a terrible misunderstanding.'

'Stay out of it, Tiff.' Her voice is remarkably calm despite the panic riding sky high within her. It's as if it's detached itself from her body. 'You have no idea.'

A whimper comes from the corner of the room. Karen and Jacqui clutch each other like two lost children.

'Think of Leo, please,' Tiffany pleads.

Violet's heart jolts. This woman has made such an effort with her over the past two weeks. She's the only friend she's ever had. But there's no time for sentiment now.

She continues directing the gun from one brother to the other. 'So, which one of you shot my mother that night? She's never recovered, you know. She's been housebound ever since. And non-verbal. And she's never walked.' She raises her voice. 'Which one of you was it, then? Because I know it was one of you. One of you murdered my baby sister.'

Lewis steps forward with what appears to be an air of confidence, as if he believes that if she hasn't used the weapon by now, she's unlikely to do so.

He doesn't know how wrong he is.

'Your mother wasn't innocent in it all,' Lewis says.

She aims the gun at his chest.

'I met her a couple of times. She tried to get me to rob your family. But I had nothing to do with it.'

'You're lying!' she screams. As if her mother would do that! 'One of you is lying.'

'She was as batty as hell,' Lewis says.

'Don't you dare talk about my mum in that way.'

'Stop!' Karen emerges from the shadows in the corner of the room. Her voice booms through the chaos. 'You don't know what you're doing, Violet. You've got it all wrong. It was me. I shot your mother.'

62

VIOLET

Violet turns the gun on Karen. 'Oh, come on. You don't expect me to believe that.'

Karen steps towards her. 'Give me the gun, Violet. We can work this out.'

'You're lying to protect your sons.' Violet blinks hard. Her chest tightens. She's struggling to breathe. 'That's what mothers do. They protect their children.'

'I'm not lying.' Karen tugs the sleeve of her silky blouse. 'Look. My sons and I, we all have the same tattoo. We had them after my son Ross died.' Her voice breaks. 'He had a bracelet that he wore all the time. We replicated the same design as tattoos.'

Visions from that night fifteen years ago flash in her head like fireworks. Bang. The noise is unbearable. The tall intruder with long arms and legs, hiding behind the sofa, but then all she can see is Mum lying in a disjointed heap at the bottom of the staircase, blood seeping through her white nightie. 'It was a man. A man shot my mum.'

'It might've looked like a man to a nine-year-old girl, but it was me. I promise you.' Tears pour down Karen's face. 'But it was an accident, Violet. A terrible, terrible accident.'

Pressure builds in Violet's head. Her eyes feel as if they are going to pop out of their sockets. It's so bright in here. As if someone has turned up the lights high. She raises her spare hand to shield her eyes from the dazzle.

Karen continues, but her voice has become all distorted. 'Your mum. She persuaded me to do it. She was a manipulative woman.'

'What the hell are you on about, Mum?' Will interjects.

Karen holds a hand up to him. 'Quiet.'

Will looks at her in alarm.

Karen continues, 'Your dad played your mum and I off against each other for far too long.'

Violet looks at Lewis, and then at Will. Her body aches. She's tired, so tired.

Karen continues through hysterical sobbing. 'I was meant to shoot your father that night. Over the short time I knew your mother, she worked me up into a frenzy of hatred. I couldn't see straight. I'd literally have done anything she said. We planned to split the proceeds from the contents of the safe and the insurance money from your father's death. We hated him for what he'd done to both of us. But it all went terribly wrong.' Her cries turn to wails. 'I'm so sorry, Violet. I mistook your mother for your father.'

63

ROSE

A sharp crack-bang of a gunshot explodes into the air. 'No, V. No.'

A black puppy runs at us, barking at my feet. I scoop it into my arms, and we run to the house. I bang on the glass doors, screaming my sister's name. Panic plays out from inside. I try my luck and wrench the door handle. It opens. 'V!' The sound of my voice rips through the stillness of the night, ragged and cutting, slicing through the freezing night air like a shard of glass.

My sister pushes past me, blinking like a maniac, and escapes into the garden.

I stumble after her. 'What have you done?'

The puppy is barking loudly.

'It was her.' Her voice carries into the night. 'That woman shot Mum.'

Jamie tears through the doors. I falter, not knowing

whether to go after my sister or to follow him. A pregnant woman screams hysterically. It's Tiffany. I recognise her from the photo on V's bedroom wall.

'Jacqui. Go upstairs. Take the dog, and make sure Leo doesn't come down here,' Will commands a woman I've never seen before.

Will looks different from when I met him after the accident. His hair is significantly shorter, and he's smartly dressed. He drops to his knees beside the woman lying on the floor.

I stand looking on, trying to process what my sister has done. 'Karen,' is all I can breathe. 'Karen!'

Another man, who I'm guessing is Lewis due to the resemblance to his brother, takes the space opposite him. 'Stay with us, Mum!' Will repeatedly shouts.

'Go, Jacqui,' Tiffany screams.

Jacqui dashes from the room, whimpering.

'Get an ambulance, Tiff,' Will orders. 'And the police. Now. Call them now.'

Tiff grabs a phone from the breakfast bar. Her shaking finger taps the screen.

Jamie rips off his coat and tends to Karen. He covers the entry wound from her abdomen now seeping with blood. 'We've got to keep this covered and apply pressure. We have to stem the flow of blood.' He meets my gaze, shaking his head in the same disbelief that's tormenting me.

'She's gone!' Will cries. 'Look, just look at her face.'

'No! No! No!' Lewis cries. 'Mum, no. Stay with us.'

Tiff's urgent cries for help boom around the room. 'Ambulance. Quick. Someone has been shot. You need to help us. Police – we need the police, too. There's a girl loose with a gun. You have to get here quickly.' She speaks for a while, answering questions.

I can't believe I'm standing watching Jamie and these two men, my half-brothers, trying to save their mother who shot my mother fifteen years ago.

Blood seeps through the fabric of Jamie's coat and onto his hands. He instructs Lewis to start CPR. 'We can save her. Do as I say.'

Tiffany, shaking like a frightened bird, passes the phone to Will. 'They're going to talk you through what to do.'

I should be doing something, but I don't know what. Jamie has taken charge. He is calmly performing CPR on Karen's frail body. Will is applying pressure to the gunshot wound.

V. I have to go after my sister.

I need to save her from herself. There are enough people here.

'I have to go after her,' I tell Jamie. 'Give the police our address.' He shouts something at me, but I'm not listening. I'm too scared my sister is going to do something else stupid. I run from the scene, dashing across the garden, my boots squelching in the wet grass.

The black Mercedes is nowhere in sight. I run to my car, calling my sister's number again. She's still not answering. I can only think she's gone home. Morbid thoughts rush around my mind. 'Please don't do anything stupid, V!' I cry in desperation.

I call Auntie Audrey as I drive home.

'This is awful. What should I do?' she says.

'Lock the doors. If she comes back, don't let her into the house. The police will be there soon.'

The roads are relatively clear. Normal people are at home

celebrating Christmas Eve with their families. What I'd do for some normality in my life.

My driving is erratic. The tyres slip and slide as I turn corner after corner way too fast. I put my foot on the brake. I can't afford to have another accident. V needs me more than ever. Mum as well.

It seems to take an age, but I finally reach home.

But the black Mercedes is not there.

64

VIOLET

'It's all done, Mum. I did it.' Violet glances up at the ceiling, to Bean looking down at her with that cute smile on her chubby baby face. 'Revenge is so sweet.'

She sits holding her mother's hand, gently caressing the prominent veins. The radiator is still chucking out heat, but she remains wrapped in her coat, stone cold. 'I'm whispering, Mum, because Auntie Audrey can't know I'm here. Not yet. I slipped around the back.'

'There's a clever girl,' Mum replies in her beautiful Irish twang. A warm, full-bodied accent Violet could listen to all day long.

'It got a bit muddled, Mum.' Violet shakes her heavy head. 'But I got the person who did this to you and our Bean.' She raises her hand and strokes the side of her mother's face. 'You didn't tell me everything, though, did you? You didn't tell me about Karen and what you'd planned with her. How brave you were to try to get Dad after what he did to you both. I admire you more for that, Mum. You should've told me, though. But it doesn't matter now.'

A dim light from the bedside table lamp glows across the room. It shines on the weariness embedded in her mother's face. She looks older than Violet recalls. As if she's aged overnight. But everything is so blurred. Her world is collapsing, brick by brick, and nothing she can do can stop that now. It's too far gone.

'You would've been proud of me, Mum. So would Bean. I only wish you could've been there to watch it all. It was better than any episode of those soaps you watch.'

She describes the details of the evening to her mother with extraordinary calmness, as if she's now at peace with the world. 'I never harmed Tiffany in the end. But never mind. It's for the best. The main culprit is gone.'

'You naughty thing.'

Violet smiles at her mother's sense of humour and gently squeezes her hand with affection. That's what she remembers the most about her beautiful mother. She always adored her playful nature.

'There was so much blood, Mum.'

Nothing. Silence.

'And you'll never guess what else. Rose turned up. I wasn't expecting that! She must've broken into my room and seen all my plans. That's the only way she could've known where to find me. But it doesn't matter now.'

Mum stares at her fingers, twiddling them in her lap.

'You can rest in peace now, Mum. You can go and be with Bean, hold her tightly.'

Her mother is no longer speaking. She knows the time has come.

Violet reaches into her coat pocket and digs out her cigarettes and lighter. 'I know what you've wanted me to do for so long, Mum. But I couldn't do it. I tried. I promise you I did. But it's time now, because they'll come for you. You know that, don't you? The truth will come out that you and that Karen woman planned to kill Dad that night and split the contents of the safe and the insurance money. They'll put you in prison, Mum. And it'll be worse than one of the homes Auntie and Rose have been looking to dump you in.'

She lights a cigarette and takes a deep drag, blowing smoke circles into the air. 'You'd hate that. Prison, Mum. Can you imagine? No. No. We can't have that. It's time to release you from your wreck of a body.'

Ash spills onto the duvet. She brushes it onto the floor and grinds the cigarette out with the heel of her boot. What a mess. But it doesn't matter anymore. Nothing matters anymore.

'It's time to free us, Mum.' She quietly places the gun on the bed, reaches across to the sofa and picks up one of the many pillows used to prop her mother up, support her, make her comfortable. She brushes the soft fabric against her cheek. She wants to cry, but tears won't come. She's used her life quota in the past fifteen years. 'I'll say goodnight for the time being, Mum.' She bends over and kisses her mother's forehead. 'Hug Bean and give her a kiss from me when you see her. Tell her how much I love her, won't you? How much I've always loved her.'

She lowers the pillow over her mother's face and pushes down. There's no struggle. It's as if her mother were already dead. She waits until she's certain her mother's faint breathing has ceased.

'I'll be joining you soon, Mum. I have it all planned out.

See, I still have this.' She points to the gun on the bed. 'I'm going to drive into the woods. I've found a lovely spot. It's going to be a little chilly, but that's OK. At least I won't make a mess in the house. We can't have that. Rose has been through enough.'

Still holding the pillow, she straightens the bed sheets. 'Rose can be happy now. She deserves that.' She tucks her mother in comfortably. 'There. I love you, Mum. I always loved you the most. You know that. I'll see you and Bean very soon.'

'Violet?'

She turns to her sister standing at the bedroom door.

65

ROSE

I storm into the room.

V jumps and turns to me. She's holding a pillow.

Her bloodshot eyes bore into me.

'V!' I cry. 'What have you done?'

She drops the pillow and picks up the gun from the bed.

'What's going on?' Auntie Audrey's voice breezes into the room. She whimpers. 'I never heard her come in.'

'Go, Auntie, please,' I say. 'Leave us alone.'

'I can't.' Auntie Audrey shakes her head. 'She's dangerous.'

'She'd never hurt me. The police will be here any minute. Go and see to them.'

Auntie Audrey tugs at her silver cross around her neck. 'Rose! I can't leave you.'

I gently push her away and close the door slowly. 'Give me

the gun, V.' I take a step towards my sister. 'You're not well. We need to get you some help.'

Mum's face is ashen in the faint light. A smudge of blood blemishes the skin below her bottom lip. 'Oh, no. No!' I rush to the bed. The same shade of red as the smudge on her face stains the pillow V has dropped on the bed. I feel for a pulse in her neck and glare at my sister. 'Oh, V. What have you done?'

Wailing sirens startle me. Blue lights ignite the room through the side window, accompanied by the intermittent blast of police sirens. The lights cast eerie shadows across Violet's ghostly face. I half expect her to threaten me with the gun, or to flee the room as she did earlier after shooting Karen.

Surprisingly, she does neither. She sinks back into her chair. Her shoulders slump, and she has a look of resignation about her. I walk around the bed and gently remove the gun from her grasp.

'I had to do it. You understand, don't you, Rose? That Karen woman ruined our lives. She took our mother away from us. Our childhood, too. It wasn't fair. She couldn't get away with it.'

Now's not the time to explain she has just killed not only her own mother, but also shot the mother of her half-brothers. 'V,' I say gently. That's what she needs now. Gentleness. 'The police will come in here soon. It's important you don't do anything stupid. No one else must get hurt. Do exactly as the police say. Let's talk to them together. Do you understand me?'

My sister nods her head. 'I had to do it.'

Those five words are the last I hear my sister clearly speak.

66

TWELVE MONTHS LATER

ROSE

'Thanks for bringing me. I hate driving at this time of the year.' I squeeze Jamie's hand.

He laughs. 'You hate driving full-stop, Titch.'

I laugh and nod in resignation.

The journey to the Midlands has taken forever today, but we're nearly there. We left early, but holiday traffic has been steadily picking up all morning. At least the weather isn't as bad as last year. We leave the main road and drive along the winding country roads to the secure psychiatric hospital where V now resides. Frost bonds to every plant and tree, and the fields are fringed with white. Words are scarcely shared, as is usually the case at this point of the journey. I clench my fists as the secure campus, which is surrounded by high fences topped with rolls of spiky wire, rears its ugly head.

'Here we go.' Jamie squeezes my hand as we approach the main gate and pass through the checkpoint. It's so much easier when he comes here with me. It's exhausting holding a one-sided conversation with my sister. It's harder than it was with Mum. Perhaps it's because we're not at home. I don't know. He hands over our ID and authorisation letter for the visit to the guard who registers our arrival.

Once inside, we follow the drill that I've become accustomed to on my visits. The guards search our belongings and pat us down with their metal detectors. There are moments when I feel like a prisoner myself. We're told to wait in the reception area, where a pathetic artificial tree barely dressed attempts to inject some festive spirit into the place, but it fails miserably.

I sit on a plastic chair, opposite a stressed-looking guy, his forehead crinkled with worry. I know how he feels.

'I'll get us a coffee,' Jamie says. He heads to the vending machine and returns with two paper cups of lukewarm coffee that tastes rank but is better than nothing. Thank heavens for this man. It's a hundred times worse on the occasions when he has to work and can't come with me.

A female member of staff calls our names. We discard our cups in the bin, and she escorts us deeper inside the complex through locked doors. The clunk as each door opens and shuts behind us echoes along the camera-ridden corridors that smell of the antibacterial spray V used when she used to clean the kitchen.

I've spent a lot of time this year thinking back to last Christmas, between burying my mother and father, selling our family home and buying another, and trying to come to terms with the fact that I'll probably never see my sister leave this secure hospital. If she does, it's going to take a while. How long, no one can tell me exactly, other than it will be a very, very long time. Although it's rare, her PTSD caused her psychosis, and she may never fully recover. The psychiatrists declared her unfit to stand trial, so a trial of the facts was held last month. There was no doubt in the jury's minds about the crimes she committed. But they took into account what she witnessed as a child and how this affected her. As long as I keep the faith, there's reason for me to keep fighting for her. I'll never lose hope that one day I'll be able to come and collect her and take her home with me.

She still suffers bouts of psychosis when she adopts Mum's Irish accent. I can't bear it when she does that. I have to switch off. There's not a day that goes by that I don't wish I'd caught what she was up to earlier. I should've been stronger – insisted that she let me into her room before it all blew out of control. But as Jamie says, I can't blame myself.

Two staff members escort us to a familiar, airless room where the table and chairs are bolted to the floor. V is waiting for us, along with another two staff members, who will remain for the duration of our visit. They always do.

My heart breaks a little more every time I see my sister. 'You've had your hair cut.' My jaw drops at the crew cut she now wears. I turn to the staff. 'She's worn her hair to her waist ever since I can remember.'

'She indicated that she wanted it cut short when she went to the hairdresser's the other day,' one of them says.

'And she said she wanted it cut this short?' Something stirs in the pit of my belly. It's the feeling of hope I carry for my sister every time I come here. Hope that this could signify the beginning of change. Hope that she's getting better. But, as usual, her head is dropped to her chest, her eyes staring at her fingers twiddling in her lap like Mum always used to.

'No,' the staff member says, 'she pointed to a picture in a magazine.'

'It suits you, V. I love it.'

We both take a seat opposite her. Jamie squeezes my hand. 'How are you, V?' I say.

Jamie chimes in, 'Hi, Violet, how're you keeping?'

Nothing. Not even a glimpse of recognition.

'I hear you're not eating.' Tears sting my eyes. She looks like a bag of bones. While she is mainly compliant, food remains a significant issue. 'You must eat. You'll get ill.'

'What's the food like, Violet? Good variety?' Jamie glances at me. He raises and drops his shoulders.

The same routine follows as in previous visits. Jamie relays funny stories about his sisters or what's been happening at work, filling in the awkward silences. I find it tougher than him to know what to talk about. My sister had little interest in the outside world, even when she was well enough to hide among it. But now she's like a ghost from a life I've left behind.

I wish I could get inside her head. I want to know if she really understands what she's done. When I told her that Dad had been buried, and then Mum, I wondered if the flaring of her nostrils was an acknowledgement of understanding, but I couldn't be sure. The same happened when Karen died in April from an infection from the gunshot wound. I mainly try to only talk about positive things when I'm here. Like when Isla, our half-niece, was born and my recent house move.

I don't mention our grandma's jewellery that Karen stole from the safe that night and took away with her. The jewellery she admitted to burying in her garden because she didn't know what else to do with it. After the police dug it up, they kept it for months as evidence, but I recently picked it up, and it is now safely at my new home. As Dad left everything in his will to me, it's now technically all mine. But, if the time comes, V can have her share of it, along with half of everything else Dad left me. This morning, for the first time, I put on a pair of diamond hooped earrings with a pearl drop from the collection. There are some beautiful pieces, and it seems a shame to keep them in a bag.

The money Karen stole that night has proven to be another issue. She also admitted to the police she gave it all to my half-brother Will to help him start his business, telling him she'd won it in the lottery. She told him not to tell his brother, Lewis, because she refused to see any of that money going up his brother's nose. It was why Will tried in vain to help Lewis out and gave him a job in his business. Will was mortified when he found out and immediately wrote a cheque made out to me for the sum Karen had given him. But I'm yet to cash it.

For an hour we sit like this, forging conversation

'Have you done any painting, V?'

There's no response.

It's such damn hard work. But I refuse to give up on her.

I cry when we leave. I always do. Tears for what could've been.

67

ROSE

'Are you sure you're up for this?' Jamie pulls up outside Will and Tiffany's new-build house on a small gated development with four other similar houses. Tiffany refused to remain in their old house. The harrowing memories were too much, so they sold up and moved here in the summer. 'We could just go home and do this another time.'

'No. I promised Leo I'd bring his present today. Anyway, I want to see them all.' I sigh heavily. 'Jeez, this sure has been a hell of a year. I'll be glad when it's over.'

'Don't say that, hun. You're going to have the best Christmas ever.'

I smile. He hasn't stopped telling me that all year.

The front door opens as we walk along the garden path. Will steps outside and stands on the mat embossed with a cheery Santa. Leo is by his side, jumping up and down. Tiffany appears holding baby Isla, who is now a chubby and cheery eight-month-old bundle of perfection. Their dog, Ozzy, who is now as big as Leo, pants. The perfect family unit. I swallow the lump in my throat. They deserve it after everything they've been through.

Will hugs me. 'Happy Christmas, Rose.' He fist bumps Jamie. 'You too, mate.'

Tiffany kisses my cheek. Despite the crazy beginning to our relationship, after the drama died down, it didn't take long for us to bond. We've become close. As have Will and I. And I adore their baby daughter. Lewis is going to take longer. He didn't want anything to do with me at first, but we're working on it, thanks to Jamie. He and baby Isla are the glue that has stuck us all together.

The money Dad left me has allowed us to secure a substantial deposit on our new home. He had known that V had issues but he never really understood the depth of her illness. He indicated as much in a sealed letter to me, held by Auntie Audrey until after his death. He also came clean about his failings as a father in that letter. His failings as a husband, as a human being. It was a comfort knowing he felt remorse.

Lewis was put out when he found out he and Will didn't feature in Dad's financial plans, but Will soon put him in his place. Lewis hadn't spoken to Dad for years. What did he expect?

'What beautiful earrings,' Tiffany says.

I touch my ear and look at Will. 'They're a pair of Grandma's.'

He nods. 'It's good to see you wearing some of that stuff.' I know he means it. I offered to share the jewellery with him, but he flatly refused.

We enter the living room where a wood-burning stove is chucking out heat like a furnace. Tiffany has prepared mocktails in stylish glasses to toast in Christmas Eve, and an impressive display of finger foods. I remove my coat and hand her the bag of presents we've brought, swapping it for baby Isla. I sit with my niece on my knee, singing *When Santa Got Stuck Up the Chimney* as she coos and giggles in delight.

'Look what I made you.' Leo hands paper chains to me and Jamie. 'Like you have in your house.'

'Thank you, darling.' I ruffle his hair.

'Santa's bringing me a new train track, isn't he, Daddy?'

Will scoops him up. 'If you're a good boy.' He tickles Leo, who laughs affectionately. He turns to me. 'How was V?'

I shrug. 'Same.'

Tiffany hands me and Jamie yellow-coloured drinks. 'A snowball?' I say.

She shivers. 'Oh, no. I could never drink one of those again. It's a passionfruit and elderflower spritz. It's delicious.' She dishes out gold-coloured paper plates and then hands around a plate of miniature sausage rolls. Jamie and I both take one. 'Yum. My favourite,' Jamie says.

Tiffany shakes the plate under his nose. 'Take as many as you want.'

He takes another four.

'Jamie!' I say.

'It's fine.' Tiffany laughs. She has such a pretty smile and amazing white teeth. 'I've got another plate in the kitchen.'

Jamie shrugs and stuffs a sausage roll into his mouth.

'You still haven't cashed the cheque, Rose.' Will strokes Ozzy's fur.

'I can't and I won't.' I take a sip of my drink. 'I never want to talk about it again.'

Will addresses Jamie. 'Talk some sense into her, will you?'

Jamie holds his hands up. 'It's a lost cause, mate. She's not budging.'

'*She* is in the room, you know.' I glare at him mockingly.

'Well, if you won't accept it, I'm going to put the twenty grand into trust for when you two have a sprog.'

'Will!' It's Tiffany's turn to glare at her other half.

'I mean it,' Will continues. 'I'll set it up and transfer the money in the new year.'

'We still need to discuss the jewellery,' I say.

Will crosses his hands over his chest. 'There's nothing to discuss. It's all yours. And I'm the one not budging on that.'

68

ROSE

'We'd better get a move on.' Jamie turns into our driveway. 'We're running late. Everyone will be here soon.' We stayed later than intended at Tiffany and Will's house. One mocktail turned into a cocktail for me and Tiffany, while the guys stuck to non-alcoholic beer.

I smile at our new home, a semi-detached three-bedroom Victorian house dripping with ivy. It needs lots of work, but we fell in love with it as soon as we crossed the threshold. I couldn't wait to move in. It's a new beginning for me, for us. My chance to be happy. Jamie has gone to town on Christmas decorations. The day we signed contracts and moved in, he promised I'd never miss out on Christmas again. Lights blink all around the outside, and he's even erected a six-foot snowman on the roof that sways like it's drunk when the wind picks up.

Inside is no less crazy, with the nodding Santa that wishes

you a happy Christmas every time you walk in the front door. Red, green and gold paper chains hang from every ceiling, and the fireplace is heavily draped in mistletoe, ivy, and holly, with two stockings hung with love and care. And the tree! I've never seen anything like it. It's brimming with baubles, tinsel, decorative ornaments of gingerbread men, reindeer, and miniature bells, and the most adorable angel crowns the top. And at its base lie presents galore, mostly labelled for me.

'I put a bottle of Champagne in the fridge before we left.' Jamie switches on the Christmas tree lights. 'Let's open it before everyone arrives.' We have some friends from work coming over for the evening. Jamie organised it. I've started to live again these past few months, thanks to him. Auntie Audrey is coming as well, and she's staying the night. 'I'm going to get changed.' He pauses at the bottom of the stairs. 'Is that OK with you?'

I hop on one leg and unzip my boot. 'Sounds good. I'll get the food ready.' I remove both of my boots and slip my feet into my fluffy slippers.

The stairs moan and groan as he bounces up them two at a time. 'I'll be down in five,' he calls.

We're getting a new kitchen in the new year, but this one is cosy for now with its freestanding units and hodgepodge of shelves that hold pots, pans and crockery and cups and glasses. I take the cheeseboard I prepared earlier from the fridge and place it on the table that Jamie has covered with a plastic tablecloth featuring cheerful Christmas elves that he sourced online. A knock at the door startles me. A red grape rolls off the cheeseboard, dropping between the eyes of an elf. I look at the clock. It's only half-past five.

I run to answer the door. Auntie Audrey stands on the doorstep. 'I'm sorry I'm early. I finished at the church earlier than I thought.' She has lost a significant amount of weight this year and is now half the size of the woman she was last Christmas. I beckon her in, but she stays, frozen to the spot. 'Your earrings. You're wearing your grandma's earrings.'

I touch the pearls hanging from my ears. Everyone is noticing these today. 'I know. I thought it was about time I started wearing some of that jewellery.'

Her gaunt face has turned as white as the path now covered in snow.

'Are you OK, Auntie?' I open the door wide.

She steps inside. 'I'm sorry I...' She stutters. 'Whe... where's Jamie?'

'Upstairs getting changed, why?'

She shrugs. 'Just asking.'

'I'm getting the food ready.' I lead her back to the kitchen. She's acting out of character, jittery, the muscles in her face all tense. 'What's wrong, Auntie?'

Her bottom lip quivers. She's still staring at my earrings as if she's in a trance. It looks like she's about to pass out.

'You're scaring me. Jamie!' I call as I pull out a chair and guide her to sit down. She bursts into tears.

Footsteps bound down the stairs like thunder. Jamie rushes into the room like a breath of fresh air. 'What's up?'

'Those earrings, they... they... they remind me of your mother.'

'They were my grandma's.'

'She was wearing them the night she...' Her voice trails off.

'The night she what?' I look from her to Jamie. He frowns as he picks at the bunch of grapes on the cheese board and pops a few into his mouth.

Auntie Aundrey's tears continue. She gulps in air as if she's drowning.

I pull out the chair beside her and sit down. 'Talk to me.'

She shakes her head. 'There's something else I haven't told you, and I can't keep it to myself any longer.'

My body stiffens.

'Your mother was wearing those earrings the night something dreadful happened.'

The hairs on the back of my neck stand rigid. I look at Jamie again. The frown on his forehead deepens. I rest my elbows on the table and clench my hands into a ball. 'Carry on.'

She clasps her hands, holding them together as if she's praying for the courage to spill what's on her mind.

'What is it?' I say.

'There was another reason why I destroyed your mother's diary. The one from the year she was shot.'

My stomach turns. I place my hands on the table in front of me, splaying my fingers. 'Carry on.' I knew it. Instinctively, I was sure there was something else. Call it a sixth sense, call it woman's intuition. The full truth has never come out.

She continues. 'Your mum was...' She sniffles and snuffles. 'Your mum was responsible for Karen's son's death.'

69

ROSE

My mouth opens wide. So does Jamie's. 'Ross?' I whisper. My first thought is she's lost her mind. But as her words sink in, I know there's no way someone would make something like that up.

She nods. 'Yes, Ross.'

'How do you know?' I ask.

'She wrote about it in that diary.'

I grab the edge of the table.

'She felt such venom towards Karen for having an affair with your father, she couldn't see clearly. She wanted to hurt her. And what could hurt a parent more than the death of their child?'

My hand covers my mouth. I think I'm going to be sick. 'Why now? Why are you telling me this now?'

'The earrings – they reminded me of the night it happened. I've kept it to myself for so long, it's killing me. I was babysitting for you and Violet while your mum supposedly went out with a friend. She came back a mess, laughing hysterically, and then crying uncontrollably. I couldn't get anything out of her at first. When she'd calmed down and I asked what was wrong, she said she'd had a bad argument with her friend. I thought it odd that she was so upset over an argument, but your mum always was unpredictable. When I found the diary, there was a passage from that night about what she'd done. There was regret in those words she wrote, but somehow it didn't seem wholly authentic, like she meant it. The same as Violet, she really wasn't a well woman.'

'Did Karen know?' This is hell. 'Is that why she shot Mum?'

Auntie Audrey grabs a napkin from the holder in the middle of the table and wipes her eyes. 'That's what I wondered.' She snuffles. 'When Karen came out of hospital, I went to see her. Just before she died.'

'You did what?!'

'I had to find out if she knew what your mum did, so I went to see her. Karen told me that she didn't know for sure that your mum had killed Ross, but she was ninety-nine point nine per cent sure she did. Your mum had made some flippant comment, which put her at the scene. Then backtracked and lied about it. There was no mistaking who Karen went to your old house to kill that night. And it wasn't your father.'

'It wasn't an accident. She meant to shoot Mum.' I stand and walk to the patio doors. My reflection stares back at me. 'Why didn't Karen just report Mum?'

'She wanted revenge. Just like Violet. She went along with your mother's plan to rob your father and murder him, when in fact, all along, she planned to murder your mother.'

'You should never have destroyed that diary. You should've taken it to the police.'

'I know. I regret it every day,' she whispers. 'But I was an accessory. I'd be in prison now if I had.'

I screw my eyes shut. The thought of her behind bars cuts me to the core. Whatever my auntie has done, I still love her.

'I'm sorry, Rose. I didn't intend to tell you all this today, of all days. It was the earrings. They brought back all the memories. It's totally up to you what you choose to do with this information. If you go to the police, then I'm going to prison. I'll take that.'

I open my eyes. The sadness in me makes me want to join my auntie in shedding a tear. But I can't. I've shed far too many this year. I'm all cried out. 'If Violet ever got better and found all this out, it would kill her.'

Auntie nods. 'I know. And I fear it'll ruin this wonderful relationship you've built up with your new family.'

'My parents deserved each other, didn't they?'

She looks from me to Jamie and back to me. 'What do you want to do?'

Thoughts of my auntie's latest revelation race around my head. My father was a serial adulterer, and my mother was a murderer. It's going to take a long, long time for that to fully sink in.

Jamie puffs out his chest. He marches over to me and enfolds me in his arms. 'Nothing. We do nothing. We need to move forward now, not backwards. What's the point of dredging up the past? You don't want to lose your auntie. Apart from V, she's the only family you have left on your mother's side. No good can come of revealing this piece of information now.'

He kisses me. 'Come on, I promised you this is going to be

your best Christmas ever, and I'm not going to let you down. Go and freshen up, Audrey.'

Auntie Audrey scuttles out of the room.

'I can't believe it,' I say.

'It doesn't change anything, Rose. We can't change what's happened. The past needs to stay in the past. We need to move forward, celebrate the wins and put the losses behind us. Let's get that Champagne out.' Jamie reaches for the fridge door and pulls out the bottle. 'Get us some glasses.'

I take three glasses from the shelf above the sink. 'Here we go.'

Removing the foil, he untwists the wire cage and pops the cork. He tilts the bottle and fills two of the glasses. He hands one to me and picks up the other. 'To the future.' He clinks his glass against mine and kisses me. 'Happy Christmas, hun.'

A FREE GIFT FOR YOU

Thank you for reading my twelfth published psychological suspense thriller. For me, building a relationship with my readers is one of the joys of writing. Keep in touch by visiting my website: www.ajcampbellauthor.com/download
You'll receive a free copy of my novella *Choices*.

Are you on Facebook? If you are, join Team AJ, my fun reader group. We're a friendly bunch, mainly talking about our love of thrillers with giveaways and lots fun thrown in!

Join here: www.facebook.com/groups/7025352430833952

PLEASE LEAVE A REVIEW

As for all authors, reviews are the key to raising awareness of my work. If you have enjoyed reading this book, please do consider leaving a review on Amazon and Goodreads to help others find it too. It only needs to be a couple of lines.

Also, please consider recommending my books to your friends and in Facebook groups.

All my novels undergo a rigorous editing process, but sometimes mistakes do happen. If you have spotted an error, please contact me, so I can promptly get it corrected.

www.ajcampbellauthor.com/contact

Thank you for choosing to read my book.

AJ x

ACKNOWLEDGMENTS

It takes a team to write a book, and I'm blessed to have the best supporting my work. Firstly, thank you to my astute beta readers and early advance readers. Mr C, Dawn, Christine, Lindsey and June. Your observations and suggestions have helped to shape this story. Your time and continued dedication to my work are priceless.

Thank you to my brilliant editor, Louise Walters, for helping to make this book the best it can be and to Becca Allen for her excellent proofreading skills. And thank you, Tim Barber, for producing yet another cracking cover.

Thank you to my ARC team and all the fantastic book bloggers and media folk who support my work! Most of you have been by my side since my debut novel. I am so lucky to have you.

Thank you, Mr C, for your support while I write my stories. The endless cups of tea and words of encouragement. I love you more than ever.

And, last but not least, thank you to all my wonderful readers. Without you, I couldn't continue writing and publishing my books.

BOOKS BY AJ CAMPBELL

Leave Well Alone

Don't Come Looking

Search No Further

The Phone Call

The Wrong Key

Her Missing Husband

My Perfect Marriage

Did I Kill My Husband?

The Mistake

First-Time Mother

Left at the Altar

Christmas Revenge

I hope you enjoyed reading my twelfth published book *Christmas Revenge* as much as I adored writing it. If you haven't read my other novels, check them out on the following pages. They are all available to purchase from Amazon and free to read in Kindle Unlimited.

THE PHONE CALL

**SHORTLISTED FOR THE ADULT PRIZE FOR FICTION:
THE SELFIE BOOK AWARDS 2022**

A single phone call can destroy your life.

Joey Clarke has been responsible for his family since he was just fifteen. Ten years on, his only pleasure is spending time with bubbly Becca, his best friend... and the secret love of his life. She's his only escape from a dead-end job, ever-increasing debts and the fear that enforcement agents will knock on the front door any day.

So when a phone call brings Joey the chance to ease his family's financial burdens, he grabs the opportunity — even though the bags he's delivering seem suspicious. What he doesn't know can't hurt him, right?

But Joey soon finds himself party to a crime that turns Becca's life upside down, and he panics.

Should he confess to the police? Tell Becca? Or keep quiet and hope for the best?

After all, the only woman who knows the truth may never speak again...

THE MISTAKE

Is it a crime to save a life?

People would say I'm a respectable, law-abiding citizen. But my baby niece is sick. She's going to die without treatment — expensive treatment. The kind we don't have money for.

So when a friend coerces me into seducing a wealthy stranger and robbing him blind, it's temptingly simple: one act of wrongdoing in exchange for Grace's life.

It's a risk I'm prepared to take.

But after witnessing the murder of the man I set out to exploit, I'm left with two impossible choices: do I go to the police and tell all, or run with the funds to save my darling baby Grace?

Or will the killer get to me first?

HER MISSING HUSBAND

#1 in Women's Psychological Fiction and Amazon USA Top 40 bestseller in 2024

Lori Mortimer once shared a perfect life with her husband Howie and their teenage daughter Molly—until the day Howie went to work and never came home.

Now a successful author living in rural North Wales, Lori has left the city and her career as an investigative journalist far behind her. It's peaceful, even if the memories still snap at her heels.

But Lori's ordered, solitary life is about to be turned upside down. Because Frankie Evans, the man she helped convict for murder—shortly after Howie disappeared—has just walked out of prison a free man.

And Frankie wants to meet Lori. He has news of her missing husband that he says she needs to hear...

THE WRONG KEY

A mother's love.
A daughter's life.
A race against time.

London-based banker Steph Knight faces the challenge of a lifetime when she's sent to New York to cover for a colleague involved in a tragic car accident. Recently divorced, Steph sees it as an opportunity for a fresh start and to spend time with her teenage daughter, Ellie, a talented musician, before she leaves for university.

Soon after arriving, Steph crosses paths with Edward, a corporate lawyer, and they immediately click. He introduces Ellie to Jack, a bioethics student on summer break.
But as both relationships intensify, the unthinkable happens.
Ellie disappears.

Terrified and far from home, Steph is unsure who she can

trust. Not even the men they've fallen for are beyond suspicion.

Now she must take unthinkable risks to save her daughter... even if it kills her.

LEAVE WELL ALONE

A broken family.
Skeletons in the closet.
Lives in danger.

How far would you go to protect your family?

When Eva's brother Ben announces he has found their
mother, Eva is determined to have nothing to do with the
woman who abandoned them eighteen years ago to a
traumatic childhood in foster care. Eva is happy now, in a
loving relationship with rich and dependable Jim, and she is
pregnant.

Nothing can change Eva's mind. Her eyes are firmly on the
future. But when her baby is born with a serious hereditary
illness, she is forced to confront both her mother and her
past. Eva begins to find forgiveness. But as old secrets and
layers of deceit emerge, she makes a shocking discovery,
leaving her fearing for her baby's, Jim's, and her own life.

DON'T COME LOOKING

Marc O'Sullivan has disappeared.

His wife Sasha is frantic, and Eva is baffled.

They were blissfully married with three kids. The perfect couple... or so everybody thought.

Sasha begs Eva to help her find Marc. But he has given a written statement at the police station where Eva works. It's on record – when his family report him missing, Marc does not want to be found.

Ultimately, friendship and loyalty override Eva's professional integrity, and she is compelled to use her resources to delve into Marc's life, even if it means breaking the police code of conduct and jeopardising her career.

As each day passes, the mystery deepens. Murky goings-on from Marc and Sasha's neighbours heighten the tension.

What dark secrets are they hiding? And what drove Marc's inexplicable actions in the weeks leading up to his disappearance? Behaviour so out of character that Eva struggles to tell Sasha about it.

Will Eva uncover the truth before it's too late and lives are destroyed forever?

SEARCH NO FURTHER

My auntie says I'm the innocent one in this madhouse of a family…

When Sienna's beloved grandmother Cara collapses at a family birthday party, everyone thinks she's had a heart attack.

Except Cara.

The successful Italian matriarch believes someone wants her dead—and she harbours a chilling suspicion of who it could be.

Sienna is the only one she trusts to uncover the truth.

A young, single mother grappling with the tragic, unresolved death of her husband, Sienna is no stranger to life's uglier side. But when she puts their big, happy family under the microscope, she reveals disturbing secrets, decades of deceit, and shockingly serious crimes.

This is all bigger than even Cara imagined—and much closer to home.

DID I KILL MY HUSBAND?

**The police officer's voice is steady as he tells me the news.
'Your husband is in hospital.' My heart pounds. I think
about my children, safely tucked up in bed. What will
happen to us if he loses his life? And more importantly…
do the police know where I really was tonight?**

Everybody thinks Michael and I are the perfect couple. But
everybody is wrong.

Because my dear, lovely husband was at the heart of a
scandal at the school where he teaches. He was cleared of any
wrongdoing. At first I believed him. Now, I'm sure he's been
hiding something terrible.

But I can't tell the police a thing. Because my husband isn't
the only one with secrets.

So, as I stand here knowing I have to tell my children that
Michael is fighting for his life, I ask myself: what would be

worse? For my husband, the much-loved local teacher, to die? Or for him to live, and for all his lies to come home again?

In the end, the choice is easy. I know what I have to do...

I'll tell the police that I would never, ever hurt my husband. But will they believe me?

FIRST-TIME MOTHER

My family say I'm unwell. They think I can't care for my baby. But they're lying. Who can I really trust?

My delicate newborn, **Lola**, is just perfect. Seeing her gorgeous little face look up at me, I know the difficult birth was worth it. And I swear I'll *never* let anyone hurt her.

My stepchildren say they love their new little sister, and my wonderful husband **Max** is so happy. He reassures me that the blackouts I'm having are normal: I'm sleep-deprived, and I just need help.

Accidents keep happening around the house. Max and his children look at me pityingly. I know what they're thinking. *She can't cope.* But why can't I shake the feeling something else is going on?

Then one day I go to check on Lola and what I see changes everything...

Because my baby isn't there.

LEFT AT THE ALTAR

My groom is gone. It's my fault. And we are all in terrible danger.

My fiancé **Johnny** is handsome, charming and perfect. But here I am, standing in my wedding dress without him by my side. There is no way he would leave me at the altar like this. I know something terrible has happened... **and what if it's my fault?**

Because looking out at the congregation, I see a face I never thought I'd see again. I didn't invite him. **Could he know the truth about what I did all those years ago?**

He smiles, and I know *exactly* what that means. My heart pounds in my chest as I'm faced with an impossible decision.

If I ever want to see Johnny again, I know I need to confess everything.

But I *have* to keep my secret hidden. Or I'll lose more than just my husband.

With all my friends and family gathered around, **just how far will I have to go?**

ABOUT THE AUTHOR

AJ CAMPBELL is an Amazon USA top 40 bestselling author, who loves throwing characters into seemingly unbelievable situations and figuring it out from there. The result is psychological suspense thriller novels full of twists, turns, and torment, with gasp-worthy endings.

An avid hiker, AJ lives in the UK on the Essex / Hertfordshire border with her husband, sons, and cocker spaniel, Max. She is a Netflix junkie, theatre tragic, and a wine and Asian food enthusiast.

Visit AJ's website for a free copy of her suspenseful novella *Choices* and to receive regular updates on her new releases, reading inspiration and author tips.

Get your copy of my FREE novella here:

www.ajcampbellauthor.com/download

CONTACT AJ

Find AJ here:

www.ajcampbellauthor.com
www.facebook.com/AJCampbellauthor
www.instagram.com/ajcampbellauthor/

Made in United States
North Haven, CT
29 November 2025

83264754R00185